SHERLOCK HOL
WHITECHAPE
AN ACCOUNT OI
BY JOHN WA'

MARK SOHN

Paperback ISBN 978-1-78705-059-4
ePub ISBN 978-1-78705-060-0
PDF ISBN 978-1-78705-061-7

Published in the UK by MX Publishing
335 Princess Park Manor, Royal Drive,
London, N11 3GX
www.mxpublishing.co.uk

Cover design by Brian Belanger

PREFACE

Dear Reader, although it has often been my glad duty to act as scribe in the public service, namely the setting down on paper of the investigative genius of my friend and colleague Mr. Sherlock Holmes, I must confess to my part in concealing his, indeed *our*, involvement in one case of particular significance. Indeed, this one case has proved itself of utmost fascination and importance to both professional criminologists and the 'armchair detectives', to say nothing of the general public.

I have wrestled with my conscience for many long hours over the years since those now far-off days of Eighteen Hundred and Eighty Eight; weighing the benefits of revelation with those of continued silence. Many will question my motives, indeed my very loyalty itself, the case as laid bare in its detail proved a singular task for my esteemed friend to unravel. There will be no no apology made for any indignancies or infelicitous errors mentioned-they are stated as they happened, and it was on the insistence of Holmes himself that I include them.

That such an eminent mind could be so terribly astray as to make false conclusions demonstrates the unique difficulties presented to the investigator of a case of such an extraordinarily horrific nature that its previous exclusion from the index of Sherlock Holmes' published exploits will have been in itself a mystery to the majority of readers. What follows from this is the full, uncensored text compiled from memory and with reference to my original notes-corroborated and, albeit reluctantly, approved by Mr. Sherlock Holmes.

CHAPTER I
A VISITOR CALLS

I awoke earlier than usual, to find the weather un-seasonably hot, Sherlock Holmes in a mood of agitated ebullience and the table laid with two breakfasts. 'Ah, Watson-Mrs. Hudson was able to obtain some of her excellent smoked salmon.' 'Poached eggs, too, eh?.' I settled myself at my customary chair. Holmes, however, seemed in poor appetite, pacing the sitting-room and pausing often to check the view of the street below. I knew that my friend was increasingly prone to finding himself without useful employment, indeed in the months following the case laid down by myself as *'A Study in Scarlet'* he had largely to content himself with only the odd minor intrigue or his interminable chemical experiments. More than once the local Fire Brigade have called at 221b to find plumes of noxious smoke billowing from the upstairs window, only to be waved off by an apologetic Holmes or an apoplectic Mrs. Hudson.

Setting down my fork, I dabbed away the remains of breakfast and could contain myself no more. 'Really, Holmes-you seem intent on leaving the carpet threadbare.' My only answer was for Holmes to stride across to the bell-pull to summon our erstwhile and patient landlady. Mrs. Hudson cleared the table, making no comment on Holmes' untouched plates save a look of resignation in my direction. 'Mrs. Hudson, we are expecting a visitor-from the police. Please would you be so good as to arrange a Hansom for his departure at nine-thirty sharp.'

'A visitor, eh?, I had no idea you had a client.' Pausing

in yet another examination of the street, my companion turned his piercing gaze to where I now sat on the sofa with this morning's *Pall Mall Gazette*. 'Not yet, Watson-I have no client *yet*. However...' he gestured towards the window and the City in general. 'I tell you that before the hour strikes nine I shall be engaged-in my unofficial capacity naturally, as a consulting detective in the solution of the most abhorrent of crimes. I shall go further; my client will be a detective from the Metropolitan or City Police of comparatively low rank yet high ambition. Our detective will, in all probability, have shaved hurriedly and be of a generally dishevelled appearance, his shoes will be dull and, despite the oppressive heat today will be wearing or carrying a rain-coat. He will be wearing a clean shirt.'

This was an excessive display even for one so accustomed to Holmes' razor-honed mind as myself. 'Come now, Holmes-even you cannot possibly have made such a series of correct guesses.' A smile showed itself for the briefest of moments below that prominent nose. 'I never guess, Watson. rather, call it a series of co-dependant deductions, each in its way to be inferred and confirmed by the other.' Pausing beside the scuttle, he selected then rejected a briar before continuing in his explanation. 'Had you read your Gazette over breakfast instead of after, you would be possessed of two of the relevant facts; namely that there has been a murder committed and that the official police are powerless to either prevent a second or to apprehend the fiend responsible.' 'Fiend, eh?-a woman or child then?.' I received a small nod of approbation. 'The former-and in a manner suggestive of great brutality.' The sound of the bell clanging from the downstairs hallway was my signal to retire, but my friend entreated me to remain, insisting I would be of use to him. Ever eager to assist, I agreed to his request, just in time for the door to open admitting our guest, a man in his middle thirties with an air of tired desperation about his pugnacious features and a macintosh draped over his left arm.

The man spoke, his broad accent marking him out as a Northerner, possibly Lancastrian of birth. 'Mr. Sherlock Holmes?.' The man looked to both of us hopefully, Holmes indicating the sofa as he seated himself in his chair, leaning across with a battered silver cigarette box. 'Why, thank you, Mr. Holmes, but-how did you know I'd not prefer a pipe?.' This was waved off by Holmes with a casual sweep of the hand. 'It is not hard to spot a sixty a day man.' He waved his long, pianist's fingers by way of explanation, the yellowing brown stains on the other man's proclaiming the extent of his habit. 'My name is Detective Sergeant Robert Sagar of the City of London police. Forgive me if I seem ill at ease Mr. Holmes, but my time is short.' 'Evidently. I have taken the small liberty of arranging a cab to take you back to your official duties. You should make it to enjoy the Assistant Commissioner's address with ten minutes to spare-enough time for proper ablutions and of course, a last minute cigarette to steel the nerves so obviously jangled by the sight of the victim and the long hours of subsequent investigation.' At Holmes' last, the young detective sergeant half rose from his seat, collapsing into it with the look of one exposed to witchcraft for the first time. 'But...but, how?. I judge myself a keen eye for faces, Mr. Holmes, but I had not seen yours present at the mortuary nor first parade this morning. How, then, do you come to know all this about me?.'

Glancing at the clock, my companion steepled his fingers together, then took a cigarette for himself. 'I shall be brief as time dictates.' Inhaling the smoke, he exhaled slowly.

'I am a practitioner of the science of deduction, of using the known facts in a case to unveil the unknown. In such methods I predicted your arrival here from the press reports of the murder of an as yet unknown woman in the District of Whitechapel two nights ago and the clumsy attempts at investigation made so far.' Holding a placatory hand up, Holmes wafted more smoke into the tense air between himself and his client. 'Of course, you have tried your best, it is your superiors that will be found wanting. I knew that, due to my previous associations with the police that a request for my assistance would become inevitable-but only from a junior officer hoping to rise in the force as no senior man would admit the need for such help. Such a man would, in all probability have spent the night on duty and would have had little time for a proper shave-I see the evidence from the cuts to your neck and chin. Finally, it was raining last night – I observe the leather of your shoes is still damp.' I interjected at this point, being fascinated with Holmes' method and the accuracy with which he applied it. 'The shirt, Holmes-you mentioned the shirt.''Quite so. Detective Sergeant, this is my friend and most trusted associate Dr. John Watson, without whose ability to clarify the mental processes I would be quite unable to proceed. The shirt he refers to is yours. I see it is freshly laundered. Ask any policeman, Watson; their business is often unpleasant and messy. Any aspiring officer with an eye to furtherance has at least one spare in his locker.'

Our visitor was seized with admiration for Holmes' uncanny perceptions, rising as he did to take my friend's hand. 'Mr. Holmes!, I must say when Inspector Gregson recommended you-I called on him at Scotland Yard, it was with no small misgivings that I agreed to call on you. I can see now how misplaced my apprehensions were; from the anticipation of my presence to the Old Man's calling us

6

together for a shellacking, you are indeed possessed of a unique mind. Will you give assistance in this matter?. I can assure you, there can be no criminal more worthy of your urgent attention than the, the beast who committed the outrage on that poor woman. Her name was Tabram, or Turner-we cannot yet be sure which.' Holmes placed a hand on the sturdy fellow's shoulder. 'You may be assured of my undivided attention to the matter. However, I must ask of you that you mention my involvement to no-one, save your immediate superior and that you provide to myself and Dr. Watson here copies of all the relevant police reports of the murders including those of the coroner's office.' 'Of course, I shall have copies made at my own expense, but did you say 'murders'?.' Nodding grimly, Holmes replied with a voice that betrayed a rare emotion. 'Murders there will be. I have to this moment only the distortions of the press in place of data, but enough to convince me that this was no commonplace killing. The man who wielded the knife will reach for it again, of that you may be sure. This business ends at the gallows.' As Holmes ushered him out, the detective sergeant was evidently buoyed up by his acceptance of the problem.

CHAPTER II
A GHASTLY BUSINESS

It was approaching the hour of eleven when the cab transporting both Holmes and myself deposited us at a faceless brick building in the city. Instructing the cab driver to wait, Holmes turned for the ominous double doors. Pausing at the step, he half turned, breathing deeply of the morning air as if steeling himself for the ordeal ahead. We entered to the registration counter and waited for the clerk, a harassed-looking individual hiding his chubby features behind a *pince nez*. 'This is Doctor John Watson, I am his assistant. We are to examine the cadaver of the woman known as Tabram or Turner.' The clerk looked at Holmes, then over to where I stood. 'Official police surgeons only, I'm afraid – anyway, the post-mortem has yet to be completed. All that awaits is the formal identification, should we get one.' 'There is doubt?.' I asked knowing Holmes would be interested in all the details. 'There always is when its a-*lady* of, shall we say indiscriminate association.' I was baffled, but the clerk's look eventually conveyed his meaning. 'A prostitute?' Holmes stepped forward 'The Doctor has travelled a considerable distance to examine the body, examine it he shall I think.' Holmes cut across the *impasse*, both by the tone of his words and the sovereign he slapped down on the counter.

At once, the clerk's demeanour changed. Setting down the registry book on top of the coin, he bade us sign it. As we complied-myself with my normal signature, Holmes with an unintelligible scrawl, in low tones he hissed. 'Ten minutes, not one more. If I find you... *disturbing* the body it'll cost you a whole lot more.' As I recoiled in shock from this specimen, he withdrew both book and coin. 'Come now *Doctor*, time is fleeting.' Holmes steered me towards the mortuary doors with a firm hand. Once inside, we found ourselves alone in the grim silence of a large white-tiled room, at the centre of which rested two large examination tables. The air was quite as dead as anything in this sombre place, with an air of unnatural stillness. Holmes purposefully strode across to the far wall, in which were set the smaller doors familiar to any medical student. 'Watson, I must ask you to set aside the natural emotions and examine this corpse as clinically as time permits.' I nodded, inhaling again the stifling mixture of formaldehyde and disinfectant pervading the air as if smelling it for the first time.

The memory of that examination shall haunt my memory until I, too am laid upon the mortuary slab. Had I known it was as naught to what was to come!. It is at Holmes' insistence that I elaborate further. As I spoke, his pen rapidly filled the page of his note book. 'Subject Female, Caucasian aged approximately from the late thirties to middle forties. Height five feet... four, weight around, say fourteen stones. Morbidity and lividity suggestive of death occurring as already stated. Cause of death-' (Here I removed the blanket, revealing the full extent of the atrocity.) '- Good God!, forgive me Holmes... the body has clearly sustained a most vicious attack. There are numerous deep wounds, in fact perhaps thirty in number.' I paused here to unroll a small leather wallet containing various surgical tools. Extracting a forceps and a probe I commenced a brief examination of the major wounds. 'Both lungs penetrated, consistent with wounds caused by a long straight bladed knife, single edged. Heart, liver, spleen- all destroyed. I, I-' Holmes' hand at my elbow was reassurance indeed!. 'I beg your forgiveness Holmes, I shall continue. Minor wounds, cuts and lacerations from a smaller bladed knife are present.' 'Which of these wounds was the mortal blow, Watson?, hurry, I must know!.' 'Either the unfortunate woman perished from loss of blood or the puncture wound to the heart-I favour the latter.' With that, the doors opened, the clerk standing there with a look of loathsome avarice upon his features-at which our acquaintance with the mortal remains of the unfortunate woman we know now to have been Martha Tabram was ended.

CHAPTER III
THE EVIDENCE OF A CRIME

The days following our examination were spent largely in waiting, both for new information-and for the murderer to claim his next victim. Sherlock Holmes spent a morning at the scene of the crime, the first-floor of George Yard buildings, Whitechapel. It was there, on the landing that the victim was found. A man by the name of Reeves, a stevedore had the misfortune of discovery, at which he summoned the assistance of a police officer, PC Barrett. Following interviews with both, Holmes was firmly on the scent. Early in the morning on the fateful day, PC Barrett had cause to speak with a private of Guards outside George Yard. The Guardsman informed the Constable that he was waiting for his mate. Later, another *demi-mondaine*, known by the soubriquet 'Pearly Poll', gave evidence in the matter, stating that she had been with Tabram in the company of not one, but *two* Guardsmen-one a corporal. It was in the company of the private that Tabram departed, never to be seen alive again.

I watched as the small pile of paperwork grew upon Holmes' already overspilling desk. Though I myself insisted on a tidy writing space, my associate seemed content to use his own as a unique mixture of filing system and *aide memoire*, packed as it were with otherwise forgotten details of various cases. Holmes himself appeared and disappeared as was his fashion, often in the most peculiar guises. It was when he burst in dressed as a farrier that I was compelled to inquire as to progress made on the case. 'I have some news, Watson, though the identity of the killers evades me still.' 'Killers, Holmes?.' 'Yes, Watson, our criminal is in the plural-the private who went with the victim became aggressive, a scuffle ensued during which he produced a clasp knife and attacked her. He managed to smother her screams, but the commotion attracted his corporal, sealing her fate. Using the bayonet he wore as part of his walking-out dress, he struck first with two blows, one the fatal wound to the heart. To conceal the military precision of the attack, both men launched into a series of further blows.'

'You deduced all this from the facts?, surely, then, the case is as good as solved.' My optimistic remark was met with a thin smile. 'Not so. Detective Inspector Reid of Scotland Yard has taken charge of the official investigation-a more determined individual I have yet to see. I have spent some time shadowing his inquiries and even managed to insinuate myself into a special parade of all privates and corporals of the Scots Guards who had leave on the night in question. PC Barrett was unable to identify the private he had spoken to, then worse-the woman known as 'Pearly Poll' stated the men she had seen wore white bands on their caps.' At once, I remarked; 'Coldstream Guards!.' 'Precisely-the First Battalion is currently garrisoned at Wellington Barracks-yet she then identified two men whose innocence was incontestable-quite the most unreliable witness since that myopic blacksmith we questioned in that Faversham strangling.'

CHAPTER IV
A FRESH ATROCITY

That long August passed slowly for the habitants of 221b
Baker Street. I spent my days engaged in medical texts and
acting *in locum* for an associate of mine, a General
Practitioner in Knightsbridge. It was while returning from an
afternoon surgery that I saw it; a street hawker selling the
Evening Standard. His cries of 'Murder, dreadful murder in
Whitechapel-woman horribly murdered' had my blood
running cold. Purchasing a copy, I hurried upstairs to find
myself alone. I inquired as to Holmes' whereabouts from Mrs.
Hudson, but she knew nothing. Accepting her offer of a
cooked supper, I waited with the *Standard.*

The facts were laid out before me-in the early hours of
the last day of August the body of a woman was discovered in
Buck's Row. At first known only as 'Polly', the victim was
later identified as being Mrs. Mary Ann Nichols, age forty
three. Again, her death was an ordeal of such savagery that it
can barely be fit for description, but my duty compels me to
persevere. Her throat had been cut so ferociously that both
windpipe and spinal cord had been severed, as had both the
carotid arteries. If there can be any cause for palliation, it is
that death would have occurred in an instant. However, the
frenzied madman continued, with the infliction of several
wounds to the stomach and lower abdomen.

As our estimable landlady arrived to set the table, so
too did Holmes. It was entirely in keeping with her kindly
spirit that she insisted he take his seat for dinner, returning
with two bowls of a hearty mutton stew, with a tray of fancies

for dessert. Over our repast, we exchanged information, although Holmes was already fully acquainted with this latest horror. As for his day, he had spent some of it at the scene in a desperate attempt to retrieve what knowledge there remained undiscovered, before the sensation-seekers and other ghouls eradicated it by their clumsy presence.

'So, Holmes, our Guardsmen again?.' His fork paused between bowl and lip. 'Not this time-though my efforts at tracing them remain unrewarded, find them I intend to. No, this is the work of a different hand-and a much more sinister one if I am not mistaken.' 'More sinister?, but surely Holmes these are the same pair that butchered the poor wretch Tabram?.' Setting his plate aside, the great detective leant forward, his facial expression and long hands animated as he outlined his theory.
'I am afraid not. Although both women were from a shared, shall we say 'trade', in the first instance, a motive may be discerned; here there is none. The injuries are inconsistent from one case to the other. This is a solitary individual. From observation I have two theorems; in the first, the killer either laid in wait or followed the victim-the second is that, knowing her to to be a lady of the night he simply approached her under the guise of a patron.' I sniffed at this last.'Vile business, prostitution.' Instantly, I had cause to regret my insensitive comment, Holmes rounding on me with a look of disapproval. 'Perhaps so, my friend-but let us not be the ones to judge the character of the fallen. These women may well have courted their fate by their trade, but if so, what drove them to do so?, drink?, poverty?, a brute of a husband, perhaps children to feed?. No, Watson, it will not do; no woman is deserving of such a piteous end. Our duty is to them, both the dead and those still living-we must catch this fiend!..'

14

It was agreed that we might gain fresh insight to the crimes by taking to the streets of the East End as night fell. I availed myself of the opportunity to rest, taking to my bed for several hours of enervating sleep. As for Holmes, he had of late been experimenting with the possibilities for mental stimulation offered by the meditative states achieved by the Brahmin of India. Removing his socks, he first sat cross-legged on the bearskin rug, elbows on knees, fingers steepled together as if in prayer. He would then concentrate on his respiratory organs, controlling and slowing his inhalations and exhalations until his chest seemed to cease movement altogether. In such a condition, Holmes could, he assured me attain a state of the purest consciousness and intellectuality-in which he could visualise any event or scene in its totality and from every possible aspect.

During our preparations for the excursion, the mood was dark, disturbed, as if Holmes had uncovered something evil while at his meditations. When I remarked on his demeanour my suspicions were proven correct. 'I had intended to use the ascended mental faculties to re-examine the crime from a unique perspective- however, all I could see was the usual murky swirl common to anyone with closed eyelids...' Selecting his black clay pipe, he filled it with a pinch from the disreputable old persian slipper hanging from its nail by the fireplace and took a box of matches from the lampstand next to his armchair. '...However, I was seized with the most extraordinary sensation, not unlike that of drowning. I had the vivid and urgent impression of being in the most terrible danger, that my life was somehow in the process of being ended.' At this, I paused in my cleaning of my old service revolver and looked across from my desk. 'Why, Holmes, this isn't like you at all. Why bother with all this

15

Brahmin nonsense?.' With a wry smile against himself, my friend nodded abruptly. 'Indeed I shall think twice before conducting further research.' Loading the chambers of the revolver, I snapped the cylinder shut and nodded back.

CHAPTER V
THE BEATING HEART OF THE EMPIRE

The cab rattled through the streets of the great city, first taking us east along the Euston road, then south-easterly down Grays Inn Road then to Newgate Street and into Cheapside, dropping us off at Fenchurch Street. Holmes paid and we continued on foot, eastwards towards the Whitechapel Road. We had made our preparations and felt ready for whatever our expedition may involve us in. Holmes wore a dark coat and a cloth cap, while I wore my dark tweed jacket over cord trousers and a felt hat. My service revolver sat in my pocket, the weight a reassurance in itself-Holmes had availed himself of a sword-stick he had kept as a trophy of a previous case. A police-issue bulls-eye lamp sat in a cloth shoulder bag I had brought along.

The early evening crowds went about their business, providing ourselves with a splendid anonymity. Here in the very centre of the Empire, it's heart beat quickest. All life was here; the pie and mash vendors and the Jews selling beigels. Children hurried home with their fathers dinner; meat pie and a bottle of ale for the English born, 'gefüllte Fische' and pastries for the immigrant. At one corner, a crowd, a packing crate covered with cloth serving as a table for a game of 'Under and Over', the canny boy running the 'gaff' with the assistance of an accomplice in the guise of a 'punter'. We stopped for refreshment in an ale-house, for a pint of uncertain provenance, steeling ourselves for the next and most dangerous area; the notorious rookery known as Flower and Dean street. Despite the name, the rookery was known as the most dangerous area in all of London-a warren of alleyways and slum dwellings ridden with disease, crime and the most abject poverty. Here even Constables feared to tread singly, as Holmes reminded me, setting down his unfinished pint.

'Not good enuff fer ya, Mister?.' A slovenly trollop leered at Holmes through a thick pancake of cheap rouge, no doubt designed to hide an even more florid *complexion*. Holmes' reply came in the gruff, unschooled tones of the Costermonger. 'The pigs was ream enough, but me and my pal 'ere's on the fly.' This seemed to satisfy the woman, but as we left, I noticed her in conference with a villainous looking thug in a derby and chequered overcoat. 'We would do well to put some distance between ourselves and that hovel, Holmes-a nasty character was sizing us up.' My companion burst into laughter at this. 'My dear fellow, the 'nasty character' you refer to is none other than Detective Constable Marriott-one of the many plainclothes men abroad this night.' 'I see, well then, what of 'ream' and the like?.' 'The slang of the Cockney, adapted from the Romany and the Costermonger alike to baffle outsiders-'pigs' is taken from 'pigs ears'-rhyming slang for 'beer', 'ream' is 'fine' and the reference to being 'on the fly' meant we were in a hurry.'

Further into the night we found ourselves, weary and in need of refreshment, outside a public house, the Princess Alice. Inside, we found a relatively quiet nook from which to observe the establishment, a noisy, roisterous den filled almost to the rafters with a patronage of the very roughest type. I was jostled by a drunken fellow who, having spilt some of his ale rounded on me as if I were the culprit. Instantly, Holmes' fist was around the ruffian's throat, steel-like fingers pressing into the windpipe to stifle the man's cry of misplaced outrage. 'No, no offence guv'nor-just some drink spilled is all it was-nuffing to get in a lather about...' Without a word, Holmes withdrew his hand and clapped the fellow on the shoulder in companionable fashion. As the drunkard withdrew I whispered across.'What can we possibly learn in a dive like this, Holmes?.' Sipping his pint with a frown, my erstwhile companion replied with a thin smile. 'Nothing, perhaps. However, with so little in the way of facts, we are forced onto the streets-with the risk that our very presence might alert our quarry.' 'How so?, we are inconspicuous enough.' 'But hardly familiar-our faces are not known to these people and that may be warning enough if the killer proves to be a native of the borough.' 'What do you propose then, Holmes?.' 'Simply this, Watson; to establish for ourselves identities that are at once familiar, yet by their nature so plausible that our true motive remains unsuspected.' Finishing his ale in one long draught, he smacked his lips and produced the clay, lighting it with the slow, considered movements of the habitual drunk. 'I can tell you one thing, however; these people are frightened of something all right.'

It was the next morning when I was given a demonstration of Holmes' idea. By means of his contacts within the official police, he had obtained for himself a Constable's uniform and foul-weather cape, with special permission to impersonate a policeman-though he was quite guarded as to the identity of these 'contacts'. Thus it was that PC 244 Melosh began his career patrolling the streets of Whitechapel that rainy and tempestuous night. As for myself, I was to set forth guised as a Temperance advocate, one of the many who gave of their time to attempt to correct the path of those unfortunates fallen through drink. With Holmes' instructions clear in my head, I first collected my pamphlets from the Temperance Hall and then took a hansom ride deep into the uncharted territory that was Commercial Street. There, as arranged, I met with a small group of activists from the

Temperance League. Foremost amongst these worthy campaigners was a formidable lady, Mrs. Shaw, wife to a certain Inspector Shaw of the City police-and the only knowing accomplice to our machinations. Under the knowing gaze of this redoubtable campaigner, I was dispatched onto the street to spread the message of moderation and sobriety, all the while on the alert for any suspicious characters or fallen women such as the killer might seek out for his next victim.

Over the next four hours, my pile of pamphlets grew steadily smaller, as my shoe leather wore thinner. There were few incidents of note, apart from when I was jeered and mocked by a gang of Irish 'navvies', deep in a drunk after their day digging the foundations for the new tramway-and then when I managed to disgrace myself, being caught mid-sip from my flask. My protestations that the brandy was purely for fortification against the elements fell on stony ground with Mrs. Shaw. Holmes himself was visible only in the odd glimpse; turning a corner here or seen as an indistinct shape in the rain. At midnight a charabanc drew up to collect a weary bunch of Temperance volunteers, finally reaching Oxford Street some time after one. I took the short walk to Baker Street and gratefully turned in for the remainder of the night and eight hours of solid slumber unencumbered by dreams.

CHAPTER VI
HOLMES ON THE SCENT

The next night was spent as a repetition of the first, with much drudgery, rain and little in the way of apparent progress. It was on the third night of my posing as a Temperance Leaguer, approaching the hour of ten when, footsore and legs leaden with fatigue, events spurred us to action. Halfway along Brick Lane, I had sight of a surly-looking man possessed of an infrequent, yet noticeable tic with partial paralysis of the lower left leg indicative of some trauma involving nerve damage. This individual was in the habit of accosting strangers in what sounded to my ears like the Russian tongue, babbling incoherently until they either turned away or placated him with coin. At the junction with Booth Street my attention was drawn to the distinct shrill of a police whistle, two short blasts and one long-it was Holmes' signal!. At once I broke into a run, my legs transporting me as fast as my clumsy feet would let them, my old wound causing me to catch my breath sharply every few steps. With lungs near to bursting, I reached the corner from whence the alert had issued, in time to see PC 'Melosh' comforting a distraught female, whose distress was immediately apparent.

'Watson, help me over!.' I braced my knee to allow Holmes to attempt to scale a formidable set of gates, which he accomplished in a lunging vault, to be illuminated by a watchman's lantern and a shouted oath. Pausing only to command the watchman to open the gates and assist the stricken woman, Holmes was off at a sprint into the yard-evidently a brewery by the barrels stacked against the wall and the carts by the stables. After a rapid examination, I concluded the woman had had the luckiest of escapes, her colourful epithets and outraged demeanour testament to her condition. I followed my friend into the yard, his silhouette visible now on the roof. Scaling the stack of barrels, I was soon on the same roof-Holmes now some way ahead in the gloom, the only light that reflected from the low clouds and the occasional glimpsed crescent moon. Picking my way gingerly along the slippery apex of the roof, I had a brief glimpse of his quarry; a be-cloaked figure darting among the chimneys.

The perilous chase continued, the going slippery and treacherous on the slime-coated slates of the houses adjacent to the brewery. The gap between buildings here was mercifully narrow, allowing even one as unsteady as myself to leap across with no more than a determined step. More than once, my feet slipped on the wet tiles. It was hard to look anywhere, but at my feet. I could not be sure, but Holmes seemed to have the beast in his grasp when, with a curse of dismay, he fell from sight. Concern for my friend impelled me to greater effort, reaching the spot where he had disappeared. The figure in the cloak had turned, waving a fist in the air in a gesture of pure spite. 'Damn you!' My whispered curse came as I drew my revolver, pausing only to take aim. Two shots rang out, shattering the very air between us. I could not be sure if the heavy bullets had found their mark; the fiend whirling around behind a chimneystack a moment after I fired. A groan from the blackness below-it was Holmes!.

A convenient drainpipe offered a route down to a small yard, where Holmes sat clutching at his ankle-a sprain, not a break I assured him, supporting his weight as he got to his feet, anger and disappointment etched into his features in that dismal light. An unlocked gate opened onto Spelman Street, the lights of the Alma public house a welcoming beacon in the darkness. Once inside, I commandeered a bench, a crowd forming around the spectacle of an injured Constable. A barmaid brought over a jug of Ale, but I ordered two double measures of brandy. The rough liquor burning our throats, I appealed for calm, thanking the patrons for their concern-though in truth a fair majority seemed concerned only that a policeman had interrupted their illicit business.

Within the space of no more than five minutes, a cordon had been thrown around the area-several Constables led by a Sergeant had responded to Holmes' whistle, the Sergeant remonstrating with him for not giving the regulation three distinct blasts!. The tumbler of whisky I bought the Sergeant, however, ended the shellacking. Soon, however it became apparent our killer had eluded us-the lack of any corpse testament to my unsteady aim. We withdrew in a police cart before suspicions about the identity of 'PC Melosh' could be aired, aided by a plainclothes Inspector who had the confidence of Holmes' mysterious benefactors. As to these, I naturally presumed them to be men of high rank indeed as impersonation of a police officer usually carried a weighty penalty, yet here was Holmes blatantly transgressing such legalities-and with the connivance of the official police!. Not for the first time, I marvelled at his influence.

Despite my protestations, Holmes insisted on venturing forth the next day, his injured ankle bandaged and tightly laced in his felt-soled boots. I was to remain at Baker Street to wait for his instructions, immersing myself in contemplation of a treatise on the medicinal properties of the plants of the island of Borneo. At around eleven, a sharp crack at the window caught my attention, soon followed by another-as if tiny stones had been thrown against the pane. Down on the pavement was a pair of wretched street arabs, no doubt part of Holmes' 'Baker Street irregulars', the little scamps who occasionally aided him in the unlikeliest of matters. I drew up the window to remonstrate with them, but to my consternation, one of the tykes produced a catapult, firing a pellet of some sort up into the room, missing my ear by a whisker. Indignantly, I retrieved it-it was a small scrap of paper wrapped around a pebble. I read the message, written as it was in a childish scrawl. 'Come at wunce, Whytechapell Stashun-Homes.' Wrapping a shilling in the paper, I threw it down, prompting a lively scramble as the urchins fought amongst themselves for their prize.

Journeying by hansom and tram, I was able to reach the station in somewhat less than an hour, thanks to the extension of the tramways with their unobstructed progress through the city. Of Holmes there was no sign, though the station itself was crowded with folk from all possible varieties. I decided to wait across the street, where it was less busy, when an uncouth lout bumped into me without as much as a hint of apology. No sooner had this occurrence taken place, natural justice exerted itself-he was himself knocked into by a gruff type with a tool bag over his shoulder. 'Got the time, Mister?'. At his request, I reached for my watch-but it was already dangling from the man's hand in front of me!. 'My watch!.' I ejaculated. 'Quite. I took it from that rogue. Really, Watson, have you learned nothing from our association?.' Of course it was Holmes-now *accoutred* as a roofer's mate.

Holmes gave a brief summation of his activities, chiefly to examine the scene of last night's chase in more detail. It was, as he conceded, largely fruitless, save some indistinct blood traces which proved insufficient for correct analysis-and some fibres found on a chimney stack. It was the latter that had proved significant, Holmes was of the opinion that they would match similar fibres retrieved from the scene of the Nichols murder. For once it was the police who had discovered them along with an incomplete footprint, which Holmes had tried-unsuccessfully-to correspond with that of the man whom he had so nearly apprehended on those rooftops. What footprints the fugitive may have left in the brewery had been eradicated by hoof-prints and the morning activity in the yard. 'So, had I shot straighter the matter would have been at an end?.' Sensing my chagrin, Holmes smiled that enigmatic smile of his. 'Your shooting may well hang a man, hence the reason for our visit.' So saying, he indicated the broad edifice behind us, that of the London Hospital.

CHAPTER VII
DR.WATSON MAKES HIS ROUNDS

Leaving Holmes to seek belated treatment for his injured ankle, I sought out the clerk of admissions, a friendly if overburdened man named Cole. Fortunately, in such a large establishment the sight of an unfamiliar doctor was not in itself cause for comment. Under the pretence of making a study of injuries related to criminal activity, I inquired as to the nature of recent admissions. Mr. Cole was most helpful, going so far as to leave me with the admissions book while he took the opportunity to avail himself of a cup of tea. I searched amongst the entries for last night, finding that none were admitted with gunshot wounds or injuries from a fall.

Thanking Cole, I left to find Holmes, eventually finding him outside the building smoking a cigarette. 'I would surmise from your expression that there were no suitable candidates admitted during the night.' I shook my head in response. 'Our task continues. It was to be expected-a clever fellow our killer.' 'Perhaps he knocked up a local doctor rather than risk drawing attention to himself.' 'No, Watson-I had one of my patrons in the force direct his men to make inquiries of the exact same nature. If it was a local practitioner, his silence may have been bought, but I think it unlikely.' Waving his cigarette in a vague gesture, my companion continued. 'Of course, there are always exceptions.' 'But, but that's-it's outrageous, Holmes. Surely you cannot suggest a man of medicine would stoop so low as to incriminate himself by accepting such payment?.' 'My friend, please accept my apology for any insult to your noble profession. There remains, however the possibility that he sought the aid of those who minister to the criminal fraternity-such as those struck off the medical list for reasons of ineptitude or shoddy practice. We may never know-but I fancy it is time for lunch.'

We took our refreshment at a nearby stall offering game pies, which were hot and deliciously spiced. At one sharp a hansom drew up, the driver evidently under some previous instruction. We climbed in to journey in silence, passing the magnificent new bascule bridge being constructed before at length crossing the river at London Bridge. As we progressed through Southwark I could scarce contain myself-but when we approached the bridge at Westminster curiosity overcame me. 'Really, Holmes, you might tell me where you are taking me.' 'There's no mystery to it. We are approaching the place now.' Holmes indicated the wide avenue that was Whitehall, the cab turning into Scotland Yard. My astonishment at finding myself at the headquarters of the Metropolitan police was short-lived, the cab depositing us at a rather shabby door to the rear of the famous building, Holmes leaving his bag of tools in the care of the driver.

A short passage led to a back stair-case, where we were met by a uniformed Sergeant who first asked if we had any weapons about us before escorting us up several flights to a rather sombre and austere corridor, then to a plain door, knocking discreetly. A voice from within rang out briskly, bidding us to enter. At once, the Sergeant flung open the door, marched in, halting three paces short of a large, highly polished desk where he snapped out a salute worthy of any Guards drill Sergeant. As the recipient of the salute returned it, in a booming voice that made Holmes wince, the Sergeant shouted out; 'Sir, beg permission to report, Sir. Doctor Watson and Mr. Holmes here as per orders, Sir.' 'Thank you, Sergeant. Dismissed.' Standing, the figure behind the desk was an impressive one, be-monocled in a simple blue tunic, the weathered features accented by a fine moustache. 'Gentlemen, thank you for your prompt attendance.' We took our seats, I for one being none the wiser as to the identity of this fine fellow, until Holmes introduced us. 'Sir. Charles, Doctor of Medicine John Watson, late of the Berkshire Regiment, Doctor, Sir. Charles Warren, Commissioner of the Metropolitan police.'

I was staggered; the Commissioner!. Nonetheless, I felt I owed it to Holmes to maintain my composure, greeting the Commissioner with as much *gravitas* as the situation merited. 'I understand you to be an amateur detective, Mr. Holmes.' 'Quite so, Sir. Charles-I would go so far as to suggest I have been of some use to the official force on occasion.' 'Indeed you have, as more than one of my detectives have readily admitted-though of your contributions the popular press remains ignorant, perhaps mercifully so.' The Commissioner reached for a silver cigar box, an offering both Holmes and myself accepted. Soon, the smoke of three fine Habano cigars was curling lazily towards the ceiling. Taking the opportunity to inspect my surroundings, I noticed a number of artefacts from the Orient and several framed photographs of Sir. Charles as a military man. As Holmes seemed content in silence, it was Sir. Charles' military background that I inquired about. The Commissioner gave us a brief list of his remarkable exploits, both in Jerusalem as an Archaeologist and in the Diamond Fields Horse in the Transvaal region.

It was Holmes who finally turned the conversation to the problem at hand. 'Sir. Charles-it is my belief that the Tabram woman and Mrs. Nichols were murdered by different hands.' The Commissioner nodded, as if in agreement.

'Continue, please.' 'An examination of the scene, combined with my inquiries strongly suggests the initial crime was committed by two men of the Coldstream Guards.' 'I see. Fine regiment, the Coldstreamers, fine regiment. Such a stain on their character could prove extremely damaging, if indeed you are correct in your theoretical assumption. However, Police work, especially that of the area of detection is perhaps beyond the reach of amateur theorising.' This last was a slur on Holmes' abilities and methods, but a look of warning from my friend was enough to relegate any protest of mine to silence. 'Of course I understand the wider implications of my statement, Sir. Charles; there is always the political aspect to be considered. Should any such allegations be made publicly, the damage to the *status quo* could only play into the hands of those who seek to subvert our liberal society.'

Sir. Charles seemed relieved that Holmes had grasped his meaning:- only the year previously had the fenians threatened Her Majesty The Queen, while it was but three years since both the House of Commons and the Tower of London had been shaken by their dynamite. 'What, then, do you propose, Holmes, for the Tabram business?. There is little chance of finding the killers without a public scandal; soldier's wives are not the best custodians of secrets.' I found this offhand remark of Sir. Charles' offensive, but merely tightened my jaw. It was not for me to comment on his views. 'What I propose, Sir. Charles, will not prove acceptable to you; namely the questioning by myself of guardsmen from the garrison. Therefore I have little choice, but to break every standard and rule by which I measure myself and leave-for the time being, at least, the matter with the official police. At the very least, I should ask that you as a military man ask a trusted officer to compile a list of all the men unaccounted for at the time of the killing.' 'And then?.' 'Perhaps the two men will be identified. If so, they can either be discharged dishonourably-discretely, of course or posted somewhere suitably remote.' 'And what of this other murderer you suspect of the Nichols woman's murder?.' 'Oh, more constables on the beat, extra detectives assigned to the area, nothing that could be said to be unreasonable when a savage lunatic is at large.' 'Would that it were so easy, Holmes, I can't even secure for my men a decent supply of good boots, let alone fill the deficiencies in our rolls. The Metropolis is woefully under-served by both uniformed and C.I.D. men alike and the Receiver will not give an inch!.'

The Commissioner rose, our signal to stand. 'Gentlemen, I must apologise. It is rare to find such discretion in matters as delicate as these heinous crimes. I have myself come to a decision that gives me cause for hope. With immediacy of effect I am instructing the Assistant Commissioner to take the unusual measure of placing this matter under a single office. You may have heard the name of Donald Swanson in the course of your investigations?.' Holmes inclined his head, replying verbally for my benefit. 'The Chief Inspector to which the Commissioner refers is none other than the man who recovered Lady Dysart's jewels and was personally responsible for preventing several fenian bombings in the capital. No finer choice could be made.' 'I am gratified you agree with my choice. You may rest assured, Mr. Holmes, I shall act upon your requests and shall ensure their fulfilment. As to the other matter, I hope we can take it that our conversation today contained no reference to any regiment of Her Majesty's Army.' Holmes gave his word for both of us and we took our leave of the great man, who had given so freely of his precious time to ensure the Empire suffered no damage from the actions of two unworthy men, cowards who had killed a defenceless woman.

CHAPTER VIII
THE HANBURY STREET OUTRAGE

The morning of Saturday the eighth of September shall remain in my memory as long as I shall live. It was on that cool morning, a westerly wind blowing away the last remnants of the showers from the night before, that I awoke to Holmes' fist banging urgently on my door. I threw on my robe and joined him in the sitting-room, where a rather nervous young fellow perched on the edge of the sofa. Holmes poured coffee for our guest, while I helped myself from the pot of tea on the dining table. At length the man spoke. 'Gentlemen, my name is Outram, Sergeant of Detectives Outram and I am currently on watch duty in the Whitechapel District.' 'Yes, Watson, the Detective Sergeant has, I fear grim news.'

Our guest had indeed come with such news. At six o'clock that morning a dreadful discovery had been made. A man named Davis, a resident of 29, Hanbury Street was entering the yard to the rear of the premises when he caught sight of the body of a woman, most horribly arranged and mutilated. 'We do not have the luxury of time, Watson, I have sent for a cab and Detective Sergeant Outram assures me the scene has been preserved intact.' 'That is correct-although the body has been removed to the mortuary.' Holmes closed his eyes at this, his jaw clenching momentarily. 'On whose orders?.' Why, Dr. Phillips, the police surgeon gave the word to remove the body, so as to allow a proper examination.' 'Hardly intact, then.' Holmes paced the room, his machine-like mind evidently tabulating at a furious pace. Pausing, he turned to the Detective Sergeant. 'Who was the senior man present?.' 'That would be Francis-Inspector Abberline-he's been working these murders on a brief from Chief Inspector

Swanson.'

At this moment Mrs. Hudson knocked, to admit a breathless young lad carrying a large envelope marked with the words 'Photographic Evidence-not to be opened unless by recipient'. One look at the lad told me he had the symptoms of shock, which was confirmed by Holmes' cursory examination of the seal upon the envelope. 'You weren't meant to have seen the contents of this. Watson, attend the boy will you?.' I did so as the youth seemed on the verge of a faint, seating him on the sofa and offering him a glass of water. After a few minutes, the lad seemed recovered, Holmes sending him on his way with a shilling.

Leaving the Detective Sergeant to find a cab home, Holmes and myself rode towards the scene of this latest atrocity, using the relative silence to examine the photographic evidence taken at the scene. A local photographer had been retained by Holmes for the express purpose of documenting the next murder, which duty he had done-with an accompanying note to the effect that his services would no longer be available. I, for one, could not blame the man:- the pictures were hideous, showing as they did a woman who had been subjected to what can only be described as the work of the devil himself.

Hanbury Street adjoins the modern thoroughfare of Commercial Street, the area being particularly busy on a Saturday. The street was packed with the curious and sight-seers from across the area, making our progress untenable. I paid the cab driver and we made for the adjoining street, where a kindly lady allowed us through to her back garden.

From there, a quick scramble and we found ourselves in the cramped yard that had so recently been host to the most awful of crimes. There was apparently little to see; a few old packing crates, a covered entrance to the cellar of the property and a passageway leading from the yard itself, door wide open. It was behind the door, however, between passage and fence that the ordinary gave way to the macabre; several bloodstains on the ground and a section of fencing bore mute testimony to the ferocity of the attack.

As Holmes made a close examination of the yard, we were interrupted by a uniformed Constable, who reacted angrily to our presence. 'This is no place for the likes of you, go find yer jollies elsewhere!.' Fortunately, we were saved further embarrassment by the arrival of a man in his middle years, evidently a senior man in his bowler hat and impressive sideburns. Prodding at the ground experimentally with his walking cane he seemed amused by the sight of two amateurs caught *in flagrante* at the scene of the crime. His voice, unexpectedly, came in a soft West Country burr, Devon or Dorset. 'Gentlemen-I hope you can explain yourselves-trespass is it?.' 'A minor transgression I assure you, necessitated by the urgency of the situation Inspector Abberline.' The newcomer seemed unsurprised by Holmes' recognition, turning his calm gaze onto myself. 'Your companion I have seen before:- he was in the third row at the Coroner's inquiry into the Nichols murder, in some silly disguise or other, but you... ah!, the Temperance campaigner. It seems, gents, you have some explaining to do after all, down at Commercial Street.' Holmes' reply was to reach into his coat, producing an envelope with a flourish. After reading the letter within, the Inspector handed it back with a look of curiosity. 'You have friends in high places, but you've none here, *Mister* Holmes. This is murder-and no place for outsiders either. You might fancy yourselves safe on these streets, but I know otherwise. I'd advise you to make your way out the way you came in:- there's a crowd outside and they're frightened. When people round here become frightened, people-*outside* people get hurt. Good morning to you both.' As the insufferable man left, the smile was back on Holmes' face.

'So, that letter you showed Abberline was one of authority?.' I asked the question as the streets slid by the windows of the hansom. 'From the Assistant Commissioner himself, drafted at the request of a friend. It grants the bearer certain privileges such as unobstructed access to areas otherwise closed. I have friends in many places, Watson-this one especially well-placed to assist us in this terrible business.' The cab ride took us to a workhouse yard off Old Montague Street, in usage as a temporary Mortuary. It was in the shed that I made an examination of the body, by then identified as Annie Chapman, of the same immoral profession as the previous victim. Even Holmes was shaken by what lay in that crude wooden box, a woman in her late forties who had been eviscerated, her womb removed-with the cause of death a massive cut to the throat that had all but severed the head from the body. We left the body in the care of the Constable guarding the premises, Holmes directing the cab driver to take us to the police station in Commercial Street. Once there, he instructed me to remain, returning after no more than ten minutes. We rode back to Baker Street, Holmes in quiet mood and myself by now thoroughly dejected by the seeming hopelessness of it all.

CHAPTER IX
AN INTERLUDE IN BEDLAM

Monday morning dawned brisk and overcast, as if the very sky was ill at ease. A convivial breakfast helped settle any feelings of lassitude remaining from the travails of the recent past, thus refreshed I sat in my chair with the Times and a bowl of 'ship's'. Holmes was in fine form, filling the room with his interpretation of an aria from *De Fledermaus,* his playing of the violin somehow both delicate and vibrant. At length he settled into his chair opposite mine, filling his briar with the pungent mixture inhabiting the persian slipper. Pausing before lighting the dreadful thing, Holmes remarked on the case at hand. 'You know, Watson, this business really is intriguing. Twice now and no doubt again the foulest of criminals strikes, leaving clues in the process, yet his identity remains as impenetrable as the Tower of London itself.' I asked of him; 'You were able to identify the men involved in the Tabram case-why the difficulty here?.' 'Ansell and Littlefield-the men concerned-had made the error of wearing their uniforms-including, with no small irony a good conduct medal in the case of the latter. It was merely a matter of elimination; who was on duty, who had leave and so forth. A child could do it. No, my friend, no-these last two murders present us with a singular challenge meritorious of a novel approach.'

I tapped out my pipe, curious on a few matters. I asked my friend both what had happened to Ansell and Littlefield-and what his remark to Sir. Charles had meant, about his being a freemason. 'Oh, there's little to tell, Watson. An elderly clerk of works was found dead from unknown causes-most probably accidental, by the Midland Railway,

35

somewhere near Rotherham. At this moment, no doubt, the two are languishing in a cell somewhere convenient to the crime, for which they will shortly be arrested, tried and hanged.' There could be no doubt these men were the killers of Martha Tabram, yet I shall never fully extinguish the feeling of disquiet at the methods Holmes and the official police employed to suppress the case. We only ever spoke of it twice-the second occasion being one of the few arguments I ever had with Holmes, who continued to insist the aid it secured him was vital to progressing the case of the Whitechapel fiend. As to Sir. Charles being a freemason, Holmes merely pointed out that the Commissioner wore a masonic charm on his watch chain, adding that many senior police officials being freemasons were bound by oath to aid each other. Thus, securing a suitable corpse for the subterfuge should not have proved too vexing a task-especially since, he claimed, provincial masons were usually keen to assist their London brethren for obvious reasons of self-advancement.

Holmes then rose from his chair to his untidy desk, reaching behind to bring out a blackboard. Rummaging in his drawer yielded the chalk, Holmes using the sleeve of his dressing gown to erase the diagram chalked on the board. He drew an oval shape to the left of the board, a doorway to the centre and a noose to the right. 'Here-' - he indicated the oval- 'We have the population of London, gathered together in a single mass. Our door here will admit just one of these millions, so acting as a filter. This individual is the one suited for the noose, the man we shall see hang.' 'But, Holmes-how do we make the correct selection?, the odds must be several million to one.' 'Let us see if we can lower those odds. How many of the mass are female?, the odds now fall considerably. How many of the remaining male population take a size eight shoe?-lower still as such footprints were present at both scenes.'

I began to see the method; with each clue Holmes was nearer to the mark. 'But your mass must still number thousands, perhaps more.' 'There you see it. The problem with this method-I call it the Application of Data Filtering, is that in itself it is hardly likely to reduce any large number enough to reveal the criminal. At most it can act as a screen to separate the innocent from suspicion.' Watson it is my contention the single factor overlooked in these crimes is that most remarkable feature of humanity-that of the human mind itself. What do you say to a trip to the countryside?.'

Barely an hour later I was enjoying the bracing air and light of a morning drive. The journey out to the notorious Lunatic Asylum at Colney Hatch took me through the North of the Metropolis, past Hampstead and the great cemetery at Highgate before the climb to the hill Muswell is named for. The Asylum gates were open and I found the drive to the entrance hall an enlightening experience. Small parties of inmates were set to work tending the gardens and the atmosphere seemed far removed from that of bedlam. At Holmes' request I presented myself to the Medical Administration Office and was presently shown through to a large room in which a single desk sat squarely beneath a tall sash window, before which was standing Dr. Milton Epshaw. A young yet eminent member of the Medico-Psychological Association, Dr. Epshaw was a leading light in his field and the man to which Holmes had entrusted the singular task of explaining the unfathomable; the workings of the lunatic mind. I presented my card... and the fellow began to eat it!. 'Sir, if this is a joke it seems in poor taste.' Smiling, the younger man rinsed down the bite of card from a carafe of water. 'What you would expect from an inmate perhaps?. There we must begin.'

Over the next hour, mostly listening and occasionally questioning I found myself humbled by the quality of intellect displayed by this physician of the mind. Before taking me on a tour of the Asylum, Milton – for he insisted always on being spoken to and by Christian names-rang for a pot of coffee and opened his humidor. We smoked and drank as befits two colleagues, albeit ones in vastly differing speciality. 'So, Doctor-Milton; what of the conditions of psychosis?-the criminal mania at work on the streets of London must be the display of a psycho-social mind?.' 'John, that is a problematic question; we do not have such patients under our care - nothing close, thankfully. Our patients-the basis for my experience, are often tortured souls driven to self-mutilation and self-destruction, harming others is actually rare in even a state of psychosis.'

Checking his watch against a clock on the wall he finished his tea. 'What I can tell you is that conditioning seems of importance; so that when a maniac attacks a woman approaching her middle years it suggests a hatred of women of that age or appearance-something about the unfortunate victim sparks uncontrollable rage and violence, as might stem from feelings of resentment concerning the childhood of the maniac.' 'So, he might be attacking, in his frenzied condition, his own mother?.' My host nodded, with an open-handed gesture towards the door and we took to the long corridor outside. 'Yes, that is one observation that is provable under laboratory conditions-the other possibilities revolve in the newly-discovered area of psycho-sexual medicine, as pioneered by the young Austrian Freud.' 'I had not heard the name.' 'Few outside Vienna have – I only know of his works through a colleague who worked at a clinic near... ah, Mary, I'm glad I found you...' A matronly nurse frowned her disapproval of the Doctor's familiar style. 'We shall visit the Male Acutes-if you could be a dear and hold the fort until our return...?'. Frostily, the nurse bowed her head to one side as we took the corridor, our footsteps resounding along the tilework.

'The Asylum is massive-how many patients can it hold?.' 'Ah, good honest facts -the cornerstone of the British psyche.' A friendly smile upon his face, the Doctor recounted the figures that he must have retained for the enlightenment of visitors. 'The place opened with twelve hundred and fifty beds-we have nearer to two and a half thousand patients here today. The Commissioners in Lunacy evidently failed to scale one of the greatest problems of any modern society. We are walking along part of a six mile corridor system in eighteen hundred and eighty-four feet of building in an estate including its own railway station, chapel and farm...'

The streets were already wreathed in fog by the time the carriage rattled to a halt outside 221b. Although I felt I had learned much about disorders of the mind, the motley collection of patients I had encountered did not seem to fit Holmes' ideas of an insane murderer. I had asked my host about suitable candidates, but with only a few exceptions the inmates of Colney Hatch were gentle souls tormented by their condition; those rare cases capable of violence had been admitted before the killings in Whitechapel had begun. Setting such thoughts aside, I smiled at the familiar gait of our landlady-Mrs. Hudson was returning from her visit to an infirm friend, but-how typical of her!-had left a salver of sandwiches. Wresting these from her grasp and declining her offer of a hot meal I took our repast up to the familiar sanctum of our rooms. Holmes himself was emerging from the direction of the bathroom, and was absent for some minutes during which I had time to both fill my pipe and peruse Holmes' chalkings. Taking the chalk I began to draw the outline of a figure hanging from the noose he had drawn that morning, writing below the doomed cartoon some ideas fashioned from some of the knowledge I had gleaned from my visit with Dr. Epshaw at Colney Hatch. HATRED OF MATERNAL FIGURES - MANIA TRIGGERED BY: LIKENESS OF FACE OR STYLE OF DRESS - PROBABLE IMPOTENCE, POSSIBLY RELATED TO PROFESSION OF VICTIMS. A clap of the hands pronounced Holmes' ablutions complete, selecting a cheese and pickle sandwich I settled myself to see if my day had been well spent. Evidently, it had; Holmes ran his finger across the bold characters as he absorbed their meaning. 'Watson. Dear, Dear Watson-you have indeed helped us progress. If these crimes are to be of any use to the science of deduction surely it lies here. The man we seek is a solitary individual, a man with a piteous childhood and unable to consort with women. Unable to satisfy the animal urges he seeks to suborn them with deeper, darker lusts. Perhaps he was once scorned by a member of the underclass of women that he now destroys.'

I puffed at my pipe to keep it lit, secretly delighted to have helped my friend with his scientific rationale of the criminal psyche. I removed it, pointing at Holmes with the stem.'If only the dead could speak.' The words had hardly left my lips than Holmes had sprung into life, frantically scribbling on a sheet of paper before ringing for Mrs. Hudson. 'Mrs. Hudson, please can you have this sent by cable?, it is rather urgent.' My ignorance must have showed, Holmes taking pity upon me. 'Not for the first time you have stimulated my brain with what you would consider an everyday remark-the dead *shall* speak, Watson, furthermore our odds will fall further as they do.' Matching action to word, he erased the oval shape on the board, replacing it with a far smaller one. Knowing better than to press him on the subject, I refrained from further comment.

I had thought we would be resuming our surreptitious patrols, but Holmes was clearly preoccupied, venturing out on some expedition of a secretive nature. Returning with an armful of parcels, Holmes then withdrew to his bedroom where he remained until, having missed supper, he set off alone and was not to return until after I had retired for the night. Tuesday and Wednesday saw me attending to my associates' patients in Knightsbridge. By now somewhat weary of moneyed dipsomaniacs and hypochondriacs, I was heartened at the sight of Holmes in the patient's sitting room, apparently in reluctant conversation with an elderly Colonel here for his bunions. The last patient of the day, Holmes came in to the consulting room, clutching his side and walking bow-legged in melodramatic fashion. 'Its me paraphenarium, Doctor, it's slipped again.' 'It's your cranium you mean-and it's incurable. Holmes, to what do I owe the honour?.' 'I have come on a mission of some importance, Watson; to relieve you from all this tedium. Tonight, we must dress for the theatre-our research takes an unexpected turn:- into the realm of the supernatural.'

CHAPTER X
THE MAGICIAN

Any thoughts of a night at Drury Lane or Covent Garden were dashed, however as our cab turned into Belgravia that evening. Eventually we pulled up outside an impressive villa standing in its own grounds. At the word from the driver, the gates were opened by two uniformed flunkies. We alighted and were admitted by a cadaverous manservant who ushered us into a tastefully furnished salon. Several other guests were present, including a prominent member of the Cabinet and at least one titled Count from one of the houses of Europe. Whatever was to occur, it would do so in noble company. We were served with drinks by girls in oriental costume, the atmosphere one of a cordial expectance. At length a gong was sounded by a muscular lascar who stood impassively, arms folded as we filed past him through a set of heavy red velvet curtains into a large room, a ball room or similar now set out as a theatre of some kind. We took our seats in the darkened space, a crepuscular green glow lighting more curtains, these last having a pair of embroidered Chinese dragons upon them.

My old friend curiosity was nagging at me, until the sounding of temple bells and a monotonous chanting began, the sound seeming to come from all around us. The curtains opened to reveal a modest stage, on which sat cross-legged a be-robed figure. As if sensing my impatience, Holmes whispered across. 'This may be instructive-try to perceive and uncover the artifice involved, Watson. It is important to ensure that this spectacle is convincing in effect.' I had little time to consider this odd request-from the assembled audience there came a collective gasp as the figure began to levitate, rising slowly from the stage to come to a rest-still sitting-some four feet above the stage!. Before my very eyes I saw it; the magician floated out from the stage, *actually passing over* the first row of spectators, then hovering back over the stage, slowly settling back down into place. With a flourish, the robe was thrown back, revealing a most extraordinary fellow. Seemingly half chinese-half caucasian the man who now stood commandingly on the stage was around six feet in height, of medium build, hair slicked back with a moustache in plaits of the oriental style. Clad in silken robes of a lustrous green there was no doubt the man had the appearance of a mystic from the far east.

'Greetings. The name I shall use tonight is Shandu:- my own name being impronouncable to mortal tongues.' As the weird figure spoke, his voice seemed to penetrate to my very core with its uncanny sibilance and resonance. My mother came from a long line of Russian Nobility, my father was a Tibetan Llama, cast out of the Temple of the Jade Cloud for consorting with someone from what is known there as the Lower Earth. Tonight I shall demonstrate before you the mind skills of the orient and the magic known only to the monks of the temple-and to myself.' Shandu then clapped his hands three times, at which a gong sounded and the lighting dimmed further, leaving only his face and hands visible. He began to chant, presumably in Tibetan, clapping his hands sharply-at which the ghost of a young woman appeared, floating in the very air before us!. Shimmering in the sepulchral light, first fading then re-appearing, the woman appeared to be reaching out to us, appealing for aid that we could not provide. 'I see the spirit of a lost soul in distress. I shall attempt to send her to her eternal rest, in the land of dreams beyond the veil of existence. To so do I must correctly name her, a task which I can only accomplish through the use of a suitable medium.' Turning to the audience, Shandu thrust his arm outwards, his finger roaming over the audience, coming to rest on the Count. 'You, Sir. Count Arno von Seydlitz, I believe.' The Count stood, bowing stiffly before resuming his seat. 'I am so.' 'Sir. My assistant will furnish you with chalk and slate. If you would, please write down the first female name that comes to mind. '

An attractive girl in a silk kimono appeared from the shadows, handing the Count a piece of chalk, which he used to write on the slate she held. The girl held the slate facing the audience, the name Gudrun visible to us. To his assistant, Shandu inquired; 'Has the Count written a name for us?.' 'Indeed he has done so, Master.' The mystic seemed lost in thought, raising a hand to his temple. 'I must ask all present to concentrate on the name the Count has given us-I shall use the collected psychic emanations in this place to read the name. I see the letter 'G', an 'N'... 'Gud, Gudrun!, the name on the slate is Gudrun-is it not so, Count?.' Holmes touched my arm as gasps of amazement and applause rippled around the room. 'Well, Watson?, what do you think of it?.' 'It's uncanny, Holmes-the man's either inhuman or the cleverest of tricksters.' 'Just so, the latter I mean.'

We sat through the rest of the performance, which included a display of abilities so wondrous that even to Holmes it must have seemed proof of the occult. Afterwards, when the other guests had departed we were granted access to the room set aside for Shandu as a dressing room. The man who bade us enter on knocking was, however clearly an Englishman-of the mystic Shandu all that remained were some silken robes on a sofa and several jars of theatrical make-up. 'Good evening, Gentlemen. My name is Maskelyne, John Nevil Maskelyne. I am, by profession a stage magician, though I have an interest in the research of the occult.' 'Mr. Maskelyne, I must introduce my colleague and friend Dr. John Watson. You will recall that I cabled you that we required a demonstration of your illusions, now that we have had such I must complement you-I have never seen the like.' 'Thank you, Mr. Holmes, it is always a pleasure to work for an *aficionado.*'

Holmes' features assumed an expression of severity then. 'What follows must remain in the strictest confidence. Are you aware of the series of murders currently being committed in the district of Whitechapel?.' Mr. Maskelyne confirmed that he had, indeed been following the story in the popular press. 'Dr. Watson and myself have been unofficially retained to attempt a resolution of these abhorrent crimes-it is my intention to draw the killer out, to compel him to reveal himself. To this end, I have arranged a suitable venue for a *séance* to take place, the result of which being announced as likely to result in the naming of the killer by means of the occult. Will you perform this séance for us?.' Mr. Maskelyne considered the request for a long moment, finally nodding. 'It would have to be arranged to my exact instruction, the optical effect involving the spirit apparition is in particular reliant on exactitude of performance.'

The great magician then broke with tradition to demonstrate how his performance that night had been achieved so convincingly, the hall now well-lit. The levitation effect was simplicity itself-the 'seated figure' of Maskelyne's Shandu character being merely a robe around a wire construct, 'levitated' by him standing-all the while wearing trousers of purest black to conceal the trickery. 'But how did you manage to float over the audience?.' My question was answered by

Maskelyne, who stood over a particular spot on the stage, calling for his hidden accomplices to raise him. A board duly rose from the stage, acting as a seat for the illusionist, the board being fed through the curtains to convey him above the seats. 'The board is both re-inforced and counter-weighted:- attached to a small frame on wheels which my assistants push to and fro. Invisible in the dimmed light, the effect is, as you can both attest, rather good.' Holmes grinned wolfishly at the chicanery. 'I assume the mind-reading trick to be a variation on the Chicago method, in which the assistant feeds the name to the performer by means of a code.' 'You seem to have an extensive knowledge of stage magic, Mr. Holmes-my assistant had to convey the name 'Gudrun' in this case; her words 'Indeed he has done so, Master' were the code. 'Indeed' beginning with 'I', two letters previous to that in the Alphabet being 'G' and so forth.' 'A numeric substitution cypher-and applied to remarkable effect. Thank you, Mr. Maskelyne-the details of the séance are contained in this letter, along with our address at Baker Street should you have any requests.' With that, Holmes passed an envelope to the magician and we left, a cab having already been called by the servants at the gate.

   With the 'séance' we had arranged due to take place on the Thursday, Holmes and myself had but a few days to complete our preparations. Firstly, the venue-the Pavilion theatre in the Whitechapel Road. The theatre had already been staging a production, but a few words from the local constabulary secured it for our usage on the night. At his own expense, Holmes had printed several hundred bills advertising the event. Under the banner line 'SEANCE-THE DEAD SHALL SPEAK', these notices stated that the noted Russian clairvoyant 'Vladimir Zukov', adviser to the Russian Imperial Court would perform the séance, using his famed powers of second-sight to commune with the dead. A further statement was that Mr. Zukov had assisted the police forces of three Continents in his naming of the culprits in several infamous murder cases. The wording of these papers would, Holmes assured me, be enough to appeal to the murderer's sense of invincibility-a common feature amongst maniacs.

Under the industrious direction of their leader, Wiggins, the Baker Street irregulars set about the East End, papering any available surface with our advertisements. I began to think they had gone too far when, while in Oxford Street a police wagon passed by me, with one of the ubiquitous bills affixed to the rear. During this period, Holmes resumed his duties as 'PC Melosh', but the streets of Whitechapel were oddly subdued by night. Returning for a few hours of much-needed sleep on the Thursday morning, Holmes remarked wearily:- 'The city is in fear, Watson, deep in the grip of the emotion. The people of the East End feel themselves safe only in numbers, yet ironically it is in those numbers that most crime is perpetrated. We must place our faith in the abilities of Mr. Maskelyne-and that Inspector Abberline remains true to form.' 'Abberline?, how does he figure in your plans, Holmes?.' 'Simply this; through means of an intermediary, I have let it be known that I have no faith in the Inspector or his abilities as a detective. He now knows that the séance will be taking place and that I shall be present. I fully expect him to accept the inferred challenge with his presence-a factor that can only assist to un-nerve our man even further, hopefully provoking him into an uncharacteristic error.'

We set out for the theatre with an hour to spare, with only myself aware that the rather drunk and elderly sailor beside me was, in fact Holmes in his latest role. For myself I

47

had chosen a threadbare raincoat, trousers patched at the knee courtesy of the Salvation Army. The early evening was unusually balmy, the air stagnant and oppressive. The jarvey dropped Holmes and myself off at opposite ends of the street, which ensured our separate arrival, part of the subterfuge necessitated by the plan. I joined the queue for the séance, composed as it was of a lively and expectant crowd. One poor girl told me she was there to find out what had become of her friend, the unfortunate Mrs. Nichols. The auditorium was reached through a long passage, the conversation loud and coarse in the way of the area. Far from being shocked, I found the experience rather refreshing, the honest and straightforward nature of these people evident.

The seats rapidly filled, with more left to stand in the aisles-underlining the importance of this to the people of the East End. Although I tried, my eyes could not make out Holmes in the dim lighting. I had to trust that my friend was present, that Inspector Abberline was also in the theatre-and that, should I have need of it, my service revolver would not fail me. The house lights went down and the curtains rose, to reveal a breathtaking sight. Under a backdrop of shimmering stars a throne-like chair sat on an otherwise empty stage. As the audience began to chatter excitedly, a green vapour began forming in the very air above us, luminous and eerie. The smoke then shot through the auditorium to hover over the chair, where it began to coalesce into a vaguely human form, finally resolving into the figure of a Russian monk, the emerald pendant around his neck the only display of opulence. This caused a hullabaloo and much gasping. The crowd only fell silent as the figure rose from the chair, standing with hands in sleeves until the silence was overwhelming. Tossing his cowl back, the face of Zukov was not recognisable as Maskelyne, the pale, gaunt features partially obscured by a long beard and eyes of an un-natural green, intense and flashing like the stone he wore.

'Here is Zukov, Vladimir Zukov of the House of Zukov, counsellor to His Excellent Majesty's Imperial Court for a thousand generations.' The voice, as with that of Shandu, seemed to come from everywhere and nowhere, the crowd now spellbound with the weird presence before them. 'I have come here to this place on the command of the dead-there is a terrible injustice in this City, a tear in the very fabric of its soul, one which must be corrected before the curtain between the living and the dead is destroyed forever.' 'Zukov' clapped his hand to his temple in dramatic fashion, staggering as he did so, to gasps of horror from the theatre. 'I must work quickly tonight, I think. The spirits are impatient tonight:- is there anyone present by the family name of Joseph?.' There was some laughter, I myself counted no fewer than five hands visible from where I sat. 'I have with me now the spirit of Ishmail, who has a message for his family.' Now there were just two hands raised. Suddenly, Zukov's features seemed to change, wrinkles appearing across his forehead as his beard began to turn a whiteish silver. In the cracked tones of an elderly man, he began singing a Russian folk tune, the words sad and full of pathos. A voice cried out from the darkness; 'Poppa!, Poppa, its me Rachel!, oh Poppa please tell me you see me!.' 'Rachel?, little Rachel? *skol'ko let, skol'ko zim!* how you have grown!, do not worry about me-I am with your mother and old friends long since passed. You will do well here in England and marry a tailor's son. I must go now, Rachel-have many children. *Dosvidanya!.*' At this, Zukov slumped back into his chair, his features returning to their original appearance as he waved away the spontaneous applause that had erupted from the crowd. Indeed, even though I knew it to be hocus-pocus and flammery I could not help but join in the laudation.

After a display of levitation came the séance proper. Assistants placed a heavy circular table on the stage and having placed Zukov's chair behind it facing the audience, set down another four slightly to the sides so Zukov remained visible throughout the proceedings. The mystic called for absolute silence, warning that any disruption would break the psychic link to the realm of the dead. Volunteers were called for, the chosen four escorted to the table by ushers. The house lighting then appeared to dim, although I knew it was actually part of the scheme, the lights on the audience slightly brighter as a radiant green glow washed over them. Somewhere in that place was Holmes, his senses no doubt primed for the unwitting killer to reveal himself. A female shriek of alarm returned my attention to the stage, where the participants had linked hands with Zukov around the table, which last was rocking and heaving as if in the grip of unseen hands.

'I, Zukov, counsellor to the Imperial Court commands the spirits present to reveal themselves, I, Zukov bid them to come forth with the invocation of the Ascended Masters and the Ancient Order of the Golden Circle. Let spirit become material, shadow become light!.' The lights flickered, then, in a flash of brilliant light a woman's form appeared over the table, her long hair floating as if in water. 'Witchcraft!, black magic!.' A man's shout of accusation rang out, followed by a struggle, two burly men wrestling the man from the auditorium with some difficulty. As the commotion subsided, Zukov spoke to reassure the unsettled crowd. 'It is to be expected. The presence of the spirits is a fearsome thing. We continue.' Speaking to the wraith above, he asked; 'What is your name, my child?.' As if from the tomb, a far-off voice answered him. 'My name was, I cannot remember my name, Sir. Such things are not needed in the place beyond life.' 'Try to remember, child-I hear the letter 'M', did your name start thus?.' The ghostly apparition seemed to incline it's head, as if in thought. 'Why, yes, Sir. Mary-I was known as Mary Ann...'. 'It's old Poll Nichols!, Mary Ann Nichols!.' This interjection came from a stout little fellow in the uniform of a Hospital Porter. 'Thank you, my friend-but, please you must return to your seat.' Zukov then raised both hands to his temple, the agreed signal that he was about to reach the vital question. It would all depend on this moment!.

CHAPTER XI
THE FACE OF EVIL

Zukov, eyes closed in apparently deep concentration appeared to be seized by some invisible force, shaking and convulsing in his chair. The spectral form seemed to collapse downwards into the magician, whose features now transfigured into those of 'Polly' Nichols. One of the volunteers, a gentleman of respectable appearance questioned the spirit. 'Were you taken by foul means?, was it murder?.' 'Nichol's' voice answered 'It was, Sir. I was cut something awful, then I was floating above meself, watching 'im wot done me-'e done wicked things to me, Sir., things as such as I can't say.' 'We are here to help you, Polly, to try to stop this beast. Tell me, my girl, can you describe him?, name him?.' Giggling in a way that sent shivers down my spine, the otherworldly voice answered. 'What's it worth?.' 'Why, child, the peace of eternal rest, of knowing that you have atoned for a life of sin and immorality.' 'Tell 'im, Pol!.' A woman's voice came from the cheap seats. Slowly, the mystic rose from his chair, his features still obscured by those of the slain woman. Raising an arm to gesture vaguely to the crowded theatre, 'Polly' spoke with a vengeful hiss. 'There he is!, thats 'im that done fer me right there!, 'im!, there!.' The audience was in uproar at this, with everyone present trying to get a glimpse of the killer. With horrifying suddenness, a whirl of rolling smoke and the cry of 'Fire!', within seconds the whole place was pandemonium, others taking up the cry as the thick choking smoke billowed down towards the front rows.

The panicked throng began fighting for the exit, hysteria beginning to spread alarmingly as the surge carried me with it. I had cause to attend a lady who, having fallen, had been trampled upon by several pairs of feet. The poor woman was suffering fractures to wrist and clavicle, the former I addressed with a makeshift sling fashioned from handkerchiefs offered by some of the shamefaced bystanders together with my own. The clanging of a bell outside announced the arrival of the first fire engine, the firemen rushing into the theatre, regardless of any risk to themselves. Seized with admiration for these fine fellows, I followed-and stopped dead in my stride, for there, up in the 'gods' the shapes of two men could just be seen, fighting for their very lives-a cap fell down from the balcony:- Holmes!. I held my handkerchief to my face, plunging into the smoke as I made my way blindly towards the stairs to the upper levels. More by feel than sight, I took the stairs, the fumes intolerable to my burning lungs.

Somehow, I managed to reach the highest tier, to see Holmes viciously kicked to the head by his assailant. Enraged, I charged forth, as Holmes rose, giddied from the blow-only to be pushed over the hand-rail!. The face that turned towards me on my shout was brutish, a brown-haired man with a thick moustache in his mid to late thirties, an appalling bruising covering the left eye. Of sturdy build, the thug was clearly possessed of immense strength and cunning to have bettered Holmes, himself no mean boxer. His eyes glittering blackly, the fiend let out a derisive laugh. 'I'll fix you, you lunatic.' My words came as a growl, my throat raw from the smoke. 'Lunatic, am I?, who the devil are you to make such a remark?.' The accent was broad Irish, the fists raised before me calloused and scarred as from years spent labouring. I raised my own, determined to make this killer pay for his pleasures, but a groan alerted me to the railing, where a hand had appeared. 'Well, my presumptuous friend-what'll it be?, save your man there or a beating from me?.' I lunged for the rail, gripping Holmes' wrist and reaching down, grasped his coat, taking the strain to enable him to find purchase on the ornately carved wood of the stalls. Heaving with all my strength, I managed to raise my colleague up to chest height, dimly aware of the noise of the Irishman's boots on the carpet as he departed. Holmes reached into my pocket, his fingers finding my revolver. 'No, Holmes-you'll fall!.' 'Watson, he mustn't get away-shoot him in the leg!.'

As Holmes tumbled over onto the front row, I snatched up the revolver from where it had fallen, whirling around into the aim, just as the thug fled through the far opening towards the back stairs and a fireman appeared in it, a fraction of a second before I would have fired. Easing the hammer down, I swiftly pocketed the revolver, following Holmes as he ran after the Irishman. We were unceremoniously grabbed by the fireman and hustled down the stairs, despite Holmes' loud protests. At the bottom, we were ordered in no uncertain terms to vacate the building. 'He went up, to the rigging gallery-I'm certain of it.' Holmes muttered to me, just as the familiar figure of Inspector Abberline stepped from the crowd of onlookers-and arrested us!.

CHAPTER XII
INSPECTOR ABBERLINE'S WARNING

The 'black maria' turned into the yard behind Leman Street police station and we were bundled into the building, to an office. In the open doorway, Inspector Abberline seemed to be involved in a heated discussion with a uniformed Sergeant, which ended with his reminding the latter that demotion was a more than likely prospect. Shutting the door with his foot, he bade us sit, throwing down a sheaf of papers upon the desk, perching himself on the edge. Regarding first Holmes then myself at length, he ran a hand over his brow, evidently a man under some enormous strain-presumably the seemingly insoluble nature of the case. The room itself was cramped, cluttered with shelves and cupboards overflowing with paper-work. There was evidently a problem with the gas, for the sole illumination came from an oil-lamp on the desk.

'Look, I'm not one for speeches-can't abide them. I'm a busy man, so hows about you two explain just how you came to be at the Pavilion, why people are seeing ghosts and the like and why I have a complaint from the Commercial Road Fire Brigade that one of their men found himself looking down the barrel of a gun?.' 'Inspector, my name is Doctor John Watson-it was I who aimed the pistol, but not intentionally at the fireman. I was aiming at the killer.' 'The killer?, that *is* handy, I'm looking for a killer too-you don't have a name for him, perhaps an address?.' Holmes, dabbing at his injured head with his handkerchief and clearly in no mood for levity answered for me. 'No name, nor address, Inspector. However, the man is Irish, County Clare and five feet seven or eight, stocky with a prominent moustache and dark brown hair, bruising to the eye. He is wearing a corduroy jacket with patched elbows and leather trim to the collar over woollen trousers, colour dark. Hobnail boots, size unknown. He is a labourer of some description, having a dark tan and calloused hands, favouring a pick to a shovel. further, he likes to fight, having extensive scarring to the knuckles, a cauliflower ear and a boxer's nose. Possibly a cobble fighter at some time, though he is somewhat out of condition. At some time he was a sailor, in the merchant marine, but he has not been aboard ship for some years.'

Abberline took all this in with a look that suggested trouble. Turning to his papers, he selected one, producing a pair of spectacles from a case in his pocket. 'Just before the Chapman murder a cab driver picked up a fare, a man about thirty, five feet six, slim, black hair, waxed 'tache possibly foreign. These others are descriptions of everything from a mad woman to me-do I really slouch?, I must do, says so here. You do see my problem, Mr. Holmes?.' 'Clearly, Inspector, but allow me to tell you why our Irishman is so significant-' A knock at the door interrupted Holmes, Abberline opening it to a Doctor waiting outside. 'Ah, Doctor, thank you-there's your patient.' The Doctor followed Abberline's pointed finger into the room, attending to the abrasions on Holmes' head and temple, cleaning then dressing the wound. Holmes took the chance to use the Doctor's spirits to remove his make-up. When he had left the room, Holmes continued:- 'The seance at the theatre was a device, Inspector, set in place as a lure for the killer. At the very moment when he was to be named, that rather convenient 'fire' broke out-a plumber's smoke rocket or the like, no doubt- (Abberline confirmed this with a nod), but not before I had seen the man both leave his seat, then return to a place from where he was guaranteed a quick exit-there being only an elderly drunkard sailor in his way, or so he imagined.'

56

'Alright Mr. Holmes, I'll play. You describe the man better than most wives could, I wonder about that-in such bad light, place full of smoke as it was. How do you come to conclusions such as the one about picks and shovels then?.' 'I first observed the man by the light of evening outside the theatre, he was smoking a cigarette.' 'And this is the basis for your remarkably complete description of the man's activities and even his trade.' Holmes continued with an even tone and studied patience. 'I should explain that I am a consulting detective, an augmentation to the official force if you like.' 'I don't, Mr. Holmes, far from it.' 'Apparently. However, among my scribblings on the subject I have produced a monograph on the influence of a tradesman's craft upon his hands-including the various patterns of callosity seen with prolonged usage of various tools.' 'And a cracking read too, I'll warrant-alright, but the years spent at sea? no doubt he bore a tattoo, a mermaid perchance, or did he wear an eyepatch and a parrot on his shoulder?.' I was outraged at this and brushed off my friend's attempt to placate my disapprobation. 'Holmes I'll not sit for it. The man nearly kills you and this... *functionary* sits on his perch in mockery. Perhaps, Inspector, you would care to earn your pay by attempting to apprehend this Irishman, or is his parrot the chief suspect?.'

As my tirade ended, the Inspector rose to his feet-and promptly burst out laughing. 'Doctor, you should have taken the silk-you'd have made a fine barrister for the defence!. All right, I've heard enough. Gents, you are free to go-there'll be no charges, this time.' Holmes rose to appeal to the Inspector. 'Charges?, really, Inspector, surely you can see the merits of our presence. Working together, we would increase the likelihood of arrest.' 'Look, Mister-*Doctor*, I've tried to make myself clear-we don't need any help from amateur bloodhounds. Besides-this Irishman is not the Whitechapel Ghoul-the reports from the theatre show he doesn't fit the pattern. At worst, he's guilty of a breach of the Queen's peace and attempted arson, but the theatre management don't need the trouble and I certainly don't need another form to fill out. Do yourselves and me a favour:- find something else to spend your time on, or I'll find something that takes up two years of it and you'll both end up in the clink. We call that a friendly chat, by the way, just so's you don't get any ideas I threatened you gents.'

With nothing to be gained from dallying further, we took our leave and searched for a cab to return to Baker Street, but as we travelled along the Marylebone road Holmes knocked up to the jarvey. 'Driver, to Bradleys the tobacconist!.' We set forth for the Tobacconist's shop, Holmes buying a pound of an especially potent blend from a mixture of turkish and kentucky shag. Meanwhile, a box of *Romeo Y Julieta,* attractively priced, caught my eye. Thus fortified, we decided on a brisk walk back to Baker Street.

CHAPTER XIII
THE IRISH QUESTION

Heavy rain lashing against the window was my welcome from sleep that Friday morning. My mood quickly adjusted to the weather, so it was in low spirits that I found Holmes had not yet risen. The timely arrival of breakfast saved me from depression, our good landlady laying down *The Star* beside my toast. As I consumed my porridge, I soon realised Mrs. Hudson's motive. The front page was filled with yet another lurid article on the Whitechapel murders, but I could not bring myself to read it. The door to Holmes' room opened, revealing that I was not the solitary malcontent present, my friend, unshaven and be-robed, shuffling quietly to the sofa on the length of which he slumped as one defeated. Despite my efforts, Holmes refused to join me at breakfast, acknowledging my existence with the curtest of grunts, a hand to the dressing on his head. Mrs. Hudson arrived to clear the table and, noticing his untouched bowl she sighed to herself. 'Why, Mister Holmes, you've not touched your porridge-can I not interest you with something else?, I've some cold beef or perhaps I could fetch in some fish?.' Holmes made no reply, so I spoke for him. 'Thank you, Mrs. Hudson-I rather think Mr. Holmes unwell, perhaps he will have regained his appetite later.'

Ever wary of Holmes slipping into one of his inactive periods, with the attendant usage of stimulants, I endeavoured to bring my companion back to the active by suggesting we spend the morning at my club, but this was ignored. Clearly, other methods were called for. I tried to direct attention to the case, reading from the *Star* article, commenting aloud on the points of significance. I had just mentioned the statement from Abberline to the effect that he was 'Following in the footsteps of the killer' when Holmes literally sprang from his repose, going to his desk where he began to search through the piles of assorted papers and documents, producing a pamphlet with a triumphal flourish, holding it above his shoulder facing backwards so I could read the title-"A Treatise Upon The Analysis of Footprints". Turning to show me a page of outlines demonstrating shoe sizes, Holmes indicated the pattern for a size eight, pulling back his dressing to reveal an angry wound, the imprint of the thug's heel clearly visible as a dark purple bruise. Taking the booklet from Holmes, I made a comparison, finally deciding on a size ten. 'As I suspected- this Irishman may be the missing link in the chain, though it seems he is not the killer himself...' Holmes re-attached the dressing, disappearing into his room to emerge after ten minutes freshly shaved and smartly dressed.

For some minutes the clatter and squeak of the blackboard was the only sound in the room. Holmes was energetically chalking onto the surface, turning to find that I was, indeed awake. 'Watson, I have it!.' Turning the board to afford me a better view, he explained the fresh workings, starting with a sketch of the Irishman. 'Here is our mystery pugilist, who so recently attempted to bring my life to a premature conclusion. We know the salient facts:- Irishman, formerly a seaman and a boxer. He is in his middle thirties to early forties, five feet seven or so, stocky of build, moustache, dark brown hair. Hobnail boots, labours with a pick.' 'Why, the man's clearly a navvy!.' 'What else?. A navvy-but why does a navvy set out to disrupt a séance at the very moment of revelation?.' 'Perhaps he feared he would be named by Maskelyne?.' 'No, my friend, we have both glimpsed the killer-albeit briefly. A taller, thinner man than our stocky Irishman. No...' Holmes turned to the window, as if gazing at something unseen. 'Watson these are very deep waters, the deepest yet. This man, this Irishman, this is someone paid or otherwise beholden to person or persons unknown to throw the performance into chaos. An *agent* or accomplice of the killer himself.' The chalk slashed an arrow from the figure to a blank outline of a man with a question mark in place of features. 'The question remains, however... of why a man would go to such extraordinary lengths to shield a brutal and savage murderer...'

I studied the board for a moment, shaking my head at Holmes. Rolling his eyes theatrically, he set the chalk aside and went to the door, pausing as if listening before opening the door with a flourish, startling our landlady who was about to knock, a parcel in her hand. 'Mrs.Hudson, thank you-I have been awaiting this package with some impatience.'

It was some half hour later when the last of the smoke from the Havana had begun to dissipate. Holmes was deep in the latest clutch of papers from Detective Sergeant Sagar and I was in no mood for further excursion. The rain drumming against the pane merely served to heighten my lethargic condition, yet my companion regained his activity with more of that interminable pacing of his. At the point of my complaining, he abruptly went across to his desk, going through his own papers with a sense of purpose, discarding some carelessly as was his custom. I too decided the time for action had come-and pulled the stopper on the decanter of port.

The clock had chimed ten, London was wrapped in cloud and the rain ran down into the gutters with no sign of cessation. In our rooms in Baker Street, we were safe-but out in the streets and alleys of the East End the women were afraid to venture out-those that did went about in pairs, seeking the comparative safety of numbers. Holmes had sprawled himself over the settee, and sensing his unease I joined him in contemplation of the collage of discards he now had on the carpet before him. 'Well Holmes?'. 'Well indeed. Here we have the press cuttings and the reports from the Nichols and Chapman murders. Observe these women were both prostitutes and both met their end in somewhat similar fashion. What strikes you about the wounds?.' 'Both were savagely attacked, disembowelled in fact-the Chapman woman had parts of the *viscera majora* removed, along with the bladder. Other than that, no purpose can possibly be served by such savagery.' 'Yet a purpose exists. Such purpose?, that eludes me. Not the work of a commonplace maniac. The execution of the second case is notable-the increased violence and removal of organs, as if...' Breaking off from his reverie, Holmes regained his chair and lit one of the turkish cigarettes that sometimes served as an aid to his cogitational processes.

CHAPTER XIV
McGINTY MAKES HIS MARK

Amongst the hundreds of pubs, gambling dens and illegal drinking clubs of the East End there were a few catering to the many Irish navigators working on the underground railways as they expanded out from the City of London proper. Hard working, hard drinking, these 'Navvies' were as ready with their fists as their legendary Gaelic wit. I had woken rather late to find Holmes had left instructions for me to meet him at a Whitechapel public house, the White Hart on the high street. The establishment was filled with Navvies, the place having been practically taken over by them as they worked on the nearby District Railway underground line. I fought my way through the good-natured crowd to the bar and laid down a penny for a quart of ale. A fair bit of my beer sloshed out of the glass as I looked for Holmes; a dark-skinned navvy lurched into me and I pushed him back down onto a bench in disgust.

Even though I was privy to Holmes' scheme, it was still a shock when I bumped into him-the ginger-haired apparition had not the slightest resemblance!. It was all I could do not to pull at the ludicrous orange bushy eyebrows and hairy ears he had put on. 'Well, really-I should think you are taking the image of the Irish a little far, don't you think?.' 'Now what would you mean by that, pally?.' Just then the sunburned navvy grabbed hold of me by the lapels and yanked me nearly off my feet towards him, growling in a heavy Southern Irish accent. 'I think he means, this isn't the place for him and he's to be on his way.' Fuming at the man's insolence, I knocked his grip free with my stick. 'Unhand me you, you yokel-or you'll wake up surrounded by a concerned crowd!.' It was when the man winked at me that I saw it; *this* was Holmes!. 'Ho-' my carelessness was interrupted by the ginger man spinning me round with one hairy fist, the other raised and ready to strike. Suddenly, Holmes let out a bellow of laughter, clapped the insolent fellow on the shoulder and in his heavy accent cried out 'Mary! whiskey girl, but be quick about it; Pat's all for laying this poltroon out, when any fool can plainly see he's not the full shilling.' Luckily, this mollified the red-haired buffoon and we were able to slip outside, leaving him in the hands of the barmaid, a feisty cockney girl who was not to be denied payment.

Walking along, Holmes lit his clay and, not being partial, I smoked a cigarette. 'Any luck, Holmes?.' 'If I rely on luck, my dear Watson, I should be a fortune teller. No, I have made little progress, but I have had some intriguing offers.' 'Well?' 'Well, for one, I have been offered work digging tunnels, the address of a shebeen... and Mary, the barmaid at the establishment we have just left, has invited me to take supper with her at a place she knows.' I let out a chuckle at this, but was none the wiser as to what a shebeen was, until Holmes told me. We went to the South West, to the Red Lion to try our luck there. Arthur, the landlord was known to Holmes and had helped him on a blackmail case once, though Holmes did not reveal himself to him on this occasion.

Ordering two pints of ale, we went to the snug at the back of the pub and insinuated ourselves into the lively company we found there. Holmes seemed interested in a man at the rear of the bar, a surly chap with narrow eyes and a nervous watchfulness about him. A slovenly trollop was attempting to persuade this fellow to buy her some gin, but he seemed to be waiting for someone and paid her little mind. After what must have been the fifth time, however, he simply swung his arm and knocked the hapless woman to the floor. At once I was on my feet, prepared to mete out the justice of the street, but Holmes had anticipated this and was over and on the brute in a heartbeat, throwing out his fists in pugilistic fashion and fairly beating the swine in some style. It took no more than three blows to the face and stomach before the beastly cad slid to the floor, Arthur the landlord throwing a bucket of water over him and, with a jerk of his head, signalled his regulars to throw the unconscious wretch out onto the street. He ended up strewn across some manure.

'Well, well, well! Cocker gets his comeuppance-and from a paddy, no less!.' Holmes, remaining in the character he had chosen, flared visibly at the epithet, but the newcomer held both hands up in placatory fashion. 'Please, join me; landlord, ale please for my friends here.' This man clearly commanded respect as, at his approach, the patrons at a table hurried to leave it clear. We sat and drank. 'My name is Tobias Webb.' Leaning forward, I decided to speak first; 'Should that mean anything to us?.' 'Well, you're not from round here, but if you were, you'd learn the name quick enough.' In his soft lilt, Holmes drawled casually-'Well, I'm quick enough, Mister Webb and I've learned your name. Now, perhaps you would explain why it is you're after the pleasure of our company this fine day.' Webb slapped his hand on the table and laughed, his smile not reaching his eyes. 'Pleasure it is, gents; never business, though sometimes the two can be found amicable and side by side. I have a friend...' 'Oh, he has a friend. I like that, don't you, John?' - I nodded and smiled back at Holmes, hoping I appeared suitably tough for our new friend's benefit. 'Yea-well, like I say, I have a friend and he puts on, *entertainments*. Perhaps you'd like to come down and meet my friend, put on a little entertainment of your own. From what I've just seen, you'd make a few bob out of it. You get where I'm coming from, Mister?...' 'McGinty.' 'Just McGinty?.' His eyes narrowing, Holmes looked over the hand he wiped across his mouth. 'Just McGinty. This here is John.' Smiling, Webb reached into a pocket and withdrew a much-thumbed Sporting Times, writing an address on the back page, which he ripped off and handed to 'McGinty'. Friday night, nine. You'll be watched as you come in so no clever ideas or they'll find you floating out by Limehouse reach. Don't worry about gloves-you won't need any. Oh, the knock.' He rapped on the underside of the table three short knocks, a pause then two short. I copied this and Webb nodded slyly. It seemed we had made progress.

CHAPTER XV
A PROFESSOR OF CRIME

We had returned to Baker Street. Holmes then handed me a handful of snippings. 'Now, would you be so good as to peruse these clippings from the press-all dated within the last three years to the present.' I did as asked, the articles being an apparently disjointed series of reports on criminal acts conducted in England, the Continent and two in New York City. Warehouse robberies, extortion rackets, bookmaking, arson and murder, all were present and detailed. 'You seem to hint at a common factor, Holmes, some invisible thread that runs through these crimes perhaps.' The glimmer in Holmes' eye encouraged my speculative imaginings and, emboldened by his tacit approval, I continued. 'The crimes all seem to be monetary-all involve profit, save the murders and one of the fires.' 'Yes, the Bowery fire that claimed the life of the watchman and caused serious injury to two members of the local fire company. The building was due to be condemned as unfit for habitation-the land just happened to be vital to a city works project, selling for some $20,000 as I recall. As for the murders, in each case there was a beneficiary-a family member or associate who stood to gain. In the Mapley case, for instance, Oliver Mapley claimed he was robbed of jewels to the value of two thousand pounds on the night of his brother's murder-whereas in the Finchley fire it was the victim herself who had drawn the same amount from her bank the preceding day.'

I saw what Holmes was suggesting, but could not bring myself to accept that such a thing was possible, or even likely. 'Surely you do not suggest all these crimes were the work of a single hand?.' 'In a way-but the commonality is in the planning rather than the execution of these acts. Watson, for some time now I have had cause to believe in the improbable-the existence of a mind so exceptional, so well-trained in the sciences and the doctrine of criminology as to be Master of the Arts.' The suggestion was fantastic!. 'A Professor of crime?, someone who-for a fee-advises the various criminal elements perhaps?. How would such a man escape detection by the police?.' 'The fact that he *has* is proof in itself, Watson. Absence of evidence is not evidence of absence. Clearly, this 'Professor' as you style him uses a variety of *nom de guerres*, no doubt arranging to receive his payments through an inventive variety of methods.' 'Then, how does this *éminence grise* fit with these ghastly Whitechapel murders?.' 'As yet, Watson, I have only a vague notion-call it intuitive reasoning. Is it reasonable that a frenzied murderer, no doubt in some cases drenched in blood, could evade the police *and* the residents of so close-knit a precinct as Whitechapel?. Surely the murderer has an agent, one who does not baulk at the nature of the evil business.' I let my mind digest this thought with a growing sense of disquiet. We turned in for the night and I noticed a smog had formed outside. It was if the city itself had been keeping a terrible secret, warning us from further investigation. I put the thought out of my mind, unable to suppress a shudder.

CHAPTER XIV
THE FIGHT OF THE NAVIGATOR

Just before eight-fifty we gave the knock Webb had shown us, the grate in the door sliding open to show a dark pair of eyes. We had come down by the Millwall docks to the address on Webb's paper, a grain warehouse. The door creaked open and we were inside a vast, dark space, at the far end of which a single overhead lamp burned dully. The Malay behind the door smiled, showing teeth darked with betel nut. Pointing at the far end, it was clear this was our destination. Walking past row after row of sacking, we became aware of a crowd roaring, which became louder as we approached the steps at the far end, which led us out into a courtyard of sorts. At least a hundred men, many Irish and Lascars were heatedly betting on the outcome of a fight in the makeshift ring that had been set up on the cobbles, some straw thrown down the only cushion to a fall and the lighting provided from several oil-lamps that had been strung up around the place. Webb himself was at the centre of it, a one-eyed giant of a man stood next to him, a leather-covered cosh in his belt. Spotting us, our host waved up and the crowd parted respectfully as the pugilists fought on; a pair of bantamweights already lathered in sweat, blood and straw.

'Hello, boys, good to see you.' Turning to a Lascar who was evidently acting as a corner man, Webb called out 'Oi, Chen, get this man ready.' The Lascar ran across and took Holmes through to an outbuilding, presumably to strip for the fight. I only hoped his dark colouring had been applied below the collar. In the ring, one of the fighters was clearly dominant, a towheaded lad who had evidently had some schooling in the art of boxing. This, however was *not* boxing, as I saw when his opponent suddenly gave a low blow, doubling the fair lad over for a knee to the jaw that saw him sprawled out on the cobbles. I wasted no time introducing myself to the proceeding, surrounded as I was by the cheering and jeering throng, I followed suit crying foul. The referee, however-a short man with glasses gave it to the man left standing. Webb stepped forward, evidently the master of ceremonies to announce the next bout. This was to be a heavyweight contest, grossly mismatched, between a hulking brute of a docker and an overweight, pallid man who appeared more than slightly drunk. Each round was three minutes or so, which was clearly as close to the Queensberry rules as this sham would get. Halfway through the second round, the docker knocked his pale opponent clean over the single rope that had been lashed around the ring. For the rest of the round, the sallow fellow contended himself with avoiding further punishment, but at the start of the third he surprised us all by lifting the stronger man clean off his feet with an eyewatering upper-cut that cracked his teeth and left him out cold. It was as an outraged Lascar who had lost his shirt was being unceremoniously coshed by the cycloptic giant, that Webb called out 'Mauler' Monahan versus 'The Dublin Demolisher, Mister McGinty!'

'Mauler' Monahan seemed aptly-named, a collossus of a man some six feet and four, easily eighteen-stone of muscle and sinew. Holmes came out and I was relieved to see he had applied his walnut stain liberally, as he was, like his opponent, stripped to the waist. Now, as readers may be aware, the goddess Chance has long been a mistress of mine and I Her servant. It seemed only right to back my companion and I put a fiver on him with a grotesquely fat man who had fistfuls of markers and a pencil behind one grubby ear. This, I was given to understand was 'Fat-but-Fair Frank', although from the look of it I would not ordinarily have trusted the man with a ha'penny. Pocketing his marker, I turned back to see the fight.

There was no way of helping Holmes now, but I could give my fullest and most vocal support.

Round one started badly for 'McGinty'. Monahan was possessed of a particular talent for a devious left hook, which caught my friend to the ribs at least twice before he learned to counter it by turning into the blow and delivering a straight left to the man's cauliflower of an ear. It was with some relief that I heard the bell-really a hammer struck against a hanging bar of metal-and Holmes was able to take to his corner. His corner-man was an old cockney who dispensed a wet cloth with some words of advice I could not hear above the roar of the crowd. Holmes has made a study of the art of pugilism, even going so far as to spar with the great John Oliver, but the second round soon descended into a low brawl as his opponent grabbed Holmes by the belt and delivered a blow to the throat with his forearm. My language by this stage would have made a sailor blush, so vehemently did I protest at this unwarranted abuse of the spirit of sportsmanship. I need not have worried, however, as Holmes delivered a savage butt with his head that split Monahan's nose, following this up with an elbow to the sternum that sent the man reeling back into the corner 'post'-in actuality a barrel. Roaring their approval, the crowd began to warm to what they believed was an Irish navvy, and I was quite hoarse by this stage.

Looking across as the fighters returned to their corners, I saw Webb deep in conversation with an Irishman I had seen earlier placing a bet. This man was evidently a foreman of some kind and was older than most present. Feeling this might be the man to lead us to the man who had attacked Holmes at the theatre, I began pushing through the crowd towards him when a sudden ruckus alerted me to the fact that Holmes was on the rope and in trouble once more. This time, Monahan's ham-fists were pummelling Holmes' ribs, while my friend could not slip away as his rival had his leading foot firmly on top of his, preventing his escape. Without thinking of the consequences, I grasped the rope and pulled it smartly, propelling Holmes forward. Luckily, his reactions were quicker than his opponent and he took the chance to deliver a stunning straight right to Monahan's wide chin. As the crowd registered their disapproval of my intervention, Holmes followed up with a haymaker of a left to the same point and the fight was over. 'Fair Frank' was deluged with angry punters demanding their money back and I was facing Webb's one-eyed friend.

CHAPTER XV
A WEBB OF INTRIGUE

We were bundled unceremoniously into one of the delivery carts from the warehouse stables, guarded by the cyclops and Holmes' corner man, whose friendly manner remainded unchanged despite the wicked-looking billhook he was holding. Sat on sacks of grain we had a surprisingly comfortable ride. At length, perhaps after forty minutes or so, we followed the cockney down and along an alleyway, the towering figure behind us precluding any attempt to run. Some rickety stairs at the back of a building led us up to the kitchen of what appeared to be a flat and we were told to sit at the single table. From below came the unmistakable sounds of merriment, of singing and boisterous drunken revelry. After a while, Webb came through from the other room and laid down a bottle of scotch. 'Right. First things first, gents. You can start by telling us who you are and who it was that put you onto me in the first place.' I was in no mood to talk, although my irritation at having been abducted in this way was tempered with, I am ashamed to admit, a gnawing fear at the pit of my stomach.

Holmes, however was more inclined to eloquence. 'My name is Sherlock Holmes. This is my friend and colleague Doctor John Watson.' 'Sherlock who?.' This came from the diminutive cockney, who frowned in bemusement at the name that should have sent fear running through him. 'The detective, Jem-he's a mutton shunter, only not proper, more amateur like.' The wizened little man raised his brows at this, but said nothing. 'So, why the gammon?.' Apparently, Holmes understood all this, though I certainly did not. 'Forgive the deception, Mister Webb, but I should very much like to speak to you in confidence.' Going over to a dresser, Webb found a cracked glass and pulled a chair up. Pouring a good few fingers, he set it down and perched on the edge of his chair. 'Well, I'm fairly confident that if you don't tell us Ginzer here...' -he indicated the mute figure of his bodyguard- 'Will tear your head off for you.' 'Perhaps. But as I have no interest in cobble fighting, or in fact any activity you may be involved in, I really would recommend you indulge me.' Webb thought this over, then nodded at his confederates. 'Go on boys, go down and keep an eye on the place while I have a chat with Mister 'Olmes and his pal wots a Doctor.'

Once we were alone, Holmes put it to our jailer that as the women of Whitechapel were in such terrible danger, it might be advantageous to help with our search for the unknown Irishman. Finally, taking a mouthful of his whisky, Webb wiped his mouth and pulled at his chin. 'I don't bark and I'm not a nark.' At this, I made to speak, but he held up his glass with a finger pointed in my direction and I stayed silent. 'However... however. This Leather Apron has got the whole town gripped and no mistake.' I had, of course heard of the suspect known by that soubriquet. Webb continued. 'By rights I should have you both weighed in for that business today-god knows how much Frank lost when it all went to cock, not that that piking old swindler won't come out ahead in the long. Mind you, you gave the Mauler a taste of ointment and no mistake. Suppose I do agree to nose-it won't be laid at my door?.' 'I can assure you, Mister Webb-your name will not leave this room.' This seemed to satisfy Webb, who finished his glass. 'Good. Because Ginzer is a first-class punisher and you never know who you might bump into in Baker street.' Holmes merely smiled and I was not about to interrupt. 'Good. Peachy. Now, as all bets were off the minute the Doctor here pulled the plug I don't expect he'll want his bees-that's *money* to you, Doc. The fiver you've lost, call it a sweetener. I'll put the whisper out, if this Patrick of yours is daft enough to still be in the smoke he'll be found. Now, I've a spieler to run and you've a fair old walk ahead of you. You won't find a cab 'til you get to Cheapside and maybe not then.' With that, Webb went to the door and held it open. We went to leave, Holmes pausing at the step. 'How will you get word to us if you find him?.' 'I'll send a hoister I know, works up West, up your way. She's a jemmy little saucebox, name of Sally.' The door closed behind us and we were left to find our own way back.

The weekend passed without further incidents of note. Holmes and myself deciding that restraint was the best tactic for the time being, we spent the time in study. Whilst I refreshed my knowledge of pulmonary disease and the diseases of the tropics, my friend looked for more evidence to corroborate his theory of a criminal potentate and researched alternative disguises for possible usage in the case. At nine sharp on the Monday, the ringing of the bell preceded the delivery of a thin assembly of papers from Detective Sergeant Sagar, who, as good as his word, had furnished us with the latest reports into the killings. Holmes tipped the delivery boy, tearing into the bundle to devour its contents with relish. These latest included a smaller bundle marked 'Letters received; copies prepared from Mimeographs of the original articles ', but Holmes tossed these aside without a glance.

Gradually, however, his expression turned to one of disappointment and bitterness. 'Well?.' 'We have failed, Watson. The police have him-and our actions have only served to divert the attention from the killer.' I stepped forwards, unable to believe Holmes capable of such abject failings. 'Surely we were at times within arm's length of the fiend?.' 'Not so. This is the man we should have stalked.' The file Holmes handed to me was that of a Swiss, Jacob Isenschmidt, his photographic likeness included-taken during one of his periods of incarceration at Colney Hatch Asylum. The man had been a pork butcher, his shop in Holloway, but the business had failed due in no small part to his mania for sharpening butcher's knives at the oddest hours. The man was subject to seasonal bouts of madness, brought on by sunstroke and was described as 'Exceptionally dangerous with a propensity for irrational violence.' Delusions of grandeur were also present. Attached to the file was a statement made by Inspector Abberline for the consumption of the press, part of which read:- *'He appears to be the most likely person to have committed the crimes and every effort will be made to account for his movements on the dates in question.'*

I was unable to watch as Holmes reached for the hated morocco leather case, pausing only to collect my hat and a few of my cigars. I set off on foot for the Regent's Park, hoping to find succour in the expansive greenery there. My walk took me past the boating lake, on which gay couples made the best of the fine weather, the men rowing their bonneted ladies to the accompaniment of carefree laughter. A balloon hung in the unusually still air, tethered to the ground by a stout rope. Craning my head, I could see the operators were using some sort of scientific equipment involving a telescope of some kind. I continued, invigorated and encouraged by the light-heartedness of it all. Pausing to allow a young man to pass on his bicycle, I noticed a man who seemed to be watching me with rather more than the casual glance of a park-goer. Remembering Holmes' advice on dealing with such unwanted attention, I feigned ignorance of any undue attention, merely increasing the pace of my stride as one seeking exercise. A turn of the head confirmed that the man was, indeed, following me. Heading North, I made for the grounds of the London Zoological Park, reasoning that I might be able to evade the tiresome fellow in the morning crowd. I joined the queue for admission, paid my shilling and purchased a guide, turning quickly to the map. I decided to follow the mass of visitors, there being safety in numbers. With a burst of *chagrin* I thought of my revolver, snug in the draw at Baker Street.

The Lion's House was wonderful, so much so my attention drifted inexorably to the magnificent beasts, some slumbering in the cool building, others pacing their cage eyeing the curious humanity outside with lofty disdain. All at once, he was there again-a man in his early forties, dressed for the town in a brown suit and well-worn shoes, highly polished. The man was clean shaven, with the easy authority of a military man or the like. He turned from my scrutiny, allowing me the chance to attempt to elude him.

I set off at a trot for the Bear Pit, in which a large furry shape was fast asleep. Quite without thinking, in what I later described as a moment of temporary madness, I vaulted the rail, dropping down into the pit. Shouts of alarm went up-and to my horror, so did the hackles on the 'sleeping' bear-a veritable titan, who stood on his hind legs to rear up before me. Now, I am not a short man, but this brute threw a shadow over me, letting out a stentorian bellow that froze the marrow in my bones. A second roar-another bear!, this newcomer being grey-haired and of a rather battered appearance, missing as he was part of an ear with a nose scarred from a lifetime of battles. I had no intention of remaining for the next. Fear finally overcame inertia, my legs carrying me towards a cave set into the rocky wall. A loud yawn sounded from the darkness within, but by then I was climbing the rockery at a rate that would have done justice to any mountain ape. Scaling the top, I had a glimpse of an ursine dispute that would have stopped even the rush hour traffic in Piccadilly, the grey delivering a vicious reprimand to the younger. Looking back, I saw my follower as he threw his hat on the ground in dismay. 'Ha!, follow me now my friend.' Chuckling to myself, I scaled the far wall and heaved myself over the railings, walking through the astonished crowd in search of the nearest exit. Hailing a cab, I called to the driver to take me to Baker Street, a sharp pin-prick at my neck. My neck. My neck... neck...

CHAPTER XVI
A FRIEND IN NEED

The dark blur became lighter as the marsh-mallow man sang to me down the speaking tube again. The spray from the waterfall became a gout, the water cold, shocking as it enveloped me, carrying me back to the realm of the conscious. I was bound hand and foot to a chair in a dimly-lit room, Chinese in appearance with carven wooden screens and silken drapery, the place reeked of opium, the sickly-sweet smell confirming that this was an opium den. Two heavily muscled thugs stood, arms crossed by the entrance, a Western woman reclined on a divan nearby, her eyes dark and glassy, her expression far away.

I looked around, to see a familiar figure-the Irishman who had attacked Holmes!. 'Well, so's it's the man thinks me a lunatic. I rather think you'll live to regret your presumptions about me, so I do.' I struggled for clarity, clutching at something Holmes had once said; *'The more a criminal talks, the more he incriminates himself and those around him.'* 'The police have you marked-you might as well give yourself up.' His laughter was not reassuring. 'The police aren't looking for me, Doctor-they're much too busy chasing a madman, a will o'the wisp, a shadow in the fog. I'm just a poor *Oyrish* navvy, come here to build a tramways for the good folk of London town.' The tramway!, we had been right in our supposition!. Of course... half of the city was being dug up to extend the reach of the infernal things. 'What are you to do with the Whitechapel murders?, why did you disrupt the *seance* at the theatre?.' 'Why, for the money in my pocket, good money too I might add. I've no interest in ghosts nor whores Doctor Watson. Yes, I know you, you and your friend Mister Sherlock Holmes, you both being the reason I've to stay in places like

79

this, hiding like a rat from daylight.' 'Perhaps if you had not chosen to live like one, then?.' I immediately regretted my defiant remark, O'Connor bending down so his face was inches from mine, before delivering a staggering blow to my mouth with his enormous fist. It was the first of many, the blows raining down on my helpless face and body until, thankfully, unconsciousness claimed me once more.

By Holmes' estimate, I must have awoken between nine and ten that night. Still bound-and now hooded, I could neither move nor see my surroundings. A reverberating dripping sound was the first clue to my surroundings, apparently somewhere cavernous, with the cloying dampness of the subterranean. From somewhere above came the faint rumble of some heavy machinery, which faded away abruptly. At length, the sound of footsteps announced the approach of several people. The hood was wrenched from my head, affording me with a view of a dank brick arch, lit at intervals by lamps affixed to brackets bolted into the walls. Pain masked my face, the left eye swollen and of little use to me. Meanwhile, my jaw ached terribly, the copper-tang of blood on my tongue. I was surrounded by crates against which were piled the tools of the navvies trade-picks, shovels, lamps and such. There were several carriages too, covered with tarpaulins. Turning, I saw a curious group of villains, one as burnt as an island native and an extraordinary top hat, adorned with beads and feathers. My Irish pugilist was there, along with several other rough types. The man that followed them into the gallery, however, was of an entirely different species. Thin to the point of malnourishment, even standing with a slouch this cadaverous creature was easily six feet and two, with eyes hooded in their sockets below a pronounced forehead. Oddly, this ghoul had something of the school-master about him, but could just have easily been an

80

undertaker from the morbidity of his features and funereal attire.

The thin man's mannerisms only served to increase the sense of abnormality, a curious, bird-like motion of the head was much in evidence and the eyes hinted at a barely concealed mania, in all probability a Napoleon complex with a definite hint of persecution complex for bad measure. I decided to seize what advantage there was to be had, if any. 'This is an outrage. I have been abducted and assaulted!. Release me at once you arse!.' If I had hoped to provoke the man, I had to admit failure-those dark eyes merely flickering malevolence in my direction for a second. When he finally spoke, it was indeed a voice from the asylum-the pitch raising and lowering alarmingly, as if controlling his thoughts was a herculean effort. 'I see Mister O'Connor has had a lapse of self-discipline. It is symptomatic of his race. The Irish are a reminder of times long passed, when tribes went to war with each other and the great chieftains reigned supreme.' The words came through ill-shapen teeth flecked with decay. Turning to his gang, he addressed them in that horrible voice. 'I wish a man's death-which of you will oblige me?'.

So this was it!. After all my adventures my life was at an end. All of the men stepped forward, to the evident satisfaction of their master.'So many-*volunteers*. You two.' Reaching into his coat with the thin fingers of a pianist or surgeon, he withdrew two phials of colourless liquid, handing one to each of the men he had indicated before returning his attention to me. 'Chemistry; a weakness as well as a passion. Long hours spent at the workbench produce their delights.' Holding the tubes up as if in admiration, this fearsome man seemed lost in a black fascination. 'These are the agents of death, Doctor-ingested separately, harmless and inert. Together, however, when mixed there follows a violent if brief reaction, forming both acid and base of what I have named Hyper-Fluorocarbonic Acid. Gentlemen, you will each pour your phial down the throat of Mister O'Connor. In this fashion, neither of you will yield to the temptation of confession, as to condemn either is to condemn both.' Realising I was to be spared-however briefly, I slumped in temporary relief, but the reprieve was to be horrifically short.

The Irishman backed away, eyes narrowed. Nodding as he wiped a hand across his mouth he gave the amateur chemist a look of pure malice. 'So, it's a drink for your pal, O'Connor then?. Well, there'll be a few bones to be broken first, of that you can be advised.' Stepping forward the weird figure seemed to grow even taller. 'Why, my dear friend-there is surely no requirement for violence. There is no need for anger. No need...' The glimmer of a coin flashed in the air as the repellent voice increased in sibilance, somehow at once more emollient and persuasive. I had to blink to be sure, but yes-*the coin was spinning in mid-air!*. Several inches above the uncanny figure's outstretched palm it hovered, turning end over end and in all possible angles of rotation in some hellish conjuror's trick. 'You see, Michael, now you see. Look deep into the metal as it spins, deep into the surface and through it, deeper now as the metal becomes liquid-a mirror made of liquid metal at the end of the World, the end of it all. What need have you to go back now that you have come so far?.' The Irishman's expression had become most oddly pale, eyes heavy as if drugged. I could see that some type of devilish mesmerism was being applied. 'Of course, you must be thirsty having come so far-why not take a drink?, what harm could come of it-a cool, refreshing drink?.' The evil at work here was shocking, even to one accustomed to the darker practices of the Jezailis such as myself. I opened my mouth to attempt to break the influence of this madman, but with extraordinary perception he had produced a small derringer pistol in his free hand, which he pointed at me in a warning as clear as any spoken.

My duty compels me to complete my account of events in that dark place, so, Dear Reader, I implore you to forgiveness and to fortify yourself for the resultant text. The two murderous henchmen approached their unwitting victim with the malicious creeping step of their kind. The poor man, yes, I say this even as I recall his brutality-the poor man allowed the first to pour his phial down his throat. Then, the second. After perhaps five seconds, an ominous fizzing and hissing began to sound from the man's stomach as, unseen, the acid reaction began. O'Connor's jaw dropped open as a rush of steam burst from his throat, a low keening wail uttering from the doomed man as he began to convulse, clutching at his chest and stomach. The wail became a scream, a high-pitched bubbling shriek such as I had never heard previously-and now cannot expunge from memory. Frantically, he tore at his shirt, ripping it open to reveal a stomach that was literally dissolving, his fingers plunging into his innards before he pulled his hands clear, fingers now claws of bone. Sinking to the floor in his death agony, his scream faded to a ghastly rattle, the flesh at his throat melting away, his clothing now smouldering as it began to burn. 'For God's sake, shoot him!' My plea could not be contained, even at risk of a bullet. Mercy, however was not in the lexicon of this monster, who merely smiled thinly as his wretched victim writhed on the ground in flames. I vowed then and there to see justice done to this abomination and his band, if I survived myself, that is.

CHAPTER XVII
THE PINKERTON MAN

(For this part of the narrative, Sherlock Holmes writes in his own words his account of the events following the kidnapping of Dr. Watson, this being considered the fullest possible explanation of the incident to hand.)

I was in the rooms at Baker Street, recumbent and in a state I might describe as a somnial euphoria. I had lapsed, the morphia lifting me gently from the defeat I had sustained, the image of the butcher Isenschmidt fading from my imagination to leave me in the transient peace of the needle. I was dimly aware of being shaken, roused from my torpor by an urgent voice, combined with the pungent tang of smelling salts. Eventually, my senses returned to me, revealing to me the presence of Dennings, the Pinkerton Agent. Immersal in water, a cigar and a pot of tea from our landlady completed my revival and I was able to interrogate Dennings on his activities. Unable to avoid the conclusion that the crime syndicate would take ruthless measures to protect itself, I had enlisted the aid of the European branch of the famous detection agency to supplement my own modest resources. Red-faced, Dennings revealed how Watson had first identified his presence and then made his daring escape through the Bear Pit. 'Honestly, Mr. Holmes, further pursuit was improbable at best-but the blame must rest with myself, attempting a follow through a large open space without additional agents was foolhardy, but I had expected the Doctor to follow his normal routine and hail a cab, an eventuality for which I had made preparations.' 'Yes, the random element is the true nemesis of any detective. You are retained until the end of the week, as I recall-it suits me to keep this so, events being unpredictable. Thank you, Mr. Dennings, I shall send word if I need you.'

I should need to act quickly to find Watson; there being no doubt that he was in mortal danger. A search of the umbrella stand yielded a penny terror and a tattered brolly. Opening the bow window a few inches allowed me to push out the rocket, which I kept in place by using the handle of the umbrella. Striking a vulcan on the sole of my shoe I lit the fuse paper, which smoked fussily for a few seconds. With a sudden shriek, the terrible thing shot skyward, terminating in a bang that rattled the slates. Going to the door I awaited for the inevitable indignations of Mrs. Hudson, with my corresponding promise never to repeat the offence. It was at her outraged exit that the bell sounded, further audible dismay heralding the arrival of 'Lame-leg Bobby', one of the smaller of the Baker Street irregulars, who, despite an obvious limp, took the stairs two at a time, whipping off his cap and snapping to attention. 'Reporting as ordered, mister 'Olmes Sir.' 'Very good, Bobby-here is a shilling and a crown. The shilling is yours, the crown should more than cover the cost of expenses. Summon the rest of the irregulars and see if you can find out the number of the strange cab that was working the rank at London Zoo today. When you have it, leave the number here at once. There's a guinea for the lad finding that cab.'

All I could do was wait; until I knew the number of that hansom I was powerless to intervene. However, a frantic hammering at the front door was followed by a commotion and a shriek; a cry from our landlady; it was Watson!. I hastened down to aid my wounded companion to the stair. 'Water, hot water and towels please Mrs. Hudson-and send for the locum at my dear friend's practice at once.' 'No, no need; it is not more than a few bruises and all I shall require are the water and the towels.' How very like him!, how noble!. 'Come up at once and tell me all' I implored of him.

Clearly Watson had been under considerable duress these last long hours; clear too the signs of his ordeal, from the residual dampness of his clothes to the trace of brick-dust at his collar and knee. Lichen too I perceived, as the smell of decay that clung to him and there were scuff marks upon both elbows and his heels where, doubtless, he had been dragged-I suspected while unconscious, judging from the angle of the marks and the sheer force such an action would have required; these marks were almost unbroken in continuity, suggestive of only the merest of pauses in what must have been a herculean effort. I could not bear to amplify his distress further by what seemed needless questioning, relieving Mrs. Hudson of her towels as she set down the bowl and left to prepare two breakfasts. I watched in silence as Watson removed his jacket and shirt, my jaw setting in silent anger as his wounds were revealed. At his direction I assisted him in applying bandages to his ribcage where several were cracked before pressing a glass of brandy into his hand.

It was only after Watson had mollified a distraught Mrs. Hudson by attempting supper that we spoke. 'Holmes I am glad to be alive-you've no idea of the horrors those fiends exposed me to.' 'Was it the Irishman?-in the tunnel I mean?.' Shaking his head in wearisome chagrin, Watson's laugh was stifled by a start of pain. 'It was no tunnel, rather a brick archway, below a railway by the sound of it. The Irishman is dead, murdered in front of me in the most hideous fashion. His name was O'Connor, that is all I found out of him.' 'Really Watson-I feared you in danger, but that was before you decided to make the acquaintance of bears...' I told Watson of my Pinkerton man and how I had inferred the rest of it, by which time he was exhausted. Leaving him to recuperate, I set to work, gathering a selection of items and my disguise-bag, a much-travelled thing in the compartments of which I kept the basis of manifold personalities. For good measure I added a bulldog revolver and a leather-covered lead cosh which fitted nicely down my boot. Finally, a sword-stick cane and my armament was complete. I knew little-only that I must be prepared for every eventuality. With nothing else for me to do, I perched on the window sill and watched the street below, eyes scanning the scene for anything out of the ordinary. After nearly three excruciating hours I spotted none other than Wiggins, the head of the irregulars, pelting along as if the devil were chasing him.

CHAPTER XVIII
INDIAN TERRITORY

Hackney playt 367-the message was brevity itself, if the spelling was somewhat lacking. Paying Wiggins his guinea, I set forth for the nearby cab rank, taking the third. My answer to the jarvey's cheery 'Where can I take you today, Sir?' was the cabman's shelter at Thurloe Place in Kensington. Once there I paid the driver to wait while I bought us both a mug of steaming hot and rather excellent tea, though I could not drink mine. As Watson so often remarked my constitutional . As he waited outside the amusing little structure I entered-there being no other members of his trade there to object at this intrusion upon their exclusive sanctuary.

Bunny-himself a former cabbie until his failing eyesight lost him his licence -was preparing for the rush of trade that preceded the luncheon hour. 'Sorry, Sir- drivers only in here.' 'I see your eyesight hasn't improved. How are you Bunny?.' 'Sherlock Holmes-well, there's a turn-up for the books!.' I should explain that as I had once helped Bunny out of a spot of bother with some particularly unpleasant specimens I was certain he would help me track down the cab in which Watson was abducted, if it were possible. '367?, Three-Six Seven... lets think a moment... who might that be?... Archie; Archie Harris of Stepney. I never forget a number, famous my memory is. Strange though... old Archie has been laid up these past few months- lumbago the doctor called it. I wouldn't want to get a pal in trouble Mister 'Olmes, but maybe Archie subbed his cab out to earn a crust 'til his back cleared up.' I wrote the address down in my notebook and thanked Bunny, with the assurance his name would be kept out of any subsequent scandal. The cab-driver Harris lived some distance from Kensington and the journey seemed to take an age.

I smoked and attempted to find a logical convergence between the recent murders and the abduction of my colleague. Nothing about any of it could be made to fit any of the facts and I resigned myself to the tedium of the journey by looking at the great city as we passed through it. Everywhere the signs of normality; the bankers of the city hurrying to their next appointments, the soldiery from the corners of the Empire wondering at the heart of it all and the hum-drummery of common commerce seen in any of the world's great cities. At last we approached the environs of Stepney itself-not wishing to be indiscreet I had the cabby drop me off a few streets short of the Duckett Street tenement where Harris resided. The building itself was a modest three storey affair-a yard at the side evidently serving as a coach-house and stable. The door was answered by a char, who showed me to an apartment on the first floor. Harris himself proved to be a friendly fellow, if suspicious of me. The man's florid complexion and nose told me he was evidently fond of drink.

'367?, yes that's my hansom right enough, but why do you ask?, from the licence office eh?.' I felt no need to offer enlightenment, allowing him to continue in his assumption. 'We have received a complaint-nothing formal as yet, but I must know to whom you have subbed your cab out to. Give me a name and it won't go on the books.' 'I see-I knew they was courting trouble-I say they as it was two of them, not strangers you understand, I wouldn't let strangers look after Beth-I named her after my wife, god rest her soul. Piebald, six years old is Beth. Good earner, good worker-likes the work, see?.' I decided indulgence was the better course and commented. 'A fine animal I am sure, no doubt in the peak condition.' Sensing my patience would wear thin, Harris waved his hand in defeat. 'The Arches, Butchers row. Ask for Lenny and Indian Joe.'

Butchers Row in Aldgate was named well, lined with shopfronts adverting 'Wholesale Meats' 'Brown & Sons, Butchers of Distinction' and the like, flanked by public houses and, of all things the local Inland Revenue office. I carried on past this last to the railway Arches, which contained a variety of shops as well as a carriage repair business. It was at this place I found it; there was no sign of any horse, piebald or otherwise, but as the place seemed distinctly unfriendly I walked past, relying on the peripheral senses to aid me. 'You lost?.' The challenge came from a surly creature of villainous countenance, who stood brazenly before me barring further inspection of the premises. 'I hope not. I'm in the market for a hansom cab-I was told Lenny or Indian Joe would be obliging.' I affected the manner of a potential customer, hoping to gain admission. Indicating with my sword-stick I could see several carriage-sized shapes in the back of the place, largely covered with canvas, the side of one unveiled showing a lantern. 'Never 'erd of 'em, now get aht while your safe mate. Go on, sling yer 'ook.' A faltering step forward and, apparently crestfallen, I allowed the stick to fall, it's hard rubber tip scraping along the ground as I feigned the motion of losing my balance. A movement at the corner of my eye revealed a second fellow, this one with a face that could have been fashioned from leather, so dark and creased was it. Wherever this man had got such a colouration was clearly somewhere far hotter and drier than England. He wore a ludicrous old top hat with some feathers attached to the band and some sort of turquoise and silver bracelet at his wrist-this was Indian Joe, then. There would be no sense in pressing further, so with a last hard look at what I presumed to be Lenny, tipped my hat and left to find a more reputable hansom cab operator.

One look had told me everything; the scrapings of mud and moss at the first man's shoulder and boots, the mud and water around the floor beneath one of the canvasses suggesting it had needed a sudden cleaning. Add this to the fact that the lantern I had glimpsed was blackened from recent use and I was fairly sure I had my answer. Only a microscopic examination of the mud sample I had scraped onto my stick would tell. The day was ending, evening turned to night. Lengthening my stride, I headed for a public house to spend a few hours, noting an early fog coming up from the river. Hopefully, this would thicken and provide me with some much-needed cover.

At exactly eleven o'clock I set down my glass and headed for the door of the pub. Stepping out onto the junction of Church Street and the Minories, I moved quickly, but quietly along to Aldgate High Street where I waited for a while, observing and listening. The towering spire and edifice of St. Botolphs loomed above the scene as if in sombre warning of God's impending wrath. The street was surprisingly busy, groups of people stumbling home from various ale houses and hostelries, whilst others headed off for a quick pint before closing time. I knew the licence laws well, but although pubs were meant to close at midnight, it was not unknown for a landlord to bribe the Constabulary with a glass or two and 'lock ins'-where the landlord bolted the door, but continued to serve, were common in the East End. I would have to be careful. Going around to the Arches all was in darkness, the businesses there long closed. The fog had settled and the dim glow of the nearest gas light failed to illuminate the ironwork on the arch I was after.

What I was attempting would not be easy. Finding the right archway was simple, however and finding a heavy, if basic padlock and chain I set to work with my lock-picks.

I had been at work for perhaps a minute when the beam of a torch alerted me to the presence of a Constable checking the Arches were secure. Cursing my luck, I shrank back behind a pile of bricks and lay still. I could hear the sound of the Constable's boots coming closer and it was a matter of a few seconds before he would see me, though I was wearing dark clothing as a precaution. The sound of glass breaking further up the road came just in the nick of time and the policeman went to investigate, his footsteps echoing through the hollow archways as he went. Returning to the padlock another two minutes and it dropped open. Unwrapping the chain as silently as possible, I then opened the gate a foot or so to squeeze through, which it did with an un-nerving creak, before replacing the chain and leaving the appearance of the gate being secure.

Going instinctively to the side of the arch, I went down on one knee and waited there a full ten minutes, letting my eyes accustom themselves to the darkness before moving any further. I had brought with me an oil lamp, fitted with shutters that I now carefully set down on the damp ground to light. As it hissed dully, I picked it up and, using the sword-cane I tapped my way gingerly towards the middle of the space, until the ferrule came to rest against a wooden object. Reaching out, I felt the wheel of a carriage of some description, then canvas. Burrowing under the material, I risked a sliver of light, finding this was indeed a Hackney carriage. Moving around to the rear, still beneath canvas, I found what I had hoped for. *367.* This confirmed it; Watson had been abducted in this

Hansom, brought here no doubt to witness the death of O'Connor. Clearly, this had been a warning; had it been otherwise, the gang would never have released poor Watson alive. Obvious, too was the fact that O'Connor's death had been warranted by my friend's recognition of him from the theatre. I needed more answers, however, so replaced the shutter to leave myself in darkness once more.

As I progressed, I saw that there were two delivery vans beneath canvas-and nearly tripped over a pick-handle. Risking some light, I found a fair quantity of tools, such as picks, shovels and heavy rope-tackle. A pile of wooden prop shafts beyond this must have stood twelve feet high and perhaps ten wide. Clearly some tunnelling was being planned, though I could not be certain that all that I had discovered was connected. It was, however, most suggestive. The one thing missing were horses, though I had no doubt had I searched the adjoining yards I would find Beth the Piebald stabled with some hefty cart-horses. Clearly a criminal enterprise was being incorporated by this nefarious gang. A thought struck me and I checked the nearest van. It had been painted-recently with the livery of a brewery, the smell of fresh paint cloying under the tarpaulin. The other was identical. I had seen all I needed to, but a further discovery left me in a less sanguine disposition. My cork-soled boot had come down in something soft. Easing the shutter showed an area of ground some five feet across by six had been sluiced down thoroughly and covered with fresh straw. On my hands and knees, working through the area with a slow, methodical search I found a trouser button. It had been almost completely melted, as if by great heat. Pocketing this, I re-arranged the straw to conceal my presence, extinguished my lamp and slowly tapped my way back to the gate. It was a relief to be out of that place, more so when I re-attached the padlock and made my way back to the land of the living.

CHAPTER XIX
THE DOUBLE EVENT

Safely back at Baker Street I went across to the map of London and found the Arches. 'Now, it is approximately three and three-quarter miles from Butchers Row here to... the Zoological Gardens at Regent's Park. Assuming the carriage travelled no more than five miles in an hour, it cannot have been at the Arches when you set off. 'Plainly.' Clearly, Watson's stock of patience was not unlimited. 'Therefore the carriage was in the vicinity of Baker Street and followed you since you had made no plans to go to the park beforehand. It was chance that you fell into their clutches; clearly had I emerged first they would have taken me and have had no need of such a brutal demonstration.' 'They would have killed you?.' 'Naturally. That explains so much. Now let us see what science may teach us.'

Under the lens of my Powell microscope I brought the slide into focus onto a sporophytical structure. This moss had not been present at the Arches, bringing me to the inevitable conclusion; the gang was using a tunnel for their purpose. There were surely no more than thirty places in all London where such a mixture of clay, slurry and soil could be found; add the moss I was examining and you have the mouth of a tunnel or drain, which must surely reduce the number to perhaps twenty or so. O'Connor's button-who else could it have belonged to?-was next, but all I learned was that it had been subject to a chemical burn, of an exceptionally violent and acidic nature. This Watson could have told me and I abandoned my desk for the comforts of a pipe and a cup of Mrs. Hudson's excellent and revivifying coffee.

(Here Dr. John Watson resumes his duties as narrator with

thanks to his estimable colleague for his own insights.)

It was several days later-Saturday the 29th of September. A day I shall never forget and that I desperately wish I *could* forget. I slept for most of the day and, bathed and in fresh clothes I found Holmes in his chair smoking a pipe and going through the papers Detective Sergeant Sagar had sent what seemed an age ago. 'Ah, there you are Watson-I was beginning to worry.' I started at myself in the mirror; my face remained livid, the wounds from my beating beginning to turn from red to purple. I sat in my chair and Holmes rang down for some tea. He was eager to hear the full details of my evil experience whilst they remained fresh, listening with mounting horror as I detailed the scene in that awful tunnel chamber and the murder of O'Connor. 'That is all Holmes, thank God. Have you any news?.' 'Yes, Watson-a telegram from my patron within the police regarding this mysterious organisation that have showed their hand and made the capital mistake of showing themselves in the process. I have the salient facts and shall soon be in a position to lay my hand on the shoulder of the mysterious leader of the cult.' Filling my briar I reached for the matches to light it, tossing the match into the fire that Mrs. Hudson had lit for us. 'Did you say cult?.' Abruptly rising from his chair, Holmes cast down his papers and took a pull, sending a small cloud upwards. 'I did. I can think of no better word-this gang is closer to their master than any mere group of cut-throats or dockyard thieves; they operate to his direction as the zombies of Haiti or the thugee in India. Such misplaced devotion, such loyalty is hard to explain other than through the rigid code of fear and retribution which you described to me.'

Now Mrs. Hudson fussed in with tea and I had the devil of a job persuading her I was recuperating to her

96

instructions. As she left us, Holmes explained that he had been neglecting his other cases of late, such as they were. Our recent excursion to the west country had proved a most instructive one, with Sir. Henry Baskerville safe to assume both his seat and the duties of the title. True also, the Dundas matter had been cleared up to the satisfaction of both parties although the post had as yet brought no reply to his summary of the Marseilles Smuggling Problem. With what he assured me was his incomplete grasp of the business at hand and Isenschmidt safely locked away he felt sure his books would lie empty for lack of clients. If I had known what that very night would bring I could have re-assured him at least one on point; Holmes would not be idle for long.

CHAPTER XVIII
THE 'DOUBLE-EVENT'

The bell ringing across the field called us in from my adventures; my Brother, was, as always, Robin Hood whereas I Little John. I could see the doorway to our house, my Mother stood ringing the bell and calling my name. Ringing the bell and calling me... I was in my room at Baker Street, the candle lit and Holmes was there calling my name. A glance at my clock revealed it was not long after two. 'What-what is it, Holmes?.' 'Murder, Watson-another murder!.' With that, he was off down the stairs to our rooms. Dressing hastily, I was down to find him in conference with none, but Lestrade and a pair of Constables. One of these turned to me, his face ashen. 'E's done it again, another one; a Judy in Berner Street this time.' Befuddled from my sleep, I uttered the name of the lunatic Isenschmidt. 'No Watson, not he; it appears that I have made a grave miscalculation in assuming the killer safely behind locked doors.' 'I wouldn't be so hard on yourself, Mister Holmes.' Lestrade's manner was self-satisfied as he puffed himself up in front of the Constables. 'You have often been of assistance to us, but, you see there is no match for the trained mind.' Before I could box the man's ears, Holmes had smoothly stepped forward to steer the pompous oaf towards the stairs. 'Thank you, Lestrade I am indeed indebted to you for your advice.' 'Yes, well, Mr. Holmes-and Doctor. I'm wanted at Scotland Yard immediately, so I shall bid you both a good night.' Replacing their Helmets, the two Constables filed out after Lestrade.

Dutfield's Yard lies between the International Working Men's Educational Club and some tenements. The Club had been founded to promote the principles of international socialism. The club had been host to a sing-song that night, most of the patrons having dispersed at midnight-and it was the club steward, a Louis Diemschutz who had had the misfortune of discovery. As is now known, the victim Elizabeth Stride-another woman of the night was terribly murdered, her body found in the yard as the steward Diemschutz drove his pony in at one o'clock. Holmes produced his letter of authority and questioned PC Lamb, as he had been on the scene amongst the any police officials now busily trampling any clues from existence. The remaining club members had all been searched and subjected to questioning, but to little use. A long-bladed chandler's knife was recovered nearby, it's handle bound with cloth.

Constable Lamb was shaken, but determined. He told Holmes of the man Morris Eagle who had summonsed him and the subsequent horror. The woman's throat had been cut with vicious force, apart from that and the amount of blood there had been no obvious sign of struggle. Holmes thanked him and attempted an examination-I say attempted as the amount of officials prevented any useful search of the yard. The body lay where it was found-on the left side, legs drawn up in her death agony. I could see Dr. Blackwell, the physician who had been called to the scene was intent on his work, leaving him to it after a brief consultation. The patrons of the club, a mixture of Jews, Russians and Hungarians were talking excitedly amongst themselves in a smattering of tongues. Holmes was himself deep in conversation with a number of these, but to little effect. Suddenly, there was a clatter of noise as a growler came flying around the corner of the Commercial Road to the North, sparks shooting from the horses hooves as they nearly fell. The driver jumped down to steady his horses before turning to us, a card in his hand. 'I'm after a Mister Holmes.' 'I am he.' My friend stepped over the where the man was soothing his horses. Taking the card,

Holmes read it and handed it to me to read as we clambered aboard the growler, ordering the driver to take us to Mitre Street, Aldgate. The message was from Lestrade and read simply *'Another body has been discovered, Mitre Sq, Mitre Street in Aldgate. Please meet Inspector Collard of the City Police at the scene.'*

As we stepped down from the growler, Holmes attempted to tip the driver Lestrade had sent for us, but the man would not take a penny. He told us he had orders to wait for us and take us wherever we wished to go, adding that as he had a sister living in Whitechapel, he would not take a tip on principle. A small crowd had already begun to appear, including pressmen, held back by several sturdy Constables. A stocky man with a policeman's steady gait spotted us and made his way over. Holmes held out a hand. 'Inspector Collard, I presume?.' Shaking hands, the Inspector went through the facts with an impressive precision, brevity and grasp of the salient facts. It is in that spirit that I shall approach the hideous death of Catherine Eddowes with concision. Mitre Square is hard by Aldgate and St.Botolph without. Bounded by the warehouse and buildings of commercial premises as well as private dwellings, one a Police Constable's house. This was the crime that escaped discovery by a whisker-one PC Watkins was patrolling his beat, going through the square at one-thirty in the morning. Returning fourteen minutes later it was he who found the poor wretch-but this exceeded even the preceding crimes in savagery. Eddowes had been released from the drunk tank just under a half hour previously.

Holmes was permitted to examine the scene with a borrowed bullseye and even his cold, rational exterior was

100

hard-pressed to remain detached from the horror we both saw that night. The body lay on its back in the corner around from Mitre street at the farthest point from the single gas lamp which was flickering and guttering badly-as if it required attention. Another lamp across the square was burning normally at the entrance to an alleyway. Eddowes' body was laying palms up as if in supplication, but whatever she had received, it wasn't mercy. Turning from the corpse, Holmes wiped his face and laid a hand upon my shoulder. In a strained voice, he asked me to examine her professionally. Had any other asked me such a thing, I should have refused them. Here I refer to the notes I took at the time. *Cause of death; throat cut with excessive force. The face; various lacerations, deep. Massive cut to right of face at the diagonal from the top of the nose downwards. Nose itself absent; cut off. Eyelids cut in single vertical strokes. Two cuts, one below each eye in shape of inverted 'V'. Abrasions to epithelium of left cheek. Lobe and auricle of right ear cut through. Abdominal injuries-massive single cut made from area of pelvis to sternum. Cut ragged and deep. Viscera removed and bowels, intestines laid across body to either side. Probable mutilation to reproductive organs.* It was a list of madness.

Inspector Collard had not been idle, collecting various items found with the body. Holmes made a list and again I refer to this; *Three small buttons, a small metal button, metal thimble, mustard tin containing two pawn tickets, 2 clay pipes, two tin boxes containing tea and sugar, some soap, a comb, table knife and teaspoon, a red leather cigarette case with silver fitments and hidden compartment containing a tailor's receipt, an empty tin vesta case, a sewing kit...* and so forth. For reasons clear only to himself, Holmes quietly pocketed the receipt he had found in the case-all he would say on the matter when I questioned this action later was that he had found the concealment as he had looked for it-and was not responsible for the deficiencies of the police. With the exception of Eddowes' straw hat, her clothes were old and much mended. An apron she wore had been cut through, a piece missing.

Witnesses described a man in conversation with her, but his unkempt description did not tally with the subsequent discovery made by Dr. Brown, the attending physician of two shirt studs in the grisly pool. We had seen all we would see by the light from the gas lamp, but Holmes bent to pick up something beneath the gas-lamp at the corner of Mitre Street, two cigarette butts, which he carefully pocketed. 'Jack's been busy tonight' were the parting words from a pressman who stood by the entrance to the square.' 'Quite. Watson, we have learned all we can for the night. It is late and I have no wish to remain here a moment longer than necessary.' 'Good night, Inspector. I shall be grateful if you keep my name from the reporters I saw on the way in.' The Inspector nodded and shaking hands, we departed.

CHAPTER XIX
JUST FOR JOLLY

Sunday morning in Baker Street saw us up bright and early to enjoy a relaxed breakfast of toast, marmalade and jams and we put away a fair pint of coffee. We sat with our thoughts of the night before until Holmes spoke his aloud. 'Berner Street to Mitre Square in half an hour?, perhaps. But, with half the Constables in London between you?-no. It won't do.' I left this alone for a minute, but when he did not speak again I reached for my briar, filling and tamping it. I knew Holmes; my friend was dangerously vulnerable to the needle in his lowest moments. Although I felt it unlikely he would succumb-still he blamed himself for my abduction due in part to his habits-there remained the possibility. I felt I should engage the finest mind of its day to divert him from this disastrous course. 'So Holmes, with Isenschmidt acquitted, and in such a devilish fashion-how to proceed?. Perhaps those letters we received from our friend Sagar might offer some suggestion?.' 'Yes, Watson-I suppose we'd do better to cover every possibility. For myself I am unconvinced; why should a killer wish to hang himself with a signed confession?.' Having expressed doubt, Holmes then tossed over a handful of letters, retaining half for himself. We read in silence; mostly these were the work of ghouls or deranged persons, with the odd amusing suggestion for the police.

'Watson, I think I have it!' Cried Holmes, but it was immediately clear from his tone and mocking stance that he was in jest. *'Dear Sir, Please find out at once if a Red Indian is available to be pressed to service-they are good trackers.'* Signed Miss Daphne Somer of Bexhill.' Joining in the spirit of the thing, I riffled through the missives. 'I have one, Holmes. Here it goes thus; *'To the Chief Inspector of Police, London.*

Please consider placing dried grass at the corners of the roads in the area most likely to be of interest to the killer. This will help catch him, but be sure to allow your own men to wear rubber soled boots for silence.' Holmes leapt up and leant against the mantle. 'Ha!-here we have a suggestion that the killer may be a Barbary ape, or my very favourite, a missive from Mr. Eli Warner of Stoke, who suggests that detectives in female attire could entice the killer with perfume and then throw their skirts over his head to apprehend him and confound his escape. Watson-the imagination of the British public!.'

It was the next letter, however that changed our mood and lowered it dramatically. Addressed to a Tom Bullen of the Central News Agency, written in a bloody red ink, the contents of that evil bulletin are ingrained upon my very being.

RECEIVED September 27th, 1888

Dear   Boss,
I keep on hearing the police have caught me but they wont fix me just yet. I have laughed when they look so clever and talk about being on the <u>right</u> track. That joke about Leather Apron gave me real fits. I am down on whores and I shant quit ripping them till I do get buckled. Grand work the last job was. I gave the lady no time to squeal. How can they catch me now. I love my work and want to start again. You will soon hear of me with my funny little games. I saved some of the proper <u>red</u> stuff in a ginger beer bottle over the last job to write with but it went thick like glue and I cant use it. Red ink is fit enough I hope <u>ha. ha.</u> The next job I do I shall clip

the lady's ears off and send to the police officers just for jolly wouldn't you. Keep this letter back till I do a bit more work, then give it out straight. My knife's so nice and sharp I want to get to work right away if I get a chance. Good Luck.

Yours   *truly*

       Jack the Ripper

  Dont mind me giving the trade name

PS Wasnt good enough to post this before I got all the red ink off my hands curse it No luck yet. They say I'm a doctor now <u>ha ha</u>

Throwing this abhorrence from me I was left with an overpowering urge to clean my hands. With a gesture towards the loathsome missive I snorted; 'A doctor! Indeed!-the mind that produced this is clearly that of a maniac. Really, these bamboozlers!.' Holmes had reached for his church warden and I knew he would be in one of his disputatious moods as he only smoked the thing when he was subject to these. Puffing away, he produced a cloud of foul smoke and seemed satisfied with his creation, whirling on me to point at the evil letter. 'Read it again.' 'I'd just as soon not.' 'Watson please!.' The raised tone and agitation of my friend's voice persuaded me to reluctantly take up the filthy thing. Again I read those appalling words, again they meant nothing to me. All the while, Holmes' eyes glistened as he watched my face for any sign of recognition. There was none and my face must have given this away. Closing his eyes and rubbing the top of his nose betwixt thumb and forefinger, the detective sighed wearily. 'Watson, *really...* read your notes from Mitre Square.' This I did, although I would never forget a word of them for as long as I should live. Suddenly it hit me; the ear!. *The next job I do I shall clip the ladys ears off and send to the police officers just for jolly wouldn't you...* Eddowe's right ear was cut through!.

Pulling up in Mitre Street there was just a Constable on duty at the entrance to the square itself and a few loafers. Even now the spot where the Eddowes woman lay was plain-it being the only area freshly washed and scrubbed. In the middle of the unpleasant reminder stood another unpleasantry-Inspector Abberline, with a detective in attendance. His colleague nudged him with a nod to alert him to our presence. 'Ah. I thought so-taking advice is not the strongest quality you are possessed of, is it?. Well?.' Holmes was clearly in fine form, ignoring the official with magnificent disdain to stand before the still damp paving. 'Remarkable work, don't you think Watson?. Really quite unparalleled-even for the police. The more evidence that is laid at their very feet the more determined their effort to obliterate it. Come, Watson, there is nothing to look at here but old soap. Let us leave Scotland Yard's finest to guard it.'

By the time we had turned back into Mitre Street I was quite red with my attempt to hold in the laughter, yet Holmes was in no mood for levity. Reaching the corner we turned left past a shop and to where three empty houses stood forlornly as if hoping to attract tenants. At the second Holmes proclaimed a sudden lack of breath, steadying himself against the door jamb. Immediately professional concern replaced jocularity as I attended my stricken friend, placing a hand of reassurance upon his shoulder and taking his pulse-strictly a ruse arranged between us I should now reveal. Under this pretence-of a physician attending a patient with bronchial distress-Holmes had unwrapped his pick-locks and was busily working open the lock-*left handed!*. Even one as accustomed to his legerdemain as myself could not fail to be impressed by such a display. I nodded to indicate there were no apparent witnesses and we were inside.

Dust, decay and the hubris of abandon lay everywhere inside that husk. Where once perhaps laughter and gaiety prevailed was now given over to mute dankness. The place had clearly lain empty a long while, but Holmes was clearly on the scent. I took the lantern he handed me and lit it. Producing his glass he subjected the boards to a careful scrutiny and took the stairs, careful to check each first and to tread on the inside, a look to me enough to recommend I followed suit on this last. Indeed, the stairs creaked alarmingly beneath our combined weight, such that it was with relief we found ourselves on a modest landing. Suddenly, Holmes threw up a hand in warning-I extinguished the light and prepared myself for fisticuffs. There was a bedroom here, the door ajar. Creeping forward using the outside edge of his feet heel to toe Holmes was silence personified, my breath caught as the tension in the foetid air became intolerable. A distinct noise reached us, a knock and a scrape as of a chair being pushed back. Holmes' hand was upon the knob-and he thrust the door open with such force that he was in the middle of the room before anything could be done about it, with me on his heels.

The room was clearly in use, by the look of it, two chairs and a table and a bare wooden bed-frame with a few patched blankets in a roll. A ragged mattress beneath the bed completed the spartan furnishment. Occupying this pitiable scene was a tramp, a veritable pensioner at that with a grey beard and a tangled mane of hair. Of rather more concern than

107

the man's welfare was the knife he held in his left hand. Holmes spoke, his voice even, calm. 'There are two of us-and the police Constable outside.' The man raised his blade, his voice trembling, fearful. 'Leave me alone. I've done you no harm. This is my place, see?.' I interjected. 'We are not here to evict you. We are here on other business.' 'Not the Landlord's agents then?.' 'Nothing of the sort. My friend spoke the truth.' Holmes' placations seemed to be having a calming effect. 'What do you want?.' 'To give you a sovereign. Call it back pay, sergeant.' The man stood, his head askew in confusion. 'I think you had best explain yourself.'

We sat ourselves down, Holmes on the bed-frame whilst the retired campaigner -of course, Holmes was correct- and myself took the chairs. After laying the promised coin upon the table Holmes passed over his cigarette-case and we smoked. At length, Holmes decided to enlighten us. 'No mystery really; boots worn out yet retaining signs of having been polished, gaiters worn regimentally and the few buttons remaining polished so often the device of the Royal Engineers is almost obliterated. You have a carved wooden stick resting in the corner which, if I am correct, was made for you as a much-prized keepsake in a market in Afghanistan. Even with that injury to your left side you retain the unmistakable bearing and rigidity of spine only attained in Her Majesty's service. That is really all, apart from trivia; blankets rolled in case of a hasty evacuation, and everything not in current use packed away in your haversack which I perceived hanging on the head-board. Corporal or Sergeant was my guess.' The man gaped in admiration before slapping the table and roaring with laughter. 'I can see it when you say how it was, but for the life of me I thought you a magician. Jacobs is the name-Stanley Arthur Jacobs, formerly of the Royal Engineers. I guess you are here about the awful business last night. Shocking.'

'Indeed. I am a consulting detective engaged on the solution of these infernal crimes. As you may have heard this was the fourth such atrocity in a month. What, if anything might you have seen or heard-the hours between midnight and two may prove crucial?.' 'Not much, sir. I was in me cups deep last night-helps me sleep. I did hear something-I actually looked out the bathroom window. I've no watch, but I would say it must have been about the time you mention.'

Jacobs took us up to the next landing, where, from the papered-over and cracked window we could see the left side of Mitre Square. The murder site itself was visible only partially in that a few of the damp flags were in view. Pointing a gnarled finger across the square, the old soldier indicated the gas lamp, the very one that Holmes had observed to be failing that night. 'The lamp-it was working fine last I saw it-but when I heard the noise, whatever caused it, I looked from this window and saw him. I mean the policeman, he was climbing the lamp to warm his tea-silly sod must have knocked it into the mantle because next thing it was flaring and spluttering something chronic.' Holmes spun round to face Jacobs. 'You say Policeman – how can you be sure?, the light was, by your own admission at fault.' 'Well, sir,' The lined face was earnest 'Well, I cannot be sure. I saw the man climb, who else would do so but a copper on his rounds wanting to keep himself a hot drink?'

Back down in Mitre Square, looking back at the rear of the houses, I saw the paper at the bathroom window move as if Jacobs were blocking out the scene below-and who could blame the poor man?. Holmes looked back up at the entrance to the Square, where the Constable was keeping back some sight-seers. Handing me his homburg, Holmes shinned up the lamp-post, opening the glass and then reaching into his pocket for his handkerchief he reached in and pulled something out, passing it down to me. As he dropped back down, I opened the kerchief to find... a human kidney. Holmes seemed remarkably sanguine at this ghastly discovery, though I was horrified. 'Not the usual place to find a kidney. What else can this remainder tell us?.'

From the way it was removed I concluded the kidney had been extracted surgically, if hastily-the cuts at the ligament were crudities unsuited to any description other than barbarity. I expressed the opinion that it was probably from Eddowes, but I had been unable to examine her thoroughly at the scene. Our next call was to the Golden Lane mortuary. On second examination, the body proved to have been grossly violated. Although there had been no sign of *coitus,* the area around the reproductive organs had, indeed been ferociously mutilated. The liver had been penetrated by the point of a sharp instrument, doubtless a knife. Most of the womb had been excised. The pancreas had been cut, but what was of topical interest was the removal of the left kidney. While Holmes examined the poor woman's meagre possessions, I took the opportunity to confer with Dr. Brown, the Surgeon to the City of London police. It would be he that conducted the Post-Mortem and it was he, you may recall who found the shirt studs at the scene.

Dr. Brown gave his opinion that the first wound was to the throat and this caused death. 'Did she then fall backwards?.' 'No, no, Doctor Watson, it is my opinion that the victim was lain on the pavement before the cut-and that it was made thus...' He demonstrated a left-handed cut over the cadaver. I was not convinced. 'But, surely, if he was over the victim as you suggest, it could equally have been a right-handed man, whose cut began superficially and deepened as it trajected across the larynx to the left common carotid.' 'Ah, but you forget, Doctor.' He said, raising his finger for emphasis. 'Here our victim, God bless her mortal soul, is raised on the table, wheras on the ground...' 'The handle!; of course!.' I realised at once he was right. The cut *must* have been made with the left hand for the knife handle not to prevent such a full and extensive cut. Death would have been, we both agreed, instantaneous. The knife would have at least a six inch-long blade. It was then that Holmes coughed discreetly to draw our attention from the throat. He had placed the kidney he had found from the gas-lamp and whilst it was somewhat distorted from the flame, the fit was demonstrably perfect. This was, indeed Eddowes' missing kidney-though as Dr. Brown remarked coolly, it was hardly likely to come from another. Holmes had made detailed sketches of the possessions and questioned Dr. Brown as to the shirt studs, which had been left with the police. This done, we left the Doctor to commence the post-mortem proper, making for the Customs House at Legal Quays by the Pool of London.

The Port of London was the busiest of its type anywhere on the globe, with docks wharves and jetties that stretched around the curves of the great river for some nine miles. I had no notion of why we had come here, but clearly Holmes felt he was on the scent and we were shown into the office of the Inspector-a dry, peevish little man by the name of Eldridge. 'Well-I must say I never expected to be involved in this business.' Said he returning Holmes' much-worn letter. 'So you suspect a sea-faring man of the crime?.' 'I cannot say anything with certainty; merely that a chandler's knife was discovered at the scene of one of the crimes-as for the relationship between the trade of the victims and men of the sea...' Chuckling at the shared indiscretion, Eldridge professed amusement with eyes that showed none. The official's tone became stern. 'Now. We've had our joke-but I am a busy man, gentlemen, and you are after a grain of rice in a warehouse full of it. You come here with your amateur's nose and tell me you've sniffed at a knife-shall we spend the rest of the century asking along the river for a knife that won't be claimed unless it was stuck through a bundle of fivers?. You are a joker, and no mistake.' Holmes rose and placed his hands wide across the edge of the popinjay's desk. 'Inspector; I have spent the last month up to my shins in bloody gore. I have no wish to repeat or extend the experience. Should you care to assist Doctor Watson and myself you may find yourself with an uncertain future-perhaps a happy one involving gold braid and a proud Mrs. Eldridge-it is not for me to say. Otherwise I assure you of *these* certainties; You will find yourself in a customs shed on the very fringe of Empire with only memories of London to sustain you and the knowledge that I was *not*, not in the slightest joking.'

The remainder of the hour passed with remarkable expedition. Holmes and myself checked the ledger of the major docks to compile a list of those vessels tied up on the days of interest, complete with their number of registration. Every request, no matter how insignificant, was furnished with a servility that had been quite lacking before. Indeed, Eldridge could not have done more for us, even to the point of whipping up a tray containing tea and coffee. Thanking him for his co-operation we proceeded to the City, to Lloyds the Insurers to spend a long couple of hours engrossed with the Registry of Shipping. The list of names in Holmes' black morocco notebook had seemed hardly to fill a few lines, such was the paucity of our apparent success. At length, the verdict on our day was given and we marked its progress as a useful one. On our return to Baker Street a letter informed me of an elderly patient in the last stages of heart failure-a retired and much-decorated Colonel from the Buffs whose name was once mentioned as a future Prime Minister, but who had deferred personal ambition to devote himself to the pensioners of his regiment. The summons from his wife was fraught and the handwriting spoke of her failing nerve. With such a noble man facing an agonized end I hastened to his bed-side to make his final night a comfortable one. Holmes waved me off with a gesture of understanding.

It was mid-morning on the Monday that I found Holmes in a rare mood of levity. The blackboard was filled with scribblings and diagrams. I ate my egg and toast and sipped my tea while Holmes drank coffee. 'Anything to show for our hard work yesterday, Holmes?.' 'Oh, not much; save the killer is left-handed, uses a carriage, was in formal evening dress and smokes specially-made cigarettes-and although disturbed at Berner Street he was not thus hampered in Mitre Square. He is well-to-do, if not outright wealthy. He is either impotent or sexually incompetent and possibly suffering with a disease picked up from such women, such as phagadena.' Setting down my toast I let out a short bark of laughter. 'Really, Holmes, you do this too often. Now, let me see how you did it... the evening dress is simplicity itself-the shirt studs?. Holmes nodded, steepling his hands beneath his chin as he awaited my attempt at deduction. 'And left-handed-because of the direction and nature of the cuts?.' Again, a nod. 'So, a man in formal dress is not of the poorer classes, hence well-to-do...' 'Partly, but there is also the cigarette case in Eddowe's possession, doubtless picked from the pocket of a-client. Not the property of a poor man. 'Come, Holmes, how can you be sure it is his?.' 'Because I found two butts around the corner at the entrance to Mitre Street; these carry the mark of a maker in Bond Street, if I am not mistaken. These correspond with a trace of tobacco I found in the case itself, surely not too far a leap to suggest these were his and she stole the case after he was rash enough to both show it to her and where he kept it. Sadly, it is not initialled or we might use it to hang him-though the tailor's receipt I found inside the case is highly suggestive.' 'Suggestive?, of what?.' 'It is for an unusually large sum-the goods listed are a few lounge suits of the finest wool, a few silk shirts; expensive material to be sure, but hardly worth £200.' 'Did you say two *hundred* pounds?.' 'I did, but the infuriating thing is the tailor's name has been ripped from the bill, so finding it may take a while.'

'And how do you arrive at a diagnoses of sexual impotence?.' I asked. 'There too I am in the realm of probability; on none of the bodies did we observe any sign of carnal activities, the natural result of congress between a man and a woman. Yet all these women died from a cut throat, administered by a man close to them as only a patron would be. It is my contention that these women were either facing away from what they thought was a normal-shall we say *customer*, ready to begin their work or with their backs to walls and suchlike, or on the floor in the cases of Stride and Eddowes. We must assume they were less particular in their regard to cleanliness of dress.' Once more I did not follow this extraordinary man's reasoning. 'Oh, Watson, can't you see it?. The killer approaches the victim, engages her in conversation of, presumably both pecuniary and erotic nature, closes in on her, but then cannot consummate the arrangement. This fuels his rage, the insanity burns within him and he strikes.' Such a man harbours a terrible compulsion to destroy fallen women. I have also investigated the possibility of a seafaring man being involved, but the only ships I could find docked at the times of the murders were of the *Norddeutscher* line. I am currently awaiting the ships' lists from our friend Eldridge... but I fancy that I see a hansom drawing up. Quickly, Watson-this place is a mess!. We tidied as the doorbell sounded.

CHAPTER XX
JEHOVA'S WITNESS

We heard Mrs. Hudson greeting our guest and footsteps on the stair. It was Lestrade, with yet more evidence. There were several witnesses to each of the murders committed that dark Saturday night. Lestrade went over their evidence whilst Holmes sat, apprently distracted. It was when the Inspector mentioned a Jew by the name of Israel Schwartz, who insisted he had seen the murderer of Elizabeth Stride that my colleague suddenly sat still in one of his trances, for all the world a man asleep-yet I knew better. When Holmes wished to absorb and digest every detail of a case he would sit thus. This Schwartz had been interviewed by the police and the Inspector read from an account of this. At twelve forty-five in the morning, Schwartz had been returning to his family lodgings in Berner Street and, at the gateway of Dutfield's Yard saw a man stop to speak to a woman matching the general description of Elizabeth Stride. The man threw the woman down onto the pavement at which she let out several short cries. Not being the sort to interfere with a domestic squabble, Schwartz crossed the road where he saw a second man lighting a pipe. He had not seen this man until he struck his match. The first man then called across to the second, shouting the name 'Lipski', at which Schwartz hurried away. The pipe smoker then gave chase, but lost interest at the Arches. His duty done, Lestrade settled himself into the settee and proceeded to fill his pipe, seeming very self-satisfied with his morning's work.

Opening an eye, Holmes looked across to my perch and shot me a playful smile. 'Was there a description, Lestrade? Of the two men I mean.' 'Yes, oh... yes, Mister Holmes, it's in the papers here somewhere... yes. The first man, the one that actually assaulted the woman is around thirty years of age, five feet and the same in inches, fair-skinned, with dark hair. He had a brown moustache, smallish, was strongly built and wore a black cap above dark jacket and corresponding trousers.' 'Corresponding trousers?; Lestrade you excel yourself, you really do.' This last brought a hint of a blush to the Inspector's cheek, but he hurriedly moved on to the next man, the pipe-smoking pursuer. This man, Schwartz put at thirty-five, a fraction below six feet in height, fresh-faced and with light brown or reddish hair. He wore a black felt hat of aged appearance with a dark overcoat.' I had listened to all this in silence, but the name shouted by one of the ruffians had been familiar; Lipski was the name of an acid murderer who had forced a young woman to consume nitric acid. What had made the murder so much more savage in aspect was that the poor girl had been with child. I commented on this to Holmes, but Lestrade seemed to think it was clear it was the name of the ruffian with the pipe. Holmes rose, stretched and went to ring for some tea to be brought to us. When he returned he went to the window and opened it a few inches. The sounds of the busy city came in and with them that peculiar mix of smells unique to London at that time of year; chimney smoke, baked bread, brick-dust and manure.

'Lestrade, can we be sure of this Schwartz' testimony? Is he accurate in his observations?.' The Inspector was adamant on the matter and replied firmly to Holmes' question. 'Oh, yes-quite sure. He visited the mortuary and identified the body as the woman he had seen to be accosted.' 'His description of the two louts was very precise indeed-his eyesight is good?.' 'We have no reason to doubt his sight, Holmes, why dwell on the matter?' 'Perhaps an illustration. Lestrade, if you would be so kind, could you join me at the window and describe to me the fellow standing beside the newspaper stand across the road?.' With the air of a sufferer, Lestrade indulged this request, but due to the haze of the city air he was limited to a generalised attempt at establishing the man's physiognomy. 'I can see several of his features, he is certainly an Englishman and no more or less than five-feet nine.' 'He is an Ottoman Turk and certainly stands six feet in his slippers, Lestrade. His name is Mehmet and he sells Mrs. Hudson some outrageous pamphlets of a romantic nature quite unsuited to a lady of her presbytarian Scottish nature.' Lestrade was not to be disheartened so easily, waving a hand at the window. 'This fog...' Holmes cut across him '...Was heavier that night in Berner Street and it was a good deal darker, yet you say this witness was able to provide such a comprehensive report, even while being chased away by one of them?. It will not do, Lestrade!. Clearly, the name 'Lipski' was an insult, directed towards the witness-an example of *Antisemitisch*, the hatred of Jews; hardly an aspersion to be cast at a man with a fresh complexion and reddish hair.' Somewhat crestfallen by now, the Inspector shook his head. 'Well, Mister Holmes, you do make sense of it, but there is more to this matter...' With that, however, our landlady arrived and set out a tray for us. We took tea and with it a brief and welcome deferment regarding these execrable murders.

Somewhat chastened, Lestrade went for his coat and hat, leaving us with the slim sheaf of papers from which he had read. It was growing dark and he had to present at Scotland Yard, there being a general call to duty that night. Whitechapel had been thick with police before these last outrages, but now it seems the district would be awash with 'bluebottles' as they were dismissively known to the *habitué* of the area. Taking his leave of us, the Inspector departed with effusive thanks from Holmes. I knew the man better, of course and soon we were both roaring with laughter. 'Corresponding trousers!; really he's the absolute limit, Watson. Rarely have the inept risen to such heights as the detective force of London.' Mrs. Hudson bustled up to remove the tray and Holmes stated his intent to dine out that night, apologising at the waste of dinner which she had, no doubt been preparing for us. He then returned his attention to the task at hand, scraping at the blackboard with the chalk whilst I contended myself with a cigarette and perusal of the papers Lestrade had left for us. There were some witness statements from unreliable sources, statements from the Constables on duty and a curious note about some graffito which had been scrawled on a wall in Goulston street. I mentioned these all, to grunts from Holmes as he worked, but the reference to the graffito stimulated his curiosity to the extent that he fairly ripped the paper from my hand in a sudden fever.

Turning the board so that I could read it clearly, Holmes had pinned a map of the area to it, with red threads radiating out from pins indicating the murder sites. Each of these threads terminated in a flurry of chalkings in the indecipherable style he was wont to assume in moments of frenetic activity. Taking a pencil from his pocket, he indicated Berner Street. 'Stride. Throat cut; no mutilation *post-mortem.*' Now Mitre Square; 'Eddowes. Throat cut, extensive mutilation. Conclusion?; the killer was disturbed with Stride, deprived of his real goal, the mutilation and-in his mind, the debasement of the victim. He struck again because he was *compelled* to.' 'You mean to say, that his unnatural urges had yet to be satisfied?, that the killing of these women is only of secondary importance to his depravity?.' 'Quite. We are entering the mind-indeed the *psyche* of the most abhorrent creature, yet one that walks, eats, breathes and sleeps among ordinary people unobserved and unremarkable. That such a creature could exist undetected is the sole reason we have not laid hands upon him yet.' 'I still wonder how he could have slaughtered two women with so much fear abroad in the area.' 'And in so short a space of time... ask yourself this, Watson; how does a man get to here-he tapped Mitre Square-from here, in just half an hour?.' 'A carriage!, Holmes, that's it!, a carriage!.'

His eyes positively shining now, my friend shook his head. 'At night in the district of Whitechapel carriages are being stopped and the occupants questioned now, Watson. Both by the official police and the vigilance committees that have been springing up.' 'Holmes, the man is invisible!. How can he possibly elude capture?.' 'Because he *is* invisible, my old friend. I shall put it to you in the form of a riddle; a hansom is stopped on the street, but found to be empty. Who rode in it?.' 'Empty?, why, no-one then.' Leaning close to myself, Holmes tapped me on the head with his pencil. 'The cabbie!.'

My watch showed a quarter to seven. We had eaten a hurried meal at a restaurant just off Piccadilly and we still had some hours before we would move to the East End to watch the Arches. Partly to pass the time, Holmes slipped me a piece of paper. It was a hand-written copy of what is now infamous as the Goulston Street Graffito. I keep this facsimile in my papers still of that poisonous graffito; to put it as bluntly as such trash deserves it is a vile slander upon the character of those adherents to the Hebrew faith. The words themselves were scrawled above a piece of bloody cloth which was already known to be the missing piece of the Mitre Square victim's apron. I have reproduced here the graffito for posterity and the amateur detectives among you.

The Thirtieth of September 1888
Copied from Goulston Street passageway.

The Juwes are

The men That

Will not

be Blamed

for nothing

CHAPTER XXI
A CLUB FOR THE UN-CLUBBABLE

As I have had cause to lay down before, the Diogenes Club is the haunt of the most un-clubbable of men, a strange oasis of silence in the noise of the city. Step through the glass-panelled doors and onto the plush carpeting and you are at once removed from society and its cares. Attended by servants trained to muteness and forbidden- under penalty of expulsion-from even acknowledging fellow members, you find yourself oddly freed from the shackles of propriety and politeness. As befitted his status, Holmes was shown to the Strangers' Room, the one room in the club where speech was and remains permissible. With reference to the hour, he ordered a half of sherry and waited by the bow window overlooking Pall Mall. A voice from the doorway behind us; 'I see you still refuse to clean your pipe thoroughly.' Without missing a beat, Holmes turned and retorted; 'Whilst I can hardly fail to observe that while you have been working over-long hours at the Foreign Office, at least you have finally exchanged your Maid for one both right-handed and competent at needlework.' 'Ah, good evening Doctor Watson. I am sorry to see that you were helpless to retaliate whilst your assailant delivered his blows... the lack of abrasions to your own knuckles is suggestive.' The preliminaries completed, the two brothers nodded, took their seats and spent some minutes in silent contemplation of the world outside the window. Mycroft Holmes was senior to his brother in years, but in ambition very much his junior-although an indispensable figure at Whitehall, Mycroft preferred the life of ease offered by the club he had helped to found. I had heard it said that he was in some way connected with the secret service, as a consultant rather than an agent or official. The two were soon entered into deep discussion, two of the very finest minds in conclave with the single purpose of identifying both purpose and felon in the murders that seemed insoluble.

Mycroft rang the bell pull for a porter and ordered us cigars and a creditable port. While we waited, he commented on the Goulston Street writing that Holmes had showed him. 'Clearly the work of an illiterate.' Holmes seemed surprised at this, raising an eyebrow. 'You assume the word 'Juwes' a misspelling, then?.' 'Clearly, the Capitalisation of the 'B' in 'Blamed' confirms it.' Handing the paper back to his brother, Mycroft pocketed his eyeglass and waved it away. 'A simple attempt to implicate the Jews, with a piece of bloodied evidence to re-inforce the claim.' Holmes seemed to find this curious, but concealed his perplexity well. 'And the placement of the body of the Eddowes woman?. Mere happen-stance?.' Turning those grey watery eyes on his younger brother, the elder Holmes shook with an ill-suppressed snort. 'You refer, naturally to the proximity to the Synagogue?.' 'Naturally.' Mycroft raised a hand to pull at his whiskers. 'Then what follows is the killer-or an unknown, took the piece of, what was it-apron?... and wrote that appalling filth simply to alert the authorities to a Jewish lunatic?.' For answer, Sherlock Holmes merely smiled one of his thin, strained smiles. The porter arrived with a salver containing the refreshments Mycroft had solicited. However, Sherlock strode from the room, leaving me to follow with a shrug of apology to his curious brother. As I departed, I heard him mutter; 'Pity. It's a '68 at that.' We collected our top hats and the gladstone Holmes had brought and left, without further words.

The growler took us through the gas-lit streets past the revellers of Charing Cross and along the Strand, along into Fleet Street. At Holmes' insistence I had called up a carriage so that we might effect our changes the more easily. In some twenty minutes I was dressed in a sturdy, if unfashionable brown check tweed that had seen better days, an Ulster over this under a scarf and an old bowler which Holmes had had re-inforced especially. My companion was no longer Sherlock Holmes, but a street tough, perhaps a market porter, a coster or a drayman fallen on hard times. Of course, we were both armed, I with my service revolver and he with a set of brass knuckles. In addition, I carried a hardwood stick that, whilst it would genuinely aid me in walking further had been altered by the simple method of drilling, being filled with solid lead. 'One thing, Holmes, what was that about a synagogue?.' 'I refer, Watson, to the Great Synagogue in Duke Street. Less than forty feet from Church Passage... the alleyway leading into Mitre Square.' Looking out of the window at Leadenhall Street, he seemed in reflective mood. 'Clearly, Watson, someone has gone to a great deal of trouble to lay the blame for these murders at the door of the Jewish community. Someone who doesn't know the meaning of the Mitre to a certain group of people.'

CHAPTER XXII
A QUESTION OF IDENTITY

The Brown Bear in Leman Street was packed to the rafters, with a polyglot crew of blaggards, roughs and the odd groom. Keeping the peace, such peace as was left to keep was the sizable group of off-duty policemen, who kept a table for themselves by the wall. Some were in uniform, but without their distinctive duty arm-bands. My watch showed a quarter of six as I entered, pushing past a pair of slatterns who were in the beginnings of a quarrel. 'Ah, Watson London's finest enjoying a well-earned pint-and just time for us to partake; a swift stiffener before the entertainment. I can recommend the mild and the landlord assures me the stout is up with the very best.' 'Kentish Hops, Sirs, none but them will make the pint thick enough, that's the secret, see?.' Without wishing to offend our host I plumped for a half of mild, which was, I must admit, rather fine.

It was time. I was to find out the cause for Holmes' curious diversion as we entered the station opposite. Inside, a rag-tag of motleys was in a semblance of a line and at its head was Lestrade and the unsmiling countenance of Inspector Abberline. 'Come for the matinee, gentlemen?. Thought so-alright Lestrade, lets get this shambles underway.' The principle became clear; a line of several men were arrayed along a long corridor. These men were all given heavy overcoats and deerstalker hats, and each a parcel wrapped in newspaper. Each coat bore a number. Holmes accepted his coat, hat and parcel cheerfully and took his place in the centre of the line. The sight of my friend in a deerstalker in the middle of the city caused me no little amusement; for all the world he might have been on the fells. I observed each man to be of similar height and build, although Holmes was the taller by a good inch. The commotion outside was subdued by the witnesses, who were brought in from a side office by a Constable. The assemblage of pressmen, officialdom and sight-seers variously scribbled their notes, preened themselves and puffed themselves and gawped as the small group was shepherded towards the entrance to the corridor. From my position-a nook across from Holmes-I saw Lestrade leading a smallish woman along the line. The woman was nervous and distrait, yet clearly was making a concerted effort to overcome her emotion and assist the police. At the end of the line she was told to pause and then go back down, but she evidently could not identify the suspect.

Holmes himself had detailed some of the suspicious characters seen around the areas at the time of the murders. One of these, a man dressed as those in the line and of medium height, but foreign appearance notable for carrying just such a parcel had been spotted at the scene of both the Chapman and Stride killings. The next witness, another woman identified the man with the number three-hardly the result intended, the man being a sergeant from H division. So it was with the majority of the witnesses, until bottom was reached with the identification of Holmes by a stout fellow with *myopia gravis* who freely admitted he had broken his spectacles some weeks prior to the whole thing and had not the purse to replace them. Abberline came down the stair from the detectives room and, after a word with Lestrade waved off the line to the right to be dismissed. As the file clumped past, a Constable relieved them of their parcels and costume. Holmes exchanged his number for a coin at the pay clerk's box and flipped it up with his thumb to catch it in his cap. 'So much for Lestrade's chorus line-some of these 'witnesses' could not be relied upon to recognize themselves in the mirror.' Hardly had he spoken than a new line was formed,

126

these men dressed according to the reports of a seafarer.

We had already decided to spend Holmes' earnings across the road in the Brown Bear when the first witness was brought around. It was our sturdy, but short-sighted chap, who squinted at the assembled sailors before frowning blindly at Lestrade. 'They're all dressed the same-how am I supposed to tell them apart?.' Suddenly, Holmes stopped dead in his tracks, whirling round with an expression such as I had only seen when inspiration was gripping him. 'Watson, what a slow fellow I have been!-that presbyopic little fellow sees more than I; they dressed the same!.' 'They?.' 'Yes, Watson-they!, them, *those, these*... it's more than one!.' Pulling me aside so as not to be overheard, he spoke in an urgent whisper. 'We have been labouring under the assumption that a single lunatic has been at large, using a cab to convey him through the city, probably under the various guises of passenger and even jarvey-now, it is my contention that there are two or even more of them. That is why there has been no resolution to this infernal case.' 'And this explains why the police are chasing so many disparate characters?, the sailors, the men with parcels?.' 'I had thought so-it is as easy for a criminal to guise himself as another as it is for us. No, this is far more sinister, a singular occurrence in the history of recorded crime. No Watson, we are not looking for one man disguised as many, but many disguised as the one!.'

Aldgate High Street was oddly quiet, as if there was a premonition of trouble in the air. The Arches sat silently, brooding in the fog, that was, if anything, the thickest I had seen in London. Thick fog plays tricks with the ear, everyday, familiar noises transposed with the sinister; a door closing became the gallows hatch dropping, a creak of a gate hinge the groan of the rope. It was with a shudder that I turned my attention to the job at hand. Holmes had asked me to apply myself to the task of lookout and with a sense of foreboding I was now engaged in this criminal activity, in support of trespass and burglary!. He had been gone some fifteen minutes when a hand was clamped over my mouth, stifling my unwitting cry. I needn't have worried; it was Holmes. His mouth close to my ear, he whispered that the Arches were currently unoccupied, but clearly preparations had been made for a nocturnal excursion. What these where, he never had the chance to say, as a pair of shapes emerged from the murk startlingly close to us. Holmes made to sink back, but I held his arm tightly to keep him still, my old experience from Afghanistan telling me such a movement was more likely to be spotted than two motionless shapes in the mist. The men went over to the gate and we hard the rasp of a padlock being opened and the rattle of the chain. One of the men must have left then, because he emerged again with a horse, the sudden wash of light from inside the archway showing it to be a coal-black beast. 'Wait here, stay out of sight.' With these whispered words, Holmes was off into the night, only to return in rather less than two minutes, just as the horse emerged, now in harness to a hansom cab, doubtless the same that took me from Regent's Park.

We watched and waited while the Arches were locked up behind the cab and as the hansom, lights dimmed, rolled past us, turning to the right. Instantly, Holmes disappeared and I heard a wolf-whistle. Out of the night itself, a second hansom came up, driven by a gaunt-faced man I did not recognise. We leapt in. 'Straight ahead and don't get too close!.' The speaking hatch was open and the craggy face at it. 'Got a lively one, then Mister 'Olmes?.' 'Quite. Watson this is Phipps, London's newest jarvey-better known to the carriage-racing trade as Lightning Len.' I raised my bowler as we went lurching in the tracks of the first cab.

Phipps proved to be as skilful as he was fleet, taking the corners closely and keeping his horse reined in on the straights, so that the lights of the cab ahead were never more than the faintest glow. It would mean disaster for our presence to be detected. Even thought this was a comparatively well-lit road, the fog made everything seem distant, remote until we were almost on top of it. The lights ahead swung to the right and we followed into the Commercial Road. This was perhaps less brightly illumined, the lights ahead now seeming to be hanging in mid-air. Traffic was less busy here-just a tram, some carts and the pedestrians fewer as we approached the New Road, where the lights turned left. Phipps held back here as the junction was well-lit, taking us round at a slow trot. It was soemthing of a shock to see how close behind we had come, the cabman clearly visible hunched over on his seat. If he were to look behind now, we should be exposed. Holmes had already given instructions that, should this occur, Phipps was to take the next turning regardless of where it took us. By now I was thoroughly lost, but Holmes had what cab drivers call 'the knowledge' and told me we were approaching Charlotte Street, a particularly seedy and destitute part of town. The lights ahead seemed to have stopped and, unbidden, Phipps slowed his horse to a walk. This, it appeared, was it.

We clambered down slowly, noise being kept to a minimum. Holmes led the way, his crepe-soled boots a distinct advantage to my own leather soles. Later, Holmes was able to identify the jarvey as the swarthy Indian Joe, but all I saw as we approached was a large man leaning against his seat. Crossing the road behind the parked cab, we made our way unseen around the corner into Oxford Street. This was a world away from its famous namesake in the West End. Indeed, it was hard to reconcile myself that two such disparate thoroughfares could exist in the same city. The only light here was from the odd lonely street-lamp, whilst the odd warm glow from the houses showed that they could, at least, afford an oil-lamp to provide light for their families. This was the only sign of relative prosperity; the place was simply appalling, both to sight and smell. Everywhere the street was fairly piled with manure, save the odd section where a sweeper had scratched their meagre living. From where we now stood, we could see nothing of the cab we had followed, so it was safe to assume that to the jarvey, we were effectively invisible. Going to the north side of the street, we worked back towards the junction and across to Charlotte Street itself.

We were now heading roughly in a westerly direction, when we heard the sound of boot scraping on pavement. Moving forward more quickly, we could see a man-indistinct and made vague by the damnable fog. He was wearing a cloak and a top hat-quite ridiculous for this area, until you consider that only a street away the theatres of the district sad, cheek by jowl with the underground. The shadow seemed to melt away, but when we reached the spot we found a ginnel and entered it cautiously. Somewhere ahead, in the darkness, an underground train rumbled through to St. Mary's station. Which is when we heard it. A woman's scream, swiftly muffled as if by a hand. Charging forward, we came to an abrupt right-angle in the passage, which Holmes flew around. I, however, hurtled headlong into the brickwork and would have knocked myself unconscious had it not been for Holmes' foresight in providing me with the stiffened bowler. As it was, I was somewhat shaken and had to force myself to continue in my friend's footsteps, passing the stage door of the London

Theatre. I found Holmes bent over something-a girl!. She had been badly shaken, yet was evidently alive. 'Watson, the girl!. See to her!.' Although I tell you I had never wanted to continue a chase as badly in my life, my Hippocratic Oath bound me to give aid and succour to this poor young woman. I make no apology for having done so, whatever the peril I may have placed Sherlock Holmes, my friend in that wicked night.

Holmes told me all of it later, of course, as I stitched his arm. He told how he had pursued the maniac through the maze of alleyways and warrens into the Whitechapel Road itself. The fiend had fled towards the south-east, past the crowd outside the underground station and to the London Theatre itself, where, as luck would have it, a large group of patrons was in the process of leaving. Finding a man in topper and cloak would normally be child's play in the East End, but now it was nearly impossible. As so often before, Holmes' intellect and sharp wits came to his aid. The killer would be alone, so he could rule out the couples present, which left perhaps ten gentlemen-of these, four were with a friend, leaving six. Of this final six, only three were caped. One was an elder man with spectacles, the others were of the right age-and build. Going up to the first in comradely fashion, Holmes clapped him on the back, reeling drunkenly. 'Evenin' pally, how wash the show?.' 'Unhand me at once!.' The man pulled away, startled at this uncouth lout who had accosted him. Tipping his cap, Holmes sidles away and contrived to bump into the final suspect. Again, he clapped him on the shoulder-and immediately returned to the previous man, delivering a savage uppercut. This would have knocked most men cold, but the man was holding a surgical knife and Holmes had been forced to pull the punch to avoid the thrust of steel. A woman screamed and there was a commotion, with the people

131

nearest drawing back to avoid the wicked blade. Again the knife flashed out, Holmes backing away, the brass knuckles on his fist now.

By this time, I was emerging from the alleyway, supporting the girl, who was by now hysterical. We managed to reach the underground station when I saw the fight. Petitioning a kindly-looking old maid to comfort the distraught victim, I drew my police whistle and blew it, before hurrying forward and entering the fray. I saw the glimmer of light on steel as the deranged lunatic slashed down-Holmes was injured!. My blood up, I charged, stick high above my head, bringing it down onto the man's wrist, which shattered with the force of my blow. The knife clattered to the ground and a voice screamed out 'He's Jack the Ripper!.' 'It's the Ripper!.' The cry was taken up and the crowd surged forward as one towards the murdering swine. All of a sudden I heard the sound of a horse whinnying and a tremendous clattering of hooves. Turning, I saw the cab we had followed bearing down on me and it was Holmes who saved me, knocking me to the pavement just inches from those flying hooves. I just had time to see the Ripper leap onto the side of the cab, which snatched him along and away from the hands reaching out for him. Holmes pulled me to my feet and a boy in an usher's buttons came up, holding the diabolical fiend's top hat and the knife which he had left behind. Holmes took these and gave the lad a coin for his trouble. I could see my friend had sustained a cut to his arm, which was bleeding freely. Taking a kerchief from my pocket, I pressed this against the wound and told Holmes to keep a steady pressure on it with his good hand. A pair of Constables had joined the throng and began taking statements. By the time they had spoken to us-and removed the knife and hat as evidence, it was clear the murderer had made good his escape. I was all for returning to the Arches with several Constables, but Holmes pointed out the lack of any evidence against anyone there; all we had seen was a cab taking a fare-raiding the premises now would only frighten the gang from view.

CHAPTER XXIII
AN INTERVIEW AT SCOTLAND YARD

The next day I covered my rounds quickly and finally made my mind up; I would tell Holmes of my intention to wed Miss Mary Morstan. Those among you familiar with my transcriptions will doubtless recall the case in which fate decreed our entwining, but for those others I advert you to the case referred to as *The Sign of The Four*. With matrimony in mind, I spent a happy afternoon casting about for suitable practice and lodgings. Several seemed suited, though the best was rather above my means. I *would* tell Holmes–and before another day had passed. True it was that I had dreaded the dissolution of our partnership, the fruits of which had proved manifold. However, these last months had been intolerable–not only had we been powerless to prevent the brutal murders of several women, but I had been assaulted and, if I am to be honest, my heart was not in it.

The last place on my list was in the Paddington district and seemed excellent for my purpose, being adjacent to another equally busy practice. The situation of the pair seemed ideal, offering a steady stream of patients, such as the poor fellow being helped from a hansom outside. I stepped aside to allow the aged cleric past. The old chap walked with a pronounced stoop and the onset of palsy, when the glint from beneath his spectacles betrayed his interest in me. Straightening my jacket I frowned sternly; this was an intrusion too far!. 'Really Holmes, must you spy on me in such an obvious fashion?.' 'You have excelled yourself, Watson-really you have!.' It *was* Holmes, but standing behind me!. Indicating the waiting cab, he seemed happier than I had seen him in some time. 'Climb in, we have a drive ahead of us.' With a crack of the reins, the horse started off, Holmes passing across a paper of sandwiches and a flask containing some brandy. 'A toast Watson-the happy couple!.' If I had had a start already it was as none to the shock I had on noticing and reading the inscription upon the silver. *To my friend and colleague John Watson MD with the fondest regards SH* . What could I possibly say against such a man?-I was seized anew with admiration for this finest of men, resolving in future to hide nothing from him.

There are perhaps no better known streets to find a gentleman's tailor than Savile Row or Jermyn Street, yet Holmes was interested in neither. The odd receipt he had found amongst the Eddowes woman's effects was, he was convinced, a payment for something other than a few suits. As such a curiosity was unlikely to be for legitimate purposes, it was likely to belong to one of many East End tailors of less repute, of which there were many. It seemed impossible to me given the number of shops crowded into the streets, back-streets and alleys of the area that we would have any success. I had reckoned without Holmes' keen insight however. The receipt, which he now produced was on fine paper, with the items listed normally. However, the writing was unusual, the noughts were crossed through, top to bottom. This, Holmes assured me was a German trait. Further, the paper contained a watermark, which had been partially ripped through by whoever had sought to disguise its origin. This mark had given Holmes a fair run for his money, with no mention of it in the London Index. Even his trusted Continental Gazetteer had proved quite useless and he had begun to despair.

In the end, it was a rare piece of luck; the image on the paper was the stamp of the Junker Sewing Machine company of Karlsruhe. Of all people, it had been our very own Mrs.

Hudson who had recognised it!. Spotting Holmes' mood, she had enquired of it and been given short shrift. It was only when she had insisted on looking at the mark that it had seemed familiar to her. She had taken the remnants of Holmes' lunch away when she came back up, fairly bounding the stairs in her excitement. Her sister owned such a machine and she had used it herself many times. Dashing off a telegram to the company, Holmes had asked for the details of their agent in London. Finding the office, the letter of authority was brandished and the names of their customers in the environs of Whitechapel were provided to him. There were thirteen of these, the first nearby in Houndsditch. This proved not to be the place; Holmes ordered an embroidered handkerchief for himself-he was talked into buying two at a special rate. Once outside the shop, the receipt he was given matched neither in handwriting nor did the paper bear any watermarking. The next, just off Angel Alley proved likewise disappointing. In all, Holmes had bought some fifteen odd kerchiefs when, at what must have been the twelfth shop, the writing and paper were a match. This was in a tiny little kiosk of a place hard by the Mile End road.

The shop was owned by one Morris Green-at least that was the Anglicised name above his premises. Green himself was a cheerful enough chap, a short plump Jew who seemed delighted to have customers. Indeed, we were greeted as old friends and I found it quite impossible to connect this merry fellow with any wrong-doing. Holmes, however was of a differing opinion, handing over the receipt he had found, his eyes scrutineer to the man's mood. Looking up from the paper, Green's face seemed anxious, as if something were wrong. 'Mister Green...' Holmes began, but the tailor waved his hands erratically in the air. 'Mo, please, everyone calls me Mo, Sir.' 'Mo it is then. We require our order a little ahead of schedule

I'm afraid.' 'We, Sir?.' 'Myself and the colleague that placed the order with you.' 'He didn't say there were other gentlemen involved, Sir-though I knew their must have been.' 'How so?.' 'Well, you don't ask for four uniforms if there's just one of you.' 'Come to think of it, Sir.-not that I'm meaning to doubt you, how do I know you are connected with the gent that first came in?.' 'Oh, that's easy enough; I don't want the finished goods sent anywhere else; the Arches will do. Now, If I *was* a thief as you imply...' This brought a flurry of protestations and repudiations. 'Please, Sir; the Arches it is. And you say November the Ninth is too late?.' 'Oh my dear fellow, you will think me a fool. The Ninth you say?. That damn fool told me it was December!. You are sure they were ordered for November?.' 'As sure as I wrote it in my ledger, here, Sir.' Green reached behind him and patted a leather-bound volume. With another apology, Holmes doffed his hat and we departed. I was elated, my poor feet being quite blistered by the long hours spent trudging the streets, but Holmes seemed positively enervated. We set off in search of a cab for our next appointment.

Old, oily and unsavoury remains the best description for the black clay pipe Holmes produced-smoking it as if he was alone in our rooms rather than in the estimable company of Sir. Charles Warren. We were in his office at Scotland Yard and our small group was completed by the Chief Inspector of the CID, Donald Swanson. With his distinctive soft Scottish burr and direct way, he watched keenly from his chair as Holmes proceeded to lay out his evidence on the table, his left arm stiff with the bandages I had applied. Soon, the massive slab of mahogany was covered by papers and the board Holmes had borrowed was chalked to his satisfaction. 'Gentlemen-Sir. Charles-here are the cases as I see them. First'-he indicated the papers-'The murders of Nichols,

Chapman, Stride and Eddowes. These cases take us into the realms of the unusual, that of a group of what I shall term Habitual Killers as yet unknown.'

Sir.Charles would have spoken first, had Swanson not beaten him to it. 'Killers?, Mr. Holmes I would like you to clear my mind of confusion and explain yourself.' 'Certainly-after consulting my brother Mycroft Holmes I have made a Comparative Crime Site Analysis, a method in which similarity and disparity can be assessed scientifically in each case. For example; Chapman and Stride.' Holmes rapped his pipe against a chalk sketch. 'A man in a dark coat and deerstalker hat, seen by different witnesses at both sites.' Sir. Charles cleared his throat and added his thoughts to the proceedings. 'The same man, then?.' 'No, Sir. Charles-the description tallies, but different ages and heights; he's forty years of age in one report, a young man in another. 'But, Mister Holmes, you must surely be aware of the variable nature of witnesses?.' The great detective whirled round, eyes bright. 'Even so, when the reports come from police officials?-men trained to observation as second nature?. By way of example; Stride and Eddowes-a sailor or man of the sea, description; close, but with disparities-this time a knife, described as a 'Chandler's Knife with a handle of bound cloth' found at the prior site. Gold shirt studs found in Mitre Square. Just last night, Doctor Watson and myself came close to apprehending a man accoutred for the Opera, who left a surgeon's knife. I had wondered about Holmes' methods many times, but I could not see how he identified the killer at the theatre and asked him this. 'Oh, it was nothing. A mere question of temperature and dampness. The first man I laid hands on wore a cool, dry cape; clearly it had been hung in the cloakroom. The killer's cape, however was both damp and warm from the inclement weather and his exertions. And that,

138

gentlemen is what led me irresistibly to my conclusions.' Drawing himself to his full height Holmes puffed at his pipe in triumph. 'Well?, what do you see from all this, gentlemen?.'

Scraping his chair back, Chief Inspector Swanson consulted his watch, checking it against the clock on the wall before walking around the table to see the chalk with more clarity. 'Sir. Charles, with your permission?.' The Commissioner inclined his head and the Scot resumed his perusal, at length he gave his opinion. 'How did we miss this?-I had thought the reports didn't quite ring true, but this plurality theory surely remains just that; a theory?.' 'The knife!-don't you see?-a sailor, assuming him to be such commits the murder of Elizabeth Stride, and then, the alarm given he not only sprints across to Mitre Square past a veritable cordon of Police and alarmed citizens but he also produces from thin air a second knife?-no sailor carries two knives. He does not, because *he* is *they*. *They,* gentlemen... they. And their travels were not on foot. They used-and still use, a variety of carriages.'

'Holmes, you have it!, I am as sure of it as I sit here. The Chief Inspector waved his hand at the board. 'This is a most remarkable display of faculty and reasoning!.' Holmes' face had assumed a grave countenance. 'Sir. Charles, what I ask now I freely admit I have no right to, but I must make of you what must seem the most flagrant imprecation.' 'Mr. Holmes, you-and the good Doctor here-have been of the greatest possible assistance in augmenting and complimenting our own inquiries. Ask it, I can do no more than to assure you that, should your request be within my domain I shall give it my most serious consideration.' 'Then it is this; you must resign your position and retire from the office you hold.'

Holmes passed across a copy of the Goulston Street graffito, one I had not seen before. This copy had a curious addition and once more I reproduce it here.

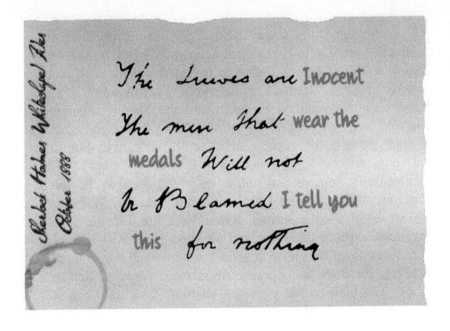

At my friend's preposterous request, I flopped back into my chair, dumbfounded. Utterly dumbfounded!. Now standing, his face still ashen from his own initial surprise, Sir. Charles turned to Chief Inspector Swanson. 'Leave us.' 'Sir?.' 'Donald, this has just been taken into the realms of affairs of state and I cannot discuss such things even with you. It is for your own sake, but you must swear that not a word of this goes through that door with you. Not one.' His reluctant assurance given, the Scot departed, with a flash of anger quickly replaced by his sense of duty to the man who had dismissed him. 'Now, I am sure Mr. Holmes that whilst you both are free citizens of the Empire you will understand why both yourself and Doctor Watson are both now prohibited from leaving this room...' He held a hand to still my protestation '...Shall we call it, voluntary abrogation of movement and communication?, temporarily, of course.' Holmes' hand was firmly grasped on my arm. 'Watson I think it best we agree to Sir. Charles injunction, with the amendment that you, Sir. Charles introduce us without delay to the secret committee to which you undoubtedly must soon report.' The Commissioner walked across to stand by the door, his face ashen. 'I can only take comfort that your talents are directed for the purpose of the good. Dear God was there ever a more uncanny mind?.'

CHAPTER XXIV
THE TWELVE O'CLOCK COMMITTEE

The coach rumbled and shook through the streets, scraped around corners and, with the power of the two massive Cleveland bays it was but ten minutes before we were taken down the steps to a waiting launch, the boiler up and ready to make way. Sir. Charles waved us aboard and we cast off into the gathering night. The launch itself was crewed by two men- I suspected them to be of the Thames Division, descended from the old River Police. Just over an hour had passed since Holmes' dramatic and enigmatic request, with hardly a word spoken since, save a series of mysterious summonses issued by Sir. Charles. He made these using Mr. Bell's machine, which he confidently predicted would revolutionize communication. My growing concern as to our destination was dampened by Holmes nonchalantly filling and lighting his pipe puffing away as if hoping to emulate the stack that rose amidships from the vessel. We were travelling downstream and with the tidal race must have done so at a good twelve knots. My eyes became dimly aware of an area of blackness darker than its surroundings up ahead of us, as I some large object sat in the middle of the river. As we approached, a single light became visible and then the outline of a large yacht, first the bows and then a wide bridge surmounted by a string of party lights adorning the railing and a tower of a funnel with a faint vortex of smoke still rising from where the yacht had clearly only recently been steaming. Holmes gave no sign of interest, yet I knew his keen mind was already hard at work to absorb the tiniest of clues as to our mysterious midstream rendezvous.

A ladder was already being lowered to the starboard and it was up this that we made our way aboard the massive yacht, a white-uniformed officer courteously bowing and showing us to a door. Determined not to embarrass my friend I nonetheless had a struggle to contain my surprise on finding ourselves in the luxurious salon within. A reception of some sort was under way, with not less than seventy people present, attended by white-jacketed stewards bearing plate trays of refreshments. The bulkheads, concealed as they were by the crowd-further by paintings and drapes, might have been the walls of a fashionable smoking room in Belgravia and the atmosphere was one of congeniality. Sir. Charles led us through the crowd with the briefest of acknowledgement to those who greeted his arrival. Ushering Holmes and myself through into a narrow corridor lined with wood panelling. Rapping a panel, Holmes kept his voice soft. 'Laurel-wood. That, in itself is not suggestive, but it does help my thoughts to point in a certain direction.' Gesturing with stern politeness, the Commissioner indicated a set of double-doors at the end of the hallway, outside which stood two more of the crew in white-tunics. Approaching these men it was instantly clear to myself that they were of military bearing-indeed such was my impression they could easily have been guardsmen as both were considerably above six feet and looked easily capable of violence should it be required. One of them stepped across to prohibit our admission with a raised hand and a polite smile that showed not the slightest sign of friendliness of warmth. 'Sorry Gentlemen-this room is out of bounds.' In a voice no more than a whisper Sir. Charles leant close to the man's ear to utter a few words, at which the guard instantly stepped back and rapped upon the door thrice. The sound of a bolt being drawn back and the click of a key and the door swung inwards.

The room was large with a low-ceiling, darkly lit with a massive oval table at the centre which reflected the light from the oil lamps hung on chains alone it's considerable length. No crystal chandeliers here, this was a room of masculinity and purpose. Seated around one side of the table were four men, some elderly, but none younger than in his fortieth year. Each man sat with a stately bearing that spoke of high position and authority, yet I sensed they were not colleagues. Sir. Charles gave the group a formal bow and took his seat beside a man who seemed most ill at ease with his new neighbour. All very strange!-I was about to introduce us when Holmes addressed the room. 'Good evening, Gentlemen. My name is Sherlock Holmes-and this is my friend and colleague Dr. John Watson, in whom you may have the utmost confidence. Please forgive the urgency of the summons that brought each of you here.' Seating himself at the table opposite the group, Holmes nodded to myself to follow suit. One of the elders sat, hands clasped before him, his face suffused with hot-tempered emotion. 'So-you are the meddler Holmes-you have the impertinence to address us?. We shall have words about this.' This last was addressed to Sir. Charles, whose demeanour was one of chagrin. Holmes rose, leaning across the table his fingers spread across its polished surface. 'Impertinence?, Impertinence Watson- indeed!. Is it not an impertinence to allow the murder of women to allow a criminal enterprise to flourish?. Is it not impertinent to misdirect the official police in their efforts to catch the madmen ravaging the East End of the Capital city of the Empire?. No, Sir it is hardly that.'

'Perhaps it were best if you share with us your understanding of the matter, Mr. Holmes.' The voice came from a clean shaven man in his prime, whose eyes seemed to indicate an intelligent curiosity and a keen grasp of affairs. 'Of course, you will be sympathetic if our committee adopts a pose of anonymity-please allow for our positions to remain obfuscated. We are rarely, if at all seen *sicut corpus* and some of our workings, should they become known to the wider public, could prove advantageous to the Nation's enemies.' 'Thank you, Mr. Matthews, Her Majesty may rest assured in the discretion displayed by her Home Secretary-although as your likeness is often caricatured most brutally in the popular press your identity was immediately clear. Would that I could say the same for the Baron Coleridge of the Privy Council, Major the Honorable Sir. Schomberg Kerr McDonnell, recently gazetted as Principal Private Secretary to the Prime Minister and, of course Sir Melville Leslie Macnaghten-whose likenesses were quite unknown to me.' This last named man banged his fist down, index finger pointed as if it were the barrel of a gun. 'How?-you must explain this, with whom have you consulted that would betray the confidence of this committee?.'

Holmes pushed back his chair and went behind the backs of the august personages arrayed around the table. 'The Lord Coleridge wears his armorial upon the signet band I observed upon my entrance, Sir. Melville's identity, however was not so simple to ascertain. I had a few suitable candidates and he seemed the most likely; the palpable disdain for Sir. Charles and the Eton tie only confirmed him to me as the owner of this yacht-in actuality a converted steam clipper-which bears his family cipher so proudly engraved upon silver and crystal in the salon through which we passed. All of which...' Holmes paused beside the last man, who gogged at him as if he had descended upon a lightning bolt. 'Brings us to the Major. The cigarette-case he has just replaced in his pocket bears the emblem of the Cameron Highlanders and the distinctive Egyptian blend that he smokes-ash and odour both unmistakable-his dress; fashionable yet not ostentatious, clearly designed to avoid undue attention on the wearer rather than the man that so obviously dictates to him. Further, he carries not one, but two pens upon his person-note that even now he sits back from the table with one leg raised; habitual in those used to writing in any and all circumstances-the staining and shine upon the left trouser leg merely supplements to the observation. If my suppositions and reasonings hold firm I can deduce the absentees are the representative of the Intelligence Branch of the War Office, and I trust that the Archdeacon will find his convalescence in Malta beneficial.'

Sir. Melville spoke, his voice one of confident coolness. 'Well, I can see you fully justify the reputation the papers accord you. Gentlemen, we have a quorum-let us proceed.' Reaching for a gavel, Baron Coleridge banged it twice before intoning the following; 'I call this meeting of the Twelve O' Clock Committee to order. As is our custom, no minutes shall be taken nor kept and no mention of our workings shall pass the lips of those present. Should the business at hand require a vote it will be by secret ballot-naturally I state that for the benefit of our guests. Now, Mr. Holmes, Doctor Watson-do you both, solemnly and without prejudice swear to the following; that you shall both, under penalty of prosecution for sedition refrain from discussion of or conveyance otherwise of the existence of this committee and the proceedings within.' After I had exchanged a glance with Holmes, we both swore our oath upon a rather dog-eared copy of the New King James Bible, Holmes flicking through the leaves with a scholarly eye. It was only later that Holmes revealed that the tome was inscribed to Nelson himself.

The purpose of the committee, it was explained, was two-fold; to both safeguard the Empire's interests and to preserve the constituent parts of both Monarchy and Parliament by any means that could be balanced against the harm done by lack of such actions. Working in secrecy, often through other agencies, the Twelve O' Clock Committee was the unseen hand in our Nation's safety. The Committee-and its predecessors have remained in the shadows since the time of Elizabeth I. The murders in London had in themselves been the province of the police, but it was apparent that more was at stake here. Before the proceedings proper, Baron Coleridge nodded to Sir. Melville, who rose to a panel and pressed the marquetry design to reveal a cleverly hidden cabinet in which several decanters were now revealed as well as a salver of crystal goblets that bore a stylised 'XII'. Filling the goblets with port, Sir. Melville placed the salver upon the table, for each man to serve himself in turn.'What good can this ritual do us, Holmes?.' I whispered across to my colleague, who shot me a look of warning before merely nodding his thanks as he took his glass.

It was clear that the yacht's illustrious owner was acting as Steward, as was the custom of many secret societies. I could see that Sir. Charles, seated nearest the door, would be the Tyler and at once I saw it; these men were all members of the fraternity of Freemasons. I had no doubt that Holmes would have already seen this for himself, so said nothing. He produced a cigarette case, but evidently smoking other than cigars was frowned upon, so we had to content ourselves with what turned out to be the most excellent Madeira and a Cuban, the band of which bore the device of the committee. Sir. Charles stood, cleared his throat and waited for Major Kerr McDonnell to unfurl a map of the City of London across the table before embarking on his explanation. 'Gentlemen. As you know I have been unsuccessful in detaining the killer of the unfortunate, *ladies of the night* who have been slaughtered in the East End. I have to report that my failure is compounded by a desire to protect the organisation to which I have sworn certain oaths.' The Home Secretary frowned at this. 'What has your being a Mason got to do with this business Sir. Charles?.' 'I can answer that, milord.' Holmes gestured with his cigar, leaving a circular trail of smoke. 'Sir. Charles was informed of some writing on a wall in Goulston Street.' Holmes indicated the street on the map. 'This writing seemed to be an implication that Jews were behind the murders. A piece of Catherine Eddowe's apron, stained with blood was found below the writing. At Sir. Charles' orders, the graffito was erased-on the pretext of his wishing to protect the large number of Jewish families in the area.' 'Pretext, you say?.' This was the Lord Coleridge. 'I say pretext because Sir. Charles' actual motive was to protect entirely another group altogether; Freemasons!.'

Holmes then detailed how he had made a visit to Goulston Street, using a special lamp with a singular lens, one that threw light from the ultra-violet spectrum of light onto the brickwork. Combining this with a specially-constructed camera, he was able to take a special type of photograph that, when developed, exposed the message in a 'negative' picture. By taking a series of pictures with plates treated with different chemicals, the most revealing image could be deciphered by shining a combination of lights of differing colours through the film itself. He was thus able to re-construct the original message, which, far from implicating 'Juwes', shone the light of blame on the 'men that wear the medals.' 'My Uncle wore things that looked like medals.' Major Kerr McDonnell's words were softly-spoken, almost wistful. 'He wore them sometimes when he came back from what he called his 'Mother Lodge.' 'He was a Mason?.' The Major nodded, answering Holmes' question as eloquently as if he had replied verbally.

'Jewels. We call them Jewels.' Sir. Charles slumped into his chair, a look of utter defeat crossing his features. 'Masonic Jewels; they are worn in Lodges and are awarded on merit or to signify some advancement within the order.' Holmes turned and addressed Sir. Charles directly. 'You knew. You, Sir. Charles knew that the message implicated Masons, you ordered it amended, then erased.' 'No, Mister Holmes-only erased. The message was altered by a junior officer who is a Freemason of his own volition. When I saw it-the altered version, I was horrified that the blame was now on the residents of the dwellings. There is a Sunday market held there and thousands of people would pass close to that message. It would have meant a return to the rioting we have worked so hard to suppress.' 'And there is also the matter of the Chapman and Eddowes killings. Both had their internal organs laid over the shoulder-in line with the allegorical Masonic punishment that, as part of ritual is ascribed to the 'Antient Symbolic Penalties'. Another of these penalties involved entrails being burnt while the victim watched-I found a portion of Catherine Eddowes' kidney in a gas-lamp.' This caused some gasps of horror and revulsion from the assembled worthies. 'Further still, there is the importance of aprons in Freemasonry-note the piece of apron that was laid below the graffito as an additional incrimination.'

Holmes now stood squarely in front of Sir. Henry Matthews. 'Finally, the place where Eddowes was murdered was originally named for the Masonic lodge that once stood on the site. As Sir. Charles can attest, the *Mitre* is an important part of the ritual or regalia central to Freemasonry. I have already demonstrated to him that these killings are the work of a group of men, using various carriages to travel undetected through London. That this group should be, at least in part composed of fellow masons places him in an untenable situation. In light of the mason's oath of fidelity, he can surely no longer serve in an official capacity. I have already identified the likely provider of the carriages involved-it is none other than the group behind the recent abduction of my friend Dr. Watson-both crimes overlap here, both co-incident and yet apparently unrelated. The murderers of women are conveyed to their crimes *by the same gang* planning a robbery of unprecedented import with no antecedents save that of Colonel Thomas Blood.' 'Dear God! You cannot mean...' 'Yes, Sir. Melville, I can and I do. This gang is engaged in the nefarious business of stealing the Crown Jewels of the United Kingdom.'

It seemed no clear agreement was to be had on what course of action be taken concerning Sir. Charles Warren's position as Commissioner of the Metropolitan force. As to the other matter, that of the Crown Jewels, the committee refused to discuss the crime with any outsiders, such as ourselves. I found this last rather galling considering without Sherlock Holmes they would never have learned of the attempt to steal the Jewels. The committee asked for some time to consider the former affair and we retired to an ante-room to await their verdict. When it came it was not in the form of a surprise. Sir. Charles would, indeed stand down, but apparently of his own accord. This would take place as soon as a suitable replacement could be found. With nothing further to detain us, we left the presence of the Twelve O' Clock Committee.

CHAPTER XXV
CUI PRODEST SCELUS, IS FECIT

It was the evening of Friday October the fifth. From my notes, I see the evening was a cool one-something of a relief after a warm day, during which I had been kept busy with my practice. The entries to my appointment book indicate I had seen the widow Pryce and treated her nervous exhaustion and the other cases were similar in their being every-day and commonplace. Holmes evidently spent the greater part of his day engrossed in the case of a strychnine poisoning. The victim's will had been the subject of dispute-it was allegedly a forgery. If I had hoped to spend a quiet evening discussing the medical points of the matter with Holmes however, I was to be sorely disappointed. At six promptly Mycroft Holmes followed the sound of the bell. I had met this unique individual but once previously-for the curious, the summings-up can be found in *The Adventure of the Greek Interpreter*-and his demeanour was unchanged. With an air of detachment he looked around the room, seeming not to focus his attention on any one thing. I let him absorb his surroundings and he allowed himself to be seated in the basket chair next to Holmes' own perch whilst I rang for a tray. 'I'm afraid your brother has not yet returned...'. 'If I know him he will be bearing the tray himself, if not he shall return within minutes of the refreshments. Doubtless he will be a coalman this time, or perhaps a ships carpenter or the like.'

Curious to see such a mind at work I leaned forward, intimating my interest. 'Doctor Watson, it is simplicity to explain yet to do so would drain me further. All I ask is my chair at the Diogenes club and the occasional problem to prevent my mind from following body in stagnation.' Hearing a measured tread upon the stair, I rose to open the door on

Holmes-bearing a tray and disguised as an itinerant docker!.
As I poured for the three of us, Holmes busied himself
resuming his own identity, removing the bushy eyebrows he
had applied and some staining from his teeth. 'What news
from the East India docks?.' 'Well-ah. I see you refer to the
spice clipper *Astrid*.' Turning his attention to the pot, Holmes
banished the smile that had formed on his lips. 'You see
Watson, my brother has seen grains of turmeric on my
clothing and possibly smelt the same. He knows, then that this
would most assuredly mean I had been at the East India docks
and, as his clandestine duties cover the Empire's seafaring
interests, he might well have learned of the spice clipper that
has visited the port for the period covering at least three of the
murders.' Raising an eyebrow, Mycroft accepted his cup from
his sibling with a snort of disdain. 'Wasting time chasing
sailors is hardly the best use of your talents, Sherlock. You
were on the right track for a while, but all these tangential
phantoms you persist on following merely distract you from
the obvious.' Steepling his hands, Holmes clapped them
together, then spread them apart slowly as if he was a fakir
enchanting a crowd. 'Then, Brother mine, I beg of you to part
the mists that have blinded me.' 'Gladly.'

Holmes and I listened, then as Mycroft told us this; a
man by the name of Kaminsky or Kaminski, working as a
boot-maker and repairer had been living in Whitechapel,
working from a shop nearby. The man had been under
observation by the city force for some time. He kept the
oddest of hours, was a solitary fellow with little by the way of
friendships. When Holmes asked who had been watching the
man, the answer came as a shock; none, but our old friend
Detective Sergeant Robert Sagar!. 'How long has the
Detective Sergeant been on this duty?.' Holmes' voice was
taut, strained even. 'Some two weeks officially, unofficially,

rather more than that. It seems...' Mycroft took a sip of his tea '...that our Sergeant of Detectives is a bright young man and had carried the suspicion of a butcher in his mind for some considerable time.' 'He did not consult me.' 'He was ordered not to.' 'You will not give the name of the author of such order?.' 'I will not. I cannot. State business, Dear Brother.' 'Confound the State and it's business!.' Holmes sprang up, fury in every syllable. 'Women are dying!, most cruelly and you find it prudent to withhold information that may lead me to a murderer?.'

Setting his cup down in the saucer, Mycroft dabbed at his lips and ostentatiously consulted his watch, a model of calm and rectitude. 'Dear me, how time flies. I must be in Whitehall in twenty minutes.' Sherlock Holmes stood rigidly, his face turned to the mantel on which he leant, his whole body tense. 'However it may appear, Sherlock, I am not indifferent to the suffering of these wretches. Perhaps if you were to confabulate with your mysterious benefactor, you would find the answers I am duty bound not to give you. Good day to you both.' And with that, Mycroft Holmes was gone. 'I say, Holmes, don't you think that was rather excessive?.'
'Oh perhaps... but for my brother to conceal such a vital suspect from me is unforgivable, whatever the reason. *State business...* indeed!.' As Mrs. Hudson arrived to take away the tray, Holmes went into his bedroom and I heard the sound that draws and wardrobe make. Suddenly, he poked his head around the door. 'Mrs. Hudson! Mrs. Hudson!-we shall require a cab. Watson, I shall need you too; would you mind awfully dressing for a meeting with an important personage?.' I hurried up to my own quarters to throw on the new suit I had rashly purchased from my tailor in Jermyn Street. Re-emerging freshly washed and attired for the city, Holmes

looked me up and down approvingly.

'Chelsea. Lennox Gardens-and a sovereign if you beat the hour!. After a most discomfiting ride in which we were thrown from one side of the cab to the opposite, the horse was lathered and exhausted and the jarvey was the richer by a sovereign. Although Holmes told me he had resolved never to do so, he was now about to call upon his hidden benefactor within the police. Number 21 was an imposing structure of red-brick and I approached it with a sense of trepidation. My own feelings were of no importance, however compared with the peril the women of Whitechapel faced. I pulled for the bell.

The butler showed us in to a comfortable and airy sitting room in which a fire was burning. Looking around, the room was surprisingly feminine, clearly designed by our host's good lady. 'Ah. Holmes. And this must be the long-suffering Doctor Watson.' We stood as the distinguished figure of Sir. Bernard Gibson entered, instantly recognisable from the many illustrations and photographs of this fine man in the press. His weight supported partially by the stick he used to ameliorate the pain from the wound he suffered leading a relief column to Khartoum. Ambushed, his men were decimated, but his fierce and tactically brilliant counter-attack saved many lives. It was while dragging his dying Sergeant Major to safety that a Mahdi spear was thrust into his leg above the knee. He only sought aid after heaving the Sergeant Major onto a cart used as a Regimental aid Post by the medical orderlies. Sir. Bernard was a handsome man, his sun-creased face speaking of his many exploits, his smile rather boyish, hinting of his easy sense of humour. 'Not here, gentlemen-this is not the place. You have been fortunate to find me here, I might have been at my country pile. If you please...' with a sweep of his arm, Sir. Bernard indicated the room at the end of the hallway and we repaired to his study.

Sir. Bernard's study was anything but feminine; rows of bookshelves bore the leading works on military campaigns, historical tomes and sombre-looking legal textbooks. Likewise the wooden panelling around the walls was fairly covered with ancient weapons, military etchings and paintings-even a tattered flag from some far-off campaign. A bronze of Artemis sat on the mantlepiece. More recent, however, was a framed certificate of some kind, which on closer inspection proved to be a parchment proclaiming our host a freemason. Holmes affected not to notice this and instead concentrated on a portrait of Sir. Bernard in Metropolitan police ceremonial dress next to a map of London. Joining me in contemplation of his own image, Sir. Bernard let out a chortle of laughter. 'Damn peacock, what?. Tunic too short and breeches you can't sit down in.' Going to a section of books on the history of viniculture, he pulled them out to reveal the door of a hidden drinks cabinet. 'Brandy?' Reluctantly, I followed Holmes' example in declining the offer. 'Pity. Got hold of some decent Napoleon-stock from his cellar, or so that blaggard at the wine merchants tells me.' Pouring himself a glass, he settled into a leather-upholstered desk chair and waved at its double across the expanse of mahogany desk between us. 'A cigar, then?.' I felt it diplomatic to accept and did so, as did Holmes after a moment's hesitation. In silence we prepared and lit our *gran coronas*. I had not tasted one before and was quite distracted by the fullness of the smoke.

It was after a sip of his brandy that Sir. Arthur looked Holmes straight in the eye and raised an eyebrow. Clearing his

155

throat-no doubt wishing he had accepted the napoleon, my friend began. 'Sir. Bernard, since you aspire to leading and reforming the Special Branch of the police, it would sit well with those set above you if you took a hand in the apprehension of a gang of ruthless kidnappers and thieves.' 'Know you of such?.' leaning forward, Holmes fixed his benefactor with a steely gaze. 'My associate and colleague, my good friend Doctor John Watson has himself been in their power. Although they released him-after a savage beating, they murdered one of their own associates when his identity became apparent.' His expression clouding, Sir. Bernard set down his glass. 'Who are these villains?' 'I have heard many names, but it is likely that there is no formal membership of this organisation, that the people in it are only assembled for specific purposes, crimes in which they variously excel. They are directed by a figure whose identity remains unknown to me, although the Doctor here has given me a full description. Sir. Bernard-these criminals are now bent on a crime that would rock England to the core, shaking both the Establishment and even Parliament itself. Does the name Colonel Thomas Blood mean anything to you?.' Sir. Bernard's face became ashen. 'The Crown Jewels?.' 'The same.' 'Have they the wit, the enterprise to carry out their bold scheme?.' 'I'm sure of it. Sir. Bernard, thus far I have kept silent as to your identity-even from Watson here, in accordance with your wishes when you decided to back me in the Whitechapel matter.

Standing, Sir. Bernard stood, arms behind his back in military fashion as he began to pace the carpet behind his desk. Finally, he stopped and turned his head to me as if weighing up some momentous decision. 'Gentlemen I must have your word; nothing of what I shall tell you must ever leave this room.' Without hesitation, Holmes gave his word and I mine-which I only break after the passage of many years and the knowledge that no harm can come from doing so.

'All across town, from St. John's Wood to Wimbledon, from Greenwich to Tottenham-all these places and every place in-between, our Detectives have been observing, watching and waiting. The combined C.I.D. establishment of both forces have spent nearly two years now, collecting and sorting information on crimes ranging from the pickpocket gangs in the West End to the smuggling rackets down at the India Docks. You name the villainy, we keep an eye on it. Now, why no arrests?, the reason is simple; the people at the top have yet to make the mistake their kind always does, that one mistake that they will spend years regretting on the moor.' This last was clearly a reference to Dartmoor prison, a terrible place where criminals were sent to rot in the quarry. 'They are a group of men that have appeared from nowhere in recent years to the point where just about every crime committed in the city, a percentage of the proceedings goes to them.' Sir. Bernard's cigar had gone out, but he continued to gesture with it for emphasis. Holmes had heard of the so-called 'Tallymen's Committee', of the 'Taxation Men' of Bow and Stepney, also known as the 'Ten Percent Men' and said as such. Sir. Bernard seemed impressed with my friend's grasp of matters. 'You have done well there, most criminals would sooner face five years breaking rocks than admit their existence. The fear surrounding these extortionists is quite unusual as most protection rackets and suchlike are reported to us by informants. Indeed, Mr. Holmes, we talk of the same group, which goes by many names. However-there is one other difference. It seems that not only do they collect, they also provide details of the jobs to the criminals they feel best suited to the-shall we say, work.'

157

This was it!, the link Holmes had sought-the syndicate's operation was sublime in it's operation. Behind it, a criminal *impresario* whose life he had dedicated to planning the most audacious, the most unlikely of crimes, but who delegated the work-and the risk, to others, content to remain unseen for a slice of the cake. And I had met the man!. Holmes puffed on his own cigar, deep in thought. I was struggling to reconcile the disparate nature of the group's crimes. Why should a criminal organisation risk exposure and destruction by conveying a group of deranged lunatics around the city?. 'Sir. Bernard' I asked 'Have you any indication that a crime of such moment is being prepared?.' 'I'm certain of it, Doctor. My men are reporting to me daily, but across the East End the reports have all dried up. Nothing, not a hint of crime save that of the meanest cut-purse and pickpocket. In such places, Doctor, the merest whisper is louder than any shout, yet no whisper is heard. Holmes has clearly discovered their outrageous plan. The Crown Jewels no less!.' Holmes had clearly gained some insight from all this, rising as if to leave. 'I have a request to ask of you, Sir. Bernard, but it may seem a curious one.' 'Ask it, then, Mister Holmes.' 'Kust this; the Jewels; increasing the Guard would only alert the gang, but if a number of your best men could be insinuated into the Tower itself, one at a time, over a period of several days, along with a trusted locksmith, the measures surrounding the jewels could easily be bolstered to great effect.' Sir. Bernard's face did not betray any surprise at such requests, and he agreed readily. Consulting his watch, Holmes pronounced himself satisfied with the meeting and we shook hands with this extraordinary man at his door. On the way home, Holmes was deep in thought once more, his only words to me that the interview had been deeply rewarding.

CHAPTER XXVI
HOISTING UP WEST

The next morning, my resolve stiffened I left Holmes to his own devices and went shopping for a suitable ring to announce my engagement to Miss Mary Morstan. The day was exceptionally fine, clear and only a few clouds in the sky. It was nearer to Naples than London and a relief after a cooler than average Summer. I took the omnibus for Regent Street and soon was lost amidst many hundreds of like-minded people, some engaged on urgent and serious business, but the many wandering aimlessly and simply enjoying the uncommon weather. No expert in matters of jewellery, I had only the vaguest idea of what to look for; Mary had expressed her love of the colour blue and a sapphire with diamonds seemed quite the thing. The first establishment I tried was ridiculously expensive and the staff quite rude. The second was more promising and it was whilst an assistant was showing me a breathtaking stone that a sudden peturbation arose outside a fashionable milliner's across the street. Going to the door, I joined the manager who seemed engrossed in the scene. A pretty blonde girl with a parasol was strenuously resisting the attempts of a shopkeeper to detain her and a shout of 'Police! Police!' went up. Suddenly, she kicked her custodian in the shins, snatched the hat he had taken from her and bolted across the street onto an omnibus, the type with stairs to front and rear. So odd was this, so likely to end in her downfall, that I quite forgot myself and stepped out into the street to watch her inevitable arrest. The shopkeeper had followed her on board and a Constable had arrived to halt the 'bus, blowing his whistle and holding his hand out to signal the driver. It was then that it happened.

Emerging on top of the omnibus, the girl hitched up

her skirts, leapt onto the handrail... and slid down it!. I could see a peculiar set of wheels on each boot and recognised them as the 'roller-skates' scandalising both sides of the Atlantic. This was the first time I had seen this American fad and was quite mesmerised. In a trice, she had crashed down to the road and was flashing along with the Constable in pursuit. Racing up to a waiting carriage, she slapped the horse on the backside with gusto and a loud cry then, as the poor beast set off with a start, she waited for the carriage to pass before hooking her parasol onto the rear and was pulled clear from the grasp of the Constable at the very point of arrest. Despite myself I was left gasping in admiration for the girl's pluck. As the carriage receded into the crowded street I suddenly remembered my errand and went back to view the sapphire for my intended wife.

It was nearly a week later when I saw her again. I had asked for-and was given, my Darling Mary's hand in marriage and was much given over to thoughts of where to live and find a new practice for myself. Holmes had absented himself for several nights to resume his watch on the Arches, but there was little for him to report. Separately, too there was our excursion down to Dartmoor to settle the affair I subsequently set down as *'The Adventure of Silver Blaze'.* Holmes returned to London triumphant and readers may well recall this to be one of his finest hours. Of the business of Kaminsky, Holmes seemed oddly negligent. The reason for this became clear only when the bell rang and Mrs. Hudson showed Dennings, the Pinkerton man up to our rooms. Dennings eschewed tobacco and had not taken well to our English obsession with tea, but took a cup of coffee. Holmes himself was rather offhand that day, seeming to prefer the dismaying screechings of his violin to human company. This was all the more galling as I had heard him give a creditable effort to the works of

160

Mendelssohn on more than the one occasion. As for Dennings, his report was stark. The boot-maker Kaminsky/Kaminski-the spelling seemed to vary for no apparent reason-had been seen abroad in Whitechapel at night and, followed by the Pinkerton man had been seen consorting with ladies of dubious virtue. It seemed his preference, however, was for photographic reproductions, rather than flesh and blood. Kaminsky was a known habitue of various illicit purveyors of erotic literature and Dennings was given to conclude the man was harmless, though disturbed to some extent. Holmes took this in with his chin propped by the violin on his knee. 'Thank you. It seems my brother has been misinformed.' I felt this somewhat unlikely, given that Mycroft Holmes was privy to the most sensitive information. 'Surely, Holmes, it is worth consideration? If there are more than one killer, might this not be one of them?.' 'Not if I know my brother. No Watson...' He set the violin back in its case and went for a pipe. 'Kaminsky is merely the latest attempt to pull the wool over our eyes. Mycroft is concealing something far, far more important than the identity of the murderers or he would merely have given us clues that... but of course!. Watson, call Mrs. Hudson-we shall dine out tonight.' Going to his desk he opened his strong-box and drew out some notes. 'Mister Dennings, you have performed your duties most admirably whilst I have been a fool!. A blind, bungling fool!.' Handing Dennings the notes, he detailed him to take over the vigil at the Butchers Row Arches. Somewhat mystified, the Pinkerton agent left us to prepare for his first long night.

With some hours until dark, Holmes took up one of his customary perches by the window and contented himself with a perusal of the passing humanity. Opting for a fresh cup of tea, I settled into a copy of the *Lancet*. It was perhaps only ten minutes when, with a flurry of crinoline, who should ascend our stairs, but the hat-thief!. I did not immediately recognise her, as she had changed her appearance somewhat, using a dark wig to conceal her golden locks. She wore a fashionable outfit in satin that would have cost a small fortune, with the flattened bustle and puffed sleeves that were, Mary assured me, 'all the rage.'. Her voice was cultured, with a playful timbre that suggested mischief. 'Mister Sherlock Holmes?.' 'Indeed. And to whom do I have the honour of addressing?.' 'My name is Sally Carter, Mister Webb commended you to me.' 'Ah!-and how is Mister Tobias Webb?.' 'He prospers, Mister Holmes. He asks me to remind you of your undertaking to him.' 'You may tell him my confidence remains inviolate, Miss Carter. But where are my manners?; here is my good friend and colleague Doctor John Watson, before whom you may speak freely.' 'I must congratulate you on your skating, Miss Carter-if not your method of procuring hats.' Favouring me with a sideways look, the girl's manner-and accent-slipped somewhat towards the common, with a remark that, for modesty's sake cannot be repeated outside of the lowest circles or a gentleman's rugby club.

With a smile, Holmes offered the girl refreshment, which was refused. 'Miss Carter' said he 'I rather doubt you came to discuss headgear. Mister Webb referred to you as a 'hoister'-I should explain to my friend here that a hoister is a person who, through varying degrees of legerdemain, contrives to remove items from shops. I had seen this young woman at work and was not impressed by the artlessness on display in Regent Street. 'A fancy name for a thief, if you ask me.' The girl rounded on me, her expression cold, save for the venom in her eyes. 'All right-*Doctor.* I'm a thief. I dare say my living compares well with yours, but do you have an idiot brother to support?. Well I do-and he gets the best care I can find for him. If it was up to the likes of you with your medical learning, Harry would be in Bedlam-or worse. Understandably rather cowed by this revelation, my opinion of the girl was somewhat altered for the better-although I cannot and will not endorse a thief. Fortunately, Holmes came to my aid by asking for her news.

'Toby-Mister Webb, told me this; the Irishman has vanished, no trace of him. His name was O'Connor.' 'Miss Carter, this is old news!, he was murdered; my friend here was unfortunate enough to be witness to the killing.' 'So he is dead, then. Thought as much.' The girl went to the window and looked down across the street. 'Looks like you have an admirer, Mister Holmes.' I would have gone to the window, but Holmes' gesture was enough to prevent me. 'Special Branch, no doubt. Since Mycroft's visit, I have noticed the odd fellow lounging around in the street and a few other places. The problem with using a small team of men is, however good and varied the disguises, they will inevitably be exposed to the trained eye.' Going into his room, he returned with his shaving mirror. He then went on all fours to the window sill, where he arranged the mirror such that a view of the street opposite could be obtained. 'As I thought. Perkins, a Detective Constable known to me only by sight. The Police, Miss Carter are not very ingenious in their methods.' Returning the mirror to its stand, he emerged to select a pipe from the rack, taking a pinch from his customary place. With an infectious laugh, our guest exclaimed that that must be where the phrase 'Pipe and Slippers' came from.

Miss Carter had a most peculiar tale to tell, but as with many thieves, she wanted something in return. It was, she said, only a matter of time and luck before she was arrested for her nefarious activities, but going 'up west' was her living and she was not about to change her ways. Respectability, it seemed was not for her. Rather outrageously, she sought a pardon-that is, if she was arrested by the police, she wanted Holmes to arrange her release without charge. Holmes wondered how she thought he was to do this-or why, indeed he should try. The girl told him that she knew all about Sir. Bernard Gibson and his patronage of Holmes and felt this would be enough to secure her freedom. When I asked how she knew of Sir. Bernard's involvement-itself still a strict secret, she declined to answer, but there was something in her manner that should have stirred a note of caution in me. I am deeply ashamed now to admit that it did not. Nor did Holmes seem unduly surprised at this news, preferring to solicit her information, which was thus; a friend of hers had turned to immoral living due to the extreme bleakness of her situation. Widowed-her husband had been killed at the battle of Ulundi-this girl had been left to starve, her husband's pension a pittance and three children to feed. She told us of a bordello in Cheapside, frequented by the nobility. One night, an extremely wealthy patron secure for himself several of the girls for what he said would be a party, to be held in a stately home in Buckinghamshire. The girls would be taken out and returned by coach, treated to the finest wines and a feast fit for Kings. They would also be supplied with dresses from a discrete *couturier* of Parisian descent. The fees alone would have paid for a year's rent-and the dresses would be theirs for the keeping, no doubt to be sold for a good price afterwards.

The party had been an unusual one to say the very least. The male guests were attired in masks and referred to only as 'Mr. Tally-Ho'. Holmes remarked on the queerness of this, but the girl seemed to be uneasy, so he fell silent as she continued. The house itself was a vast pile in its own grounds, but as the carriages had been blacked out, none of the girls could be sure exactly where they were to be taken. This was explained as a precaution to safeguard the name and reputation of their host. Once there, they were taken to the ladies' salon and outfitted with their dresses as promised. Each girl was given a substantial sum in notes and told the rules of the house. Apart from the peculiar *noms de commodité*, they were to do exactly as asked by each client, to the point where they would be effectively acting as slaves. This, understandably gave some of the girls, least not Miss Carter's friend, pause for thought, but it was too late to renege on their agreement and they agreed. After this, they were led into a dimly-lit grand hall, onto a stage of sorts, on which there was a kind of mock auction, each girl going to the highest bidder. Miss Carter's friend-she called her 'Mandy' though that was not her real name, was 'sold' to an older man of illustrious appearance and exquisite manners. Perhaps a count or baron, she had thought.

Following this auction, some of the older women were taken upstairs, but Mandy and two of the other younger girls were blindfolded and led down some curving stone stairs into a basement of some description. When the blindfolds were removed, they found, to their horror, that they were in a dungeon. It was long chamber, the only light came from a row of massive braziers that illuminated what can only be described as the tools of the devil. Manacles hung from iron rings set into the wall, tables had been placed with heavy slabs of marble for tops, chains set into the surface. There was what looked like a gymnasium vaulting horse at the far end- and, more ominous, a tiled section with what appeared to be a Gynaecologist's chair and various medical instruments. By now, Mandy was thoroughly petrified and asked to leave, but was answered with a heavy blow to the face. One of the other girls tried to run, but was tripped and sent crashing to the stone flags, before being dragged over to one of the marble slabs. As the girl told us all this, the hairs on the back of my neck rose and I could see Holmes, too was shocked although he hid it from her.

What took place in that hellish chamber I shall not reveal for the sake of you, my dear readers; suffice it to say that the instruments of torture which were wielded in that place left scars both physical and mental on the poor girls that had been enticed there. Mandy herself was whipped to the point of unconsciousness, branded with an iron and grossly violated in the most un-natural manner. Despite this, she considered herself fortunate. Of the other two girls, one was left an imbecile after her ordeal and would probably never utter another word. The other was dead, her feminine constitution unable to support the outrages perpetuated on it. Afterwards, Mandy was informed in no uncertain terms that if she breathed a word of all this she would be killed; the monster who had procured the girls knew her name and the address of her lodging house. At the end of all this, Holmes was sat in his characteristic pose, fingers steepled and eyes closed. Opening them, he looked across at me and then completed Miss Carter's dreadful tale. 'But she did talk.' 'Yes, she talked. Not only to me, but I do not know to who else.' 'I think I can venture an informed supposition. As to to her real name, this 'Mandy' of yours, would it be too great a leap to give her the name of Mary Kelly?.'

CHAPTER XXVII
AN EXCURSION TO THE COUNTRY

The shrill whistle of the guard signalled our departure. It was precisely Seven-Fifteen and I was still grumbling about missing breakfast. The train had been making steam for some minutes now and pulled away with a slight lurch, the impressive ironwork of Charing Cross now behind us. We sat in our compartment and smoked. Holmes had said little of the Carter girl's story, but seemed keen to test his theories. 'I tell you, Watson, this case is the end for me.' 'Really?, I had thought you equal to the chase, Holmes, though I confess the twists and turns it has taken have left me quite baffled.' 'And you are not alone in that. In point of fact, this is easily the most perplexing case I have ever had; just when I thought I had a workable theory, everything changes and again the work is impenetrable.'

He leant forward, his pipe in hand. 'Here is what we do know-it is simpler if we confine ourselves to that, at least. The women were murdered by a group, using transport arranged for them at the Arches by the cadaverous creature you encountered. He is also behind the attempt on the Tower. Now, it seems, these girls were killed to silence their tongues regarding this unspeakable *soirée* at the house we are currently engaged in finding. One of the women-Eddowes, was killed quite by mistake. It was on the night of September the Thirtieth. When she was discharged from the drunk tank, she left the name Mary Ann Kelly, giving a Fashion street address.' Clearly, then, she was killed in error-and by someone seeking to silence this Mary Kelly, none other than the unfortunate 'Mandy' Miss Carter told us about.' 'And what, then of this group of curs calling themselves 'Tally-Ho?'. 'This is the group we have been hunting-an ironic turn of phrase

167

given their choice of soubriquet. These, Watson, are the murderers who have been stalking the East End, these are the Whitechapel Fiends... depraved, debauched perverted creatures who no longer find pleasure in the normal fashion, but who must commit murder in the most ghastly expedients available to them.'

The train was rolling through the crowded terraces of South East London now, the smoke from the chimneys leaving a pall upon the clouds and feeding the ever-present fog. It was only as terrace gave way to suburb that I felt myself able to lower our window for some much-needed air. Holmes puffed away at his pipe for a while before returning to his theme. 'You see, Watson, they have made several elementary mistakes which shall see them tread the gallows steps. First, there are the murders themselves-committed purely to conceal two; those of Eddowes and this Mary Kelly.' Holmes shook his head irritably as I attempted to speak. 'Their second mistake was sending an outsider to kill the woman they *thought* to be Kelly-one of what I shall call the 'Upstairs Men'. These are those foolish enough to join this obscene club, but not depraved enough to enjoy the torments of the dungeon below. It was clearly one of these Upstairs fellows that went after Kelly.' I had fortified myself for this trip with a flask of medicinal brandy-medicinal in that I was a Doctor and no other sense. I offered my friend a pull, which he refused and, thinking better of it, replaced stopper and flask into my pocket. 'How can you be sure of any of it, Holmes?.' 'Simplicity itself. The girls in the dungeon were all young; you will recall Miss Carter saying this. Presumably then two things; the Upstairs men were younger men preferring older, more experienced women...' I thought back to my earliest experiences in the matters of love with a blush, which Holmes noticed with a cackle and a smile. '...Where was I?, oh yes-while the younger girls, sought after traditionally by certain men of middle-age were subjected to the grossest excesses. It follows that had one of the Downstairs Men gone after Kelly, he would have known that Catherine Eddowes, a woman in her mid-forties was not the surviving witness at all.'

Now I began to see it, but surely the 'Upstairs Men' would have known the girls to be tortured were all young?. Not if they were led upstairs and downstairs one by one, with their 'owner'. Clearly, the purpose was to obscure the details of the victims-and no member would necessarily know which girl had been given to which man. But why not simply send one of the torturers after his own victim?-he would recognise her easily and would, so to speak, be clearing up his own mess. I put this to Holmes, who, as ever, had the answer; Blackmail. The 'Upstairs Men' were men of relatively ordinary nature, but of low morals. Such men would take delight in belonging to an exclusive and secretive club that provided women for their pleasure in the splendid surrounds of a large Country house. They would then be told of what took place downstairs, perhaps even held to an oath of membership similar to that of Freemasons. By threats and coercion, they would be made to commit the murders we had been investigating, thus forever leaving them vulnerable to their blackmailers. I asked Holmes what form the payments would take and he replied it could be anything from money, family jewels and the like to property, favours of a political nature even. Political?-Holmes believed these to be men of power, wealth and influence, able to influence even a police investigation to the wrong conclusions. I had wondered at Holmes' choice of destination, but he refused to say anything other than he had made some private enquiries and was following a hunch. But by now, we were approaching our station.

The town of Tunbridge Wells perches on the edge of the High Weald, an ancient area of sandstone famous for its rock formations, where iron age farmers scraped a living and Beau Nash took the waters. Now we alighted from the train and headed for the tea hut where the jarveys stood around waiting for a fare. Finding a likely fellow, we hired him for the day and set off on a tour of the houses set around the countryside past the town. A drive of a few miles saw us at the gates of the Solomon Estate, Sir. Henry Solomon's residence. After some negotiation with the gateman, we were admitted. Sir. Henry himself had passed away some years past, but, being childless his home passed to his nephew, himself a Scientist of note. Sir. Nathan Solomon received us cordially, being in the middle of an experiment concerning electromotive force. Holmes professed to be a student of the phenomenon and we were shown to Sir. Nathan's laboratory. As his workshop was in the basement, Holmes was quickly able to dismiss the house from his inquiries. Thanking our host for his time, we left without ever explaining the true reason for our visit.

The next house we visited, Pashburn Manor, was simply too small to be the house described by Miss Carter's friend. Although her details had been infuriatingly vague, this was not the place. Onwards. We were headed to the West of town, through rural country lanes that had remained unchanged since William the Conqueror's men had marched along them. Our driver, Carter, pointed out it was approaching lunchtime and his horse, which he had named 'Dainty' was both thirsty and due a rest. With the welfare of the beast strictly uppermost in our minds, we decided to find Dainty a drink at the George and Dragon. The host, a ruddy-faced man named Fordham, came out to us with a young groom who took Dainty out of her traces and led her, without complaint, for some hay and water. This gave us, our jarvey assured us, a comfortable half hour in which to imbibe the local ale and I, for one was relishing the chance. The Inn itself was a simple, rustic affair dating back some six hundred years. Even at this hour there were the usual locals enjoying a quiet pint before returning to the fields and we were assured the locally-brewed Porter the equal of anything brewed in London. Finding a seat by a window-it was not yet cold enough for the fire, we sat and took in the place. The low beams and horse brasses were dull with the smoke from centuries of winter and it was quite the finest of those Inns that are disappearing across our nation.

It was with a sense of regret that we returned our mugs and said our farewells to Mr. Fordham, who had been more of a friend than a landlord. Dainty was already in her traces and looking much refreshed, having had a vigorous brushing-down from the groom. Back aboard, we set off on our meandering journey, which winded its way along the lanes and through the tunnels of trees. The next house on Holmes' list was Laroche Abbey, which had enjoyed brief notoriety as the Marquis De Salle had once killed a Colonel of Artillery on the terrace in a duel over his mistress. The Abbey sat in several acres of landscaped gardens, the surrounding estates having been sold off to pay off the Marquis' debts at cards. Finally, with creditors hammering on his door, he had been forced to beat a hasty retreat to his native France.

Now, we pulled up to the gatehouse and were met by a flunky, hastily buttoning his livery jacket, a ludicrous wig perched on his head as if this was renaissance Paris and not the Kent countryside. 'Are you expected, Gennlemen?.' The

171

man spoke with a broad accent quite at odds with the uniform. 'Oh I should think not.' Replied Holmes. 'We are conducting a tour of the area inspecting the local houses and are considering the Abbey for our journal.' 'Jernal?, what jernal would that be Sur?.' 'Why, what other journal could it be, but the Royal Institute's Journal of Architecture?.' This gave the man pause for thought and, without further comment he shambled off on his bandy legs to the gatehouse. I could hear the sound of a bell and surmised the gateman to be using some variant of the telephone. After a minute or so, he returned to inform us that the Master of the house was away on business and we should make an appointment. This Holmes did, giving the name Gresham and bestowing the title of Professor upon himself for the purpose. With no purpose to loitering, we decided to go back to the George and Dragon to take supper and rooms. Holmes paid Carter with instructions to return for us in the morning.

After a healthy repast of steak pie and potatoes-washed down with a few pints of the excellent local brew, we went up to our rooms and prepared for our second visit to Laroche Abbey. We set off under the pretext of being keen amateur entomoligists, Holmes stating that the local woods were the ideal habitat of the *Lepidoptera Flagrante.* Our host wished us luck and a few of the regulars raised their mugs to our endeavours. With our packs and the long net Holmes had assembled, we certainly appeared to be keen insect collectors. The walk to the Abbey took us somewhat over half an hour, through moonlit lanes that had been so cosy and amenable by daylight. Now, however, they seemed to be full of menace and hidden peril. I am not an easily frightened man, but that walk seemed no less dangerous than the alleys of Whitechapel, each owl hoot or animal call giving me a start. Eventually, however, we came to the stone wall bounding the remaining estate and Holmes showed the versatility of the pole the net had been a disguise for. By unscrewing the net, then dismantling the pole he was able to re-assemble it into a large 'H', held together by stout steel pins. With this ladder, our progress over the wall was simplicity itself and I pulled our ladder over after us. Emerging from the trees bordering the gardens, we could see the house was in darkness, save for a lonely light above the gatehouse and another in what looked to be the servant's quarters.

Crossing the lawn, I was cursing the moonlight that threatened to betray us to any watching eyes, but Holmes seemed confident and we reached the rear of the Abbey without any interference. Crouching by a large set of French windows, my friend soon had his lock-picking set unrolled and set to work on the simple mechanism that was the only barrier between us and the interior of the house. Once inside, we were in a large drawing room, but at once we saw that all the furniture was covered with dust sheets. I tapped Holmes on the shoulder and whispered that it was odd that the flunky had had to telephone the house to see if his Master was at home, even odder now that we saw the dust sheets. Clearly, the Master had not been home for some considerable time. Turning his head, Holmes muttered that the call may have been made to anywhere and not necessarily to the House itself. On we went, treading carefully lest a creaking floorboard betray our presence to the servants. The far door to the drawing room was also locked, but was soon opened out onto a large marble hall, columns forming a corridor around the perimeter of this. There was a massive sheet covering what had to be one of the largest chandeliers I had ever seen, the sole light here coming from hidden skylights around an upper level, the moon's hard, pale light streaming in to throw the most peculiar shadows. A large compass was inlaid into the floor, but we kept to the shadows for fear of discovery.

If there was a dungeon, the way down to it might have been behind any of at least five doors, but Holmes was already making his way along the wall towards the grand staircase that dominated the far end of the house. Following him, we found ourselves at the foot of the stairs, when from somewhere behind us came the sounds of a door being opened and footsteps. With no time to pick any locks, our only recourse was to take the stairs, which we did as swiftly and silently as we could, keeping to the very edges to avoid undue noise. The gallery at the top was ornamented with busts of Roman emperors and provided temporary concealment while Holmes went to work on the nearest lock. From my hiding place behind a marble bust I could see the light from a lantern and a watchman or servant of some description moving along towards the front of the Abbey. I nearly jumped out of my skin when Holmes tapped me on the shoulder and grabbed the bust, inadvertently sending it toppling. With reflexes that would do a Cossack credit, Holmes had thrown his arms around the heavy marble and I him, or he would have been dragged over the edge with it to be smashed onto the stone below. Heaving with all our might, we managed to drag the bust back into place, but at the cost of an appalling scraping sound that must have been heard at the gatehouse. Luck was with us, however, as the light did not return.

I was about to suggest we hide in the bedroom Holmes had unlocked when he froze suddenly, his gaze fixed on the floor below. 'What is it, Holmes?.' 'The compass... look, Watson!.' I did as bid, but could not see anything odd or amiss. 'Don't you see?... which way does the house face?.' Thinking quickly, I judged it to face South-and saw it at once; the

Compass was facing East!. We waited there on the gallery, Holmes re-locking the bedroom door after judging the top floor unlikely to yield any worthwhile secrets. The room, he explained, was all under dust covers and done out as a bordello, complete with a small library of the most exotic literature. This was the house!. Clearly it was used only for the occasional *soirée* and left unoccupied in between. At length, the lantern returned and the watchman's patrol was complete. Checking his watch, Holmes estimated the man made his rounds every hour or two and we crept cautiously back down the stairs to the sounds of doors closing at the servant's end.

The compass was clearly pointing to something, but what was not clear. The elaborately-worked pointer was in a line with a vase on a pedestal and it seemed that nothing would be learned from this. Holmes, naturally, thought otherwise and strode across to examine the vase. This was an alabaster urn and of little merit save antiquity and a portrait of a woman hunting. From my school days I knew this to be Diana, Goddess of the Roman hunt. It was not this, but the pedestal that fired Holmes' keen intellect; although this appeared to be a simple stand of classical Greek style, it was engraved with a Latin phrase and a curious hieroglyph depicting a man standing at the South cardinal point of a compass. The phrase read; *Extra orbem iter incohatur* Moving across the hall to a symmetrically-placed urn, we saw that this one had a depiction of Pluto, the God of the Underworld with a similar engraving, but this time there were two men, the second standing on the North cardinal. Looking back at the far end of the hall, two more urns stood. I was about to head towards the third and fourth urns when Holmes stopped me, heading for the stairs instead. As I walked with him, he explained; 'The other pedestals are irrelevant, Watson, it is clear that there is a doorway of some kind, that it is opened by four men standing on the cardinal points of that compass. *The path to the world beyond begins here...*' 'What was that, Holmes?.' 'The inscription on the pedestals; the first stated the path began there, the second that it continues... it is obvious the other two contain superfluous instruction and we have little time to waste before that watchman returns. It takes the weight of four men to unlock this door; we must remove two of these busts to make up for our deficiency in numbers.'

By the time we had manhandled and wrestled two of the busts down to the hall, we were quite exhausted. Heaving the cumbersome emperors into place on the East and West points, we took a moment to regain our breath. Holmes then stood on the Southern point of the compass and indicated I take my place at the North. Nothing happened for a long moment, but then a low shudder ran through the inlaid device and the rays of the compass began to fall away into the floor one by one, at varying depths until the most remarkable circular stairway I had ever seen was formed. 'Quickly, Watson!, we must be back up and replace those busts before he returns!.' Extracting and lighting his bullseye from his bag, Holmes led the way, down into the unknown.

CHAPTER XXVIII
THE DESCENT TO HELL

I can not, to this day dismiss the vision of depravity that lay beneath the hall of Laroche Abbey. Even the mysterious fire of 1891 that destroyed the Abbey could not erase the scene from my mind, nor would Holmes ever admit any knowledge of the mysterious Romany who was seen watching the fire with a look of satisfaction on his swarthy features. That day in 1888, we found ourselves surrounded by the implements of torture and a subterranean Hell of man's making. It was all as 'Mandy'-or Mary Kelly had described; the marble slabs, the braziers, manacles... all of it. I had lit my own lamp and was aghast at what I saw. There was no remaining room for doubt; Laroche Abbey was the scene of depravity, murder and blackmail. A curiosity among the madness; a small pile of pamphlets sat on a shelf. On inspecting these, Holmes took one for his bag. It was time to leave, but not before Holmes unveiled a further surprise from his bag; a small Bible!. This transpired to be a cunningly-concealed camera, of a type I had not seen before; so compact a device I had not known to exist, but Holmes informed me with a grim smile that it was a gift from the famous French Detective Deschamps, that took five exposures in almost any light. The dungeon, however, would be too dark even for such a versatile instrument, so Holmes explained that the ribbon of magnesium he was feeding into a tube was vital. Giving me the tube to hold aloft, he advised me to keep my eyes closed against the vivid light of the flash- even so, my eyelids were scant protection against the sudden incandescence that flared in the dark. Going over to the wall, Holmes repeated the process to secure an image of the manacles and pronounced himself satisfied.

Neither of us had accounted for the roiling cloud of

smoke that had accompanied the use of the flash ribbon, however-but the smoke had not passed un-noticed. We had barely begun to shift the first bust towards the staircase when a voice rang out, hollow against the expanse of marble. It was the watchman-and he was armed with a shotgun, the ugly mouth of which was pointed directly at my chest. 'Burglars, eh?. Well, you'll be quite dead by the time the local constable gets on his bike.' 'I wouldn't do that if I were you.' Holmes' voice was steady and clear, betraying no sign of fear. 'Your Master will surely wish to interrogate us. Wouldn't you wonder how and why we came to be here?-how we knew the secrets of this place?.' This seemed to give the man pause and I could see Holmes' hand had slipped surreptitiously into his bag.

Before the slow-witted watchman could make up his mind to shoot us, Holmes had whipped his hand out-containing the flash bar-and shouted my name in warning as he ignited it. As the hall disappeared in a blaze of blinding white light, I darted to the left as an almighty *BOOMPH* announced the man had pulled his trigger. Holmes had dropped to the floor, unslinging his bag and sending it scudding across the floor to trip the watchman, who was fumbling another cartridge into the breech of his gun. Just as he had loaded and aimed it, still blinded, I reached him and gave him the hardest punch I had ever thrown, nearly breaking my knuckles in the process. This man was made of sterner stuff, however and it was only on the second blow that he succumbed, falling to the floor in a state of unconsciousness. 'Good work, old chap!.' my colleague was delighted by my handiwork, even if it had left me in some considerable pain. Together, we hauled the man over to the compass and threw him roughly down the stairs. 'How do we close this up?' My question was answered by Holmes jumping onto the central star, which set the mechanism into operation to close up the stairs. A sudden scream from below was cut off as the last piece settled itself back into place.

There was no time to lose; the other staff would be arriving at any time, but Holmes was not finished yet. Taking up the man's shotgun, he first fired it at one of the busts, then swung the empty weapon against the other, leaving nothing but two piles of marble fragments for anyone to find. This accomplished, we ran for the drawing room, reaching its safety just as the far door to the hall was being opened, frantic voices ringing out in alarm. Holmes re-locked the door and we made good our escape unseen by the remaining staff. The ladder was where we had left it and we were over the wall and headed back to the Inn, Holmes letting out a snort of satisfaction at the fate we had left the watchman to. Unless the secret of the compass was known to others, he might still be alive when the police were finally called, which Holmes assured me would only take place once we were safely back in London.

Paying Carter and thanking him for his service, we said our farewells and I gave Dainty the carrot I had begged from the kitchen at the Inn. The train back to Charing Cross was due in twenty minutes and I went to buy a newspaper for the journey back. Holmes himself was engrossed in the odd pamphlet he had found in that awful cellar. The front page of the *Chronicle* was covered with the ongoing hunt for the Ripper-the police were, it seemed no nearer to finding what they still thought to be a solitary killer. I remarked on this to Holmes, who responded that only a few officials in the two London forces were aware of his theory concerning multiple killers. The papers were filled with speculation, both uninformed and accurate, so that it was quite impossible to tell truth from fiction in the matter. Thinking this over, I asked where this confounded case would take us next. My surprise at his answer could not be concealed. We were going, he said, to hunt a prostitute!. *Tally-Ho*, indeed...

CHAPTER XXIX
HUNTING MARY KELLY

Dennings was waiting for us at the Café Royal in Regent Street. The patrons of this famous establishment included the very cream of society and the Irish journalist Wilde was in fine form, debating the finer points of Cock-Tails with the bartender. Looking around the gilded mirrored walls I saw several prominent politicians, a junior member of the Royal Family and the painter Sickert, who appeared to be sketching for one of his paintings. Dennings had, rather wisely, chosen a quiet table-as much as could be found, at least and the waiter came over to take our order. The Pinkerton man was in high spirits and, accordingly ordered a Fancy Manhattan for himself. Holmes and I plumped for brandy and cigars for all three. Dennings' Cock-Tail took a while to arrive and we left our own glasses until it did. The waiter clipped the cigars for us and lit them with the elegant *mien* of his trade. A most convivial moment, so it was presumably with some regret that Holmes returned his thoughts to business by enquiring as to Denning's report.

Reaching into his pocket for his notebook, the detective thumbed through the leaves and cleared his throat. 'The watch on the Arches has shown considerable signs of activity within. On no less than five occasions I have seen men go back and forth in carriages, always at night. The dates and times are in the copy of my report which I have... here.' So saying, Dennings produced an envelope and passed it to Holmes, who placed it into his pocket. 'Now, the men followed the same pattern on four instances, always the same two; Leonard Martins and 'Indian Joe' Joseph Cole. These two I have identified and their lodgings are also in the report.' He paused to take a sip of his drink and a puff of his cigar, which he retained to continue reading from his notes single-handed. 'Now to the interesting part, Gentlemen. Whilst on those four occasions they left and returned with the same carriage, on the fifth occurrence a tall, thin man I have as yet been unable to identify arrived by private coach with no livery. He remained there in conference-I was able to approach close enough to ascertain this using a device I had obtained from Professor Mayer, the noted Audiologist. I have brought it along, so that you may see it's practicality in use.' The Pinkerton man looked about furtively before handing Holmes what looked to be a stethoscope with a   steel tube and a cone attached. This curious thing hardly inspired confidence-and yet when Holmes, rather self-consciously donned the earpiece he was instantly able to discern the conversation of two fashionable gentlemen across the room. I declined a demonstration for myself and Holmes handed the thing back to its owner.

I looked up and, as if I had called for him, the attentive waiter instantly appeared at my side. Ordering more drinks, I listened as Dennings recalled that he had heard the thin man described as 'Professor' and that he was definitely in charge of the proceedings. This Professor seemed impatient at the slow progress of things, seemingly anxious to set things in motion. There was much noise coming from within, the sounds of heavy objects being moved and the chink of metal upon metal. A date-either the twenty-fifth or twenty-sixth was mentioned and the word 'Bartizan', though by then the noise coming from the Arches made listening increasingly difficult. After a few more minutes, the Professor re-emerged and was gone in his carriage. Almost immediately, the lights inside were extinguished and a small group of men left Lenny and Indian Joe to lock up. Declining the waiter's offer of more cigars, we took our second round of drinks and Holmes waited for the man to leave us. 'Dennings, I have a further-and I suspect a final job for you.' 'Name it; the chance to work for Sherlock Holmes will keep my grandchildren entertained one far-off day.' 'That, I'm afraid will be unlikely. All mention of this case must, of necessity remain prohibited-and for some long years to come.'

Taking a sip of his brandy, Holmes took a map from his pocket, it was a Bacon and Company map of the East End of London, upon which I could see Holmes had made several markings. He explained that these were the murder sites, numbered in order of occurrence. Somewhere within the radius of the murders, somewhere in that vast sprawling pile of slums, tenements, lodging houses and the like was a girl, by the name of Mary Kelly. In all likelihood terrified for her life and in hiding in one of ten thousand or more places. Dennings' task was simplicity itself-he was to go to several public houses-also listed on the map and ask for her, implying an employer of great wealth and importance who wished to take her to a party in the country. This was fiendish and I protested vociferously, but Holmes said that it was vital to beat the ground for the hunters, by which he meant himself and myself. We were to follow, unseen in the Pinkerton man's wake and see what emerged, who took an interest in his presence.

CHAPTER XXX
THE RITUAL OF NUMBERS

We sat eating supper at Baker Street, as so often before. My marriage to Miss Morstan was but a few days hence and I could not keep this from my thoughts. Holmes was, as ever deep in his own realm of logic and rational thought, but had agreed to be my best man without really emerging from his own world. I sometimes despaired that this fine man would ever take for himself a wife. Surely the children of such an extraordinary lineage would rise to greatness in their own right!. However, on that day, October the Seventeenth, I was a truly happy man. I vowed never to share with Mary any of the horrors that I had experienced in this, or so many of Holmes' other cases. I was shaken from my reverie by the pamphlet Holmes had thrown across to me. 'What do you make of it, Watson?.' I could see at once it was the tract from the dungeon at Laroche Abbey and was annoyed at having my train of thought destroyed by such an evil thing. Reluctant, I looked through the paper and found it rather curious, incomprehensible to normal English. As ever, faithful reader, I share it for your consideration;

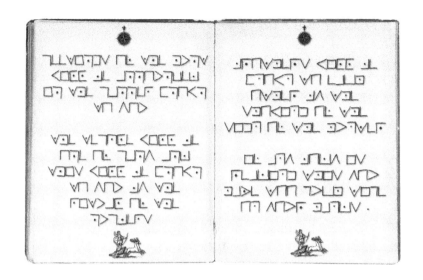

Aside from the obvious, that the symbols were the Compass and Diana, the Huntress it seemed gibberish to me. To Holmes, however, it was an easy riddle to work out. By chalking the glyphs on the board, Holmes determined the symbols to be letters and as any schoolboy knows, a simple substitution had been set in place. Working on the assumption that 'E' would be the most commonly-used letter, followed by 'T', 'A', 'O' and so forth it was relative child's-play for Holmes to work the text out. The first word soon became *EET**** and then *EET*N** before finally revealing itself as 'MEETINGS'. Thus, Holmes was able to reveal the contents of the publication as this;

MEETINGS OF THE HUNT
WILL BE ANNOUNCED
IN THE MANNER
KNOWN TO YOU

THE TEMPLE WILL BE
ONE OF MANY
AND THIS WILL BE KNOWN
TO YOU BY THE
RITUAL OF THE NUMBERS

BROTHERS WILL BE KNOWN
TO EACH OTHER BY
THE SHOWING OF THE
SIGN OF THE HUNTER

Quite what this all meant eluded me and my face must have made this plain, for Holmes had already stalked over to the paper rack and was furiously going through the day's editions. 'Meetings...will be announced...' He muttered '...in the manner...in the manner...' beckoning me to join him, which I did, we were both soon sprawled out on the hearth rug, immersed in the personal columns. I was told only to look for anything out of the ordinary, especially any advert containing references to numbers or letters that seemed out of place. Holmes stated his intention to one day compose a monograph upon the science of ciphers and secret writing. There was nothing to be found in any of today's papers, so I went to the pile Holmes kept by his workbench-this being the complete collection of newsprint stretching back for the past several weeks. Going through this pile meticulously, we were still engaged some hour later, when, with a start I realised I had found something that might be of interest. An advert in the *London Evening Standard* seemed unusual; it announced the Love of *'Mr. T.H. to Diana'* and was followed by the numbers; *1910.* Clearly, 'Mr. T.H.' was a reference to the name adopted by the members of the infernal club, that of 'Mr. Tally-Ho' and of course 'Diana' was self-evident. The numbers made no immediate sense, but Holmes was already chalking them up. I asked him what he made of it and his reply was that it was probably the date of the next 'party'. He began re-arranging the numbers with that of the following month, hence '11' became the first digits, leaving the '09' for the day. Something about the date struck me as familiar and we both blurted out the date together. November the Ninth!, the tailor!. Of course, the tailor we had visited had remarked on the date as being when his delivery was to be made!. This was surely no co-incidence and, setting this discovery aside we attacked the remaining aggregation of papers.

This time it was Holmes, again with the *Standard*, a copy from the previous Tuesday, carrying no message, but a string of obscure numbers; *6-8-26-17-21-10-2-15*. Whilst Holmes took this to the board, I continued the hunt and soon found a second, then a third string of unintelligible numerals. Using a basic and rather obvious method, Holmes attributed to each number a corresponding letter; thus '1' became 'A', but this merely produced nonsense; *FHZQUJB*. Holmes then tried various alterations, but none made any sensible message or word-until, in desperation, he tried the obvious-subtracting one from each number. He held his pipe in his hand and beckoned me over to look at the single word now on the board; *'EGYPTIAN'*. The second and third sets of numbers produced the words *'AVENUE'* and *'HIGHBURY'*. I had not heard of such a place, but Holmes was already riffling through his map drawer in search of the relevant plan. Triumphantly, he unfurled a large sheet, using an inkwell and a book to prevent it from coiling. Stabbing a finger at the map, he took his pipe from his mouth once more. 'Egyptian Avenue, Watson-a notable feature of the cemetery at Highgate. That is where the next meeting will convene.' 'But, surely there is nowhere for them to conduct their loathsome business...in a *graveyard*?.'

CHAPTER XXXI
AN EVENING IN THE EAST END

I was on the eve of matrimony when Holmes came bursting up to our rooms where I had been packing my things. Excitably, he told me that Dennings was waiting to resume his duties in Whitechapel and that, for one last time, I was needed. Emerging from my room to find a whirlwind of activity with Holmes at the centre, I was minded to refuse, but he would have none of it. Holmes simply insisted my presence was vital and promised me it would be the last such call on our friendship. With more than my share of misgivings, I retrieved my revolver from my case and reached for my Ulster and re-inforced bowler and stick, while Holmes dressed himself as a porter once more. For some nights now, we had followed Dennings from a distance as he had gone about the district in the hunt for the Kelly woman, now the sole witness to the sinister purpose of the club. I rang up Mrs. Hudson and asked her to find us a hansom.

On the journey, we went over the details of the case once more, Holmes explaining that the whole thing hinged on three women who were at the party at Laroche Abbey that night; Catherine Eddowes, Elizabeth Stride and Mary Kelly. Eddowes and Stride, being older, had been taken upstairs for a relatively normal night's work. However, Kelly being the only surviving witness to the horrors below would have to be silenced-indeed was only set free to *be* killed and by one of the 'Upstairs Men' as we had named them. This man was important enough to be blackmailed-his silence and compliance a necessity to be obtained by the extreme duress imposed by the gang behind the club-and thus our sinister Professor. In high position, he was informed of the release of a woman calling herself 'Mary Kelly' and, not knowing her likeness, murdered Eddowes in error. 'And what of the Chapman and Nichols women?-were they, too at the Abbey that night?.' 'I am certain of it. Had the gang killed them there and then, they would have had no purchase, no hold on the men Upstairs.' 'But, who are these men?. Who has such a position that losing it would destroy everything?, who would commit such brutal and foul murders just to escape exposure or punishment for being at a bawdy house?.' Lighting his pipe, Holmes thought this over and shook his head. 'No, Watson- this is not for you. In approximately...' He consulted his watch 'Fifteen hours, you are to be married. I fear this business will lead to repercussions and retribution against those pursuing it; you, my friend have earned the right to read about it from the safety of your own breakfast table some weeks hence.' As much as I tried, I could not get Holmes to change his mind on this and soon gave up the hopeless attempt.

Reaching Bishopsgate Holmes paid off the cabby and we set forth for our rendezvous with Dennings. We found the Pinkerton man outside the station, dressed like a banker-and conspicuously out of place. The plan was simple in outline; he would tour the pubs known to be haunts of Kelly, make enquiries after her and then leave. Holmes and I would be close by, watching and listening for any sign, any clue that Dennings had ruffled the right feathers. It was hoped Kelly could be located quickly and quietly, although Holmes had assured me this course of action was likely to produce results, he later confided to me that he had enlisted Mr. Tobias Webb to the colours, offering him a substantial bounty if he could locate the woman first. Holmes handed Dennings a piece of paper containing a sketched map detailing his route for the night and after consulting this, he set off in the direction of The King's Stores, a most disreputable house along where Widegate Street meets Sandy Row. Holmes warned me that the place was quite notorious for it's clientele, many of whom were cut-throats, pick-pockets and prostitutes. I was glad of the stiffened bowler Holmes had got for me and the weight of my revolver in my inside pocket and, following his directions, I went along behind the Pinkerton agent, leaving Holmes to follow.

The place was fairly packed as I entered, but it seemed half the patrons were uneasy at my entrance. Doing my best to affect ignorance of this, I pushed through to the bar and ordered a pint of beer. Looking about casually, I caught Denning's eye for an instant and he began the routine made so familiar by these past nights. The din from the crowded bar made eavesdropping all but impossible, but I could see the reactions of the women that they professed to know nothing of any woman named Kelly. One, however, seemed interested in Dennings and was clearly offering him more than information. At this time I saw Holmes outside, staggering as if drunk. I was about to venture outside when I realised he was shamming, part of his personation. The sound of a slap and sudden uproarious laughter commanded my attention and I could see that Denning's companion had been upset by something, a large red mark on his face the evidence of her disapproval. It was time to move on and I decided to leave before the Pinkerton man to allay any suspicion of our complicit nature.

Outside, I stood for a moment, looking each way before heading down Sandy Row towards a poorly-lit back street beside a school, which led into a pitch-black narrow passageway. If Dennings was to be at any risk it would be here and we had decided that I would loiter here to offer protection to our comrade. Of Holmes there was no sign, none since I had seen him stagger past the pub. I found a dark patch of shadow at the entrance to the alley and stepped back into the darkness, waiting, my weighted stick at the ready. After a minute or so, I heard steps echoing along and then a shadow. It was Dennings and he was alone. As he came up into the passage I was sure he would spot me, but held my nerve as he walked past into the narrow passage to Bell Lane beyond. Just as I was about to follow, another man appeared and hurried up silently behind our stalking-horse. As he was about to enter the alley, the end of my stick took the wind from his sails and he fell back, bellowing for air. 'Good evening; what business have you following this man?.' 'Nuffink pers-pers'nal guv... I was only gonna tickle him up an' roll him for his gilt.' 'Be off with you, or I'll blow this.' I held up my police whistle on its lanyard for him to see and the wretched thief scrambled to his feet and fled on his cork-soled heels.

Walking along Dorset Street-the irony of this was only evident later-to its junction with Commercial Street our next port of call was The Britannia, another pub known for its lively and nefarious customs. Dorset Street itself was a repugnant place and I was glad for my armament; I was whistled at by a toothless trollop, accosted by beggars who tried my pockets and it was only when I threw a few loose coins that they left me alone. I wondered aloud how landlords had such nerve as to charge people to live in such squalor. An old man leaning on a broom chuckled as I passed and his words sent a thrill down my spine; 'Good job you chucked them some change, cocksparra'. Little Henny there was marking you up for the razor.' Looking back I saw a little tyke saluting me with a cheeky smile and shuddered at the thought one of such tender years could prove so vicious. As I entered the Britannia, the noise and smoke rolled out into the busy Commercial Street to be swallowed up by the din of the late night traffic.

Once more, the establishment was packed tightly, with perhaps fifty people in a space no bigger than the average parlour. Finding myself at the bar next to a pair of sailors I caught the attention of the barmaid, a pretty girl of no more than nineteen. Ordering rum, my neighbours loudly applauded and I asked for the bottle. This, as you may imagine, made me somewhat popular and the two men-they were stokers, toasted my good health in true Naval fashion. As an old soldier, I felt safe in such good company and quite forgot my duty, until I saw Holmes ensconced with none other than Tobias Webb. The two were deep in conversation and I left them to it, looking about for Dennings, who was nowhere to be seen. Taking my glass, I went to find the W.C., a shifty specimen brushing past me on the way. I found Dennings on the floor, unconscious!. Hauling him to a relatively quiet spot by the stairs, I managed to partially revive him before returning to the saloon bar to signal for Holmes-but he was gone. Nor was there any sight of Webb. Returning to my patient, I gave him a large tot of my rum. Spluttering and coughing, the Pinkerton man looked around him then tried to get to his feet. 'Steady, old chap-you've taken a nasty knock to the head.' A large bump was rising beneath his scalp as I spoke. 'We must find him, Doctor-the cash carrier!.' When I expressed my bafflement at the term, Dennings winced and informed me that a 'Cash Carrier' was local slang for a Pimp. This must have been the man who pushed past me and I thought hard to recall his features. *Shifty features, Ginger hair, eyes close, thin moustaches...* Helping Dennings to his feet, I assisted him to the bar for another dose of medicinal revitalization.

The clock above the bar showed ten-thirty when we

192

walked out into Commercial Street, now somewhat quieter, although still far from empty. Since we had been in the pub, the ubiquitous fog had pervaded the air and crept into every crevice and doorway, creating a spectral scene. With no sign of Holmes, or indeed Webb, we soon decided to keep to the original scheme and gallantly, Dennings decided to go ahead to the next place on the route. This was the notorious Ten Bells, to the North on the corner of Commercial Street and Fournier Street. Not uncommon was the fight that was raging as we arrived, two market porters laying into a group of thugs. A bystander edged up as we approached and warned us from the corner of his mouth; 'Watch yerselves lads, them's the Nichols Gang.' I had heard of them, the dregs of the Earth that preyed on forlorn and fallen women and strode forth to assist the porters, though I had not thought to find them this far from their Bethnal Green territory. As with all gangs, cowardice is never far from the surface and after a few well-placed blows with my heavy stick, two of the fellows decided to withdraw, at which the others took to their heels and fled, to the laughter of the two porters who had taken them on. This time I went in with Dennings, anxious to protect the younger man from any more ruffians.

'So what actually transpired in the *Britannia* before the villain struck you?.' My question gave Dennings pause and a wry smile crept across his features before he answered. 'I was asking for the girl, I kept to the brief to imply a party and he said he was her agent and protector and wanted money up front. I explained she would be well paid, but only on the night-at which he coshed me and took my wallet.' 'How much did you have in it?.' 'Nothing, Doctor-just a card with a message printed on it.' 'And this message?...' 'Was *'Better Luck Next Time.'* I keep my valuables in less obvious places.' I finished my pint and with a gesture enquired if Dennings wanted another, which was refused politely. Webb was standing by the entrance looking around and I waved him over. 'Ah, Doctor-I thought I'd find you here-I've just seen Shep Malling and he says some toff just knocked three of his teeth out. I wouldn't tarry here too long as he's gone for an iron.' I knew this to be a reference to a gun and also knew that if anyone was going to be shot tonight, it would not be me. 'Where is Holmes?.' 'He's waiting for you and your pal at Baker Street. He sends his apologies, but it was urgent, so he said.' I thought this unlikely, but there seemed little alternative, but to return to 221b. As an afterthought, Webb laid down a wallet in front of Dennings. 'I believe this is yours, mate-Sandy says as how he's sorry to have laid one on your nut, but times is hard.' Dennings took his wallet without comment, but I had a question; what was this 'Sandy' to do with Mary Kelly?. The answer was nothing at all-the man was a 'chancer' and a sneak-thief, nothing more. It seemed our time in the East End was at an end.

CHAPTER XXXII
THE WEDDING GUEST

The morning clouds parted to show a clear, but solitary patch of blue and for the umpteenth time I checked my laces and buttons, pulling my tunic straight. I had obtained permission from my old Regiment and wore the dress blues of the Northumberlands, who had been kind enough to send down a piper to play us in. Holmes was best man-who else!. Even Mrs. Hudson had made the journey to All-Saints Church in Margaret Street, though her strict Scots Presbyterian upbringing must have riled against it. With her was a young girl of exceptional beauty, in her middle twenties, flame-red hair hidden beneath a bonnet. This was none other than Mary Kelly, who-thanks to Tobias Webb-Holmes had found the previous night hiding in a lodging house. She had spent the night as our guest, with Mrs. Hudson taking her under her wing. As my Beloved Mary was a catholic, although with a decidedly small 'C', we had agreed on this as the ideal place for our union. The congregation had gone in already and after a last, nervous cigarette, Holmes clapped me on the back and shook my hand firmly. 'Go to it, Watson; no woman ever had a finer man.' With these words from such a noble man ringing in my ears, I took my place before God, waiting for my bride to arrive.

The walk past friends and guests took me awhile as many old faces had to be acknowledged. Stamford, my dresser at Barts was there, as was my nephew, Charles. Surprisingly, Mycroft Holmes had taken the rare trip from his club and there, too was Lestrade, seated with Inspector Gregson. From Mary's own family, there was only her eccentric brother Thaddeus, wrapped against some imagined epidemic, with a distant cousin, a disagreeable chap named

Foster. The church choir was singing a work by Handel and the Chaplain was waiting. All that was missing was my Mary. I looked at my watch and could see she was already ten minutes late, a glance at Holmes showed he was apprehensive about something. Five minutes later I was becoming worried and Holmes seemed about to comment on this when a boy rushed up with a note for me. Taking it, I gave him a sixpence and read this;

```
We have Miss Morstan,
and shall exchange her
unharmed for Miss Kelly.
Midnight at Wapping Steps.

Fond regards,
Major T.Y. Reamis, Esq.
```

Of course, the card was in rather better condition when presented. Back then, I merely handed it to Holmes and walked from the chapel without a word spoken, save the murmur from the assemblage. Outside, I spied the delivery boy and called him back. Holmes, too, had come outdoors and questioned the boy, who professed to know nothing of the man who had given him the note, save that he was 'A right Toff'. Looking about, Holmes seemed to spot something and gave chase, running toward a carriage, which set off at a rapid pace at his approach. He tried to get a cab, but as so often when needed, none was to be found. By the time he had got back to the carriages waiting by the church, it was hopeless.

Returning to Baker Street my mood was melancholic- and I was much given to despair. Even Holmes could not console me-indeed, to my chagrin now I rather blamed him for poor Mary's predicament; had we not embarked on this fool's errand she would be safe in my arms as Mrs. Watson. Undaunted, Holmes had taken the card over to his desk and was scrutinising it closely with his glass. A tap at the door announced Miss Kelly and she came in rather hesitantly. 'It's about me, isn't it?. That card, I meant.' Turning from his desk, Holmes regarded her thoughtfully. 'Yes.' 'What will become of me, Mister Holmes.' 'Oh nothing for you to worry about; I gave my word to you that when you came to us I would see to it that you were safe.' Turning towards me, with her head bowed, Mary Kelly looked up shyly and I quite forgot her choice of profession. 'Your Wife, Doctor, she surely means a great deal more to you than a girl from the streets.' For the first time since our return I left the meagre solace of my chair and stood, fists clenched. 'By God, Miss Kelly, she means more to me than life itself, but Holmes gave his word for both of us and I would sooner die than break my word of honour.

Even though it means the worst of all fates for my own true love, I would not see you handed over to these, these beasts!.' Rising, Holmes was quite overcome as he clasped his hand to my arm. 'Stout fellow!, I never once doubted your resolve on the matter. Come over here and lets see what secrets this terrible card has given us.'

I did as asked, Miss Kelly too joining me at Holmes' side. 'See here the Type-Writer used, a popular American model of portable nature. It is both well-used and badly adjusted-see the height of the 'a's as example. Also, the letter 's' is smudged and we shall return to that. See too the dropped 'n' of 'and' contrasted with its perfectly-placed cousin in 'exchange.' We have an amateur, a tinkerer-one who loves the mechanical, yet whose practical touch is exceeded by his theoretical knowledge.' 'The Professor!' I ejaculated. 'Even he.' Tapping the stem of his pipe against the card, my friend continued. 'Those spoiled 's's are significant; the ink was thrown up even as the bar hit the card. Highly suggestive, wouldn't you say?.' Miss Kelly spoke first. 'It was moving, then-the Type-Writer I mean?.' 'Precisely. My first thought runs to a carriage-possibly the very one I attempted to fag down.' I was seized anew with conflicting passions and would have sworn, but for the presence of femininity. 'Then Mary may have been in that carriage!.' 'Yes, old friend-I'm very much afraid she would have been incapacitated in some way, possibly by use of ether.' 'The swine!.' I felt my cheeks redden and made to apologise, but to her credit Miss Kelly was made of stern stuff and merely waved my appalling manners away. 'They won't harm her, Watson-I'm sure of that at least. They need her to keep to the deal they themselves are attempting to force us into.'

'What do you make of the name, Holmes?, this man does not act as any Major I have known.' 'He's not, I'll stake my reputation on it-what's left of it after this affair.' Holmes strode to the blackboard and dashed out the name on the card. 'What does this look like to you both?.' By way of answer, Miss Kelly merely shrugged and I merely waited to hear Holmes' ideas on the subject. 'If it our Professor, we know something of his make-up, a little glimpse into his mind. As you so vividly described him, Watson, the man is a maniac, egotistical to the point of absurdity.' 'What Doctor Epshaw might describe as a Megalomaniac?.' My description seemed apt and Holmes nodded his agreement. 'So we have a man who cannot resist the temptation to demonstrate his superiority, even though any ordinary criminal would rather hang than advertise themselves.' It began to dawn on me what Holmes might be digging at and I waved my hand at the board. 'Do you mean to say that is his actual name?.' 'Yes and no. It is, I believe, an anagram. Now, Miss Kelly, be a dear, ring that bell-pull and have Mrs. Hudson bring us up some lunch.' I did not feel I should be eating whilst my poor Mary was in the clutches of these brigands and retreated upstairs to my room.

The tapping at my door shook my from my reverie and I laid down Mary's portrait upon my bed. 'Enter.' Miss Kelly came in and stood by the dresser. 'The landlady-you all, have been most kind, Doctor. She felt you would do better for some nourishment.' 'Thank you, but no.' 'Is that her?-your good lady, I mean?' I followed her gaze to the down-turned frame. Suddenly weary, I tried to nod, but my head dropped as is made of stone. Taking the photograph in her hands, she stood and regarded it for a while, before gently placing it upon the dresser. Before I could speak, she hushed me as a mother does a child and, to my astonishment, this fallen woman told me that she belonged there and not face down. She laid a hand

199

lightly on my shoulder as she left and I suddenly cursed myself for a coward. My place was alongside Holmes, bringing the business to a conclusion, not hiding away in a rum funk. Taking myself by the bootlaces, I went to my washstand for some cold water for my face and then went down to the sitting-room.

CHAPTER XXXIII
THE CALL TO ACTION

I had eaten a sandwich and taken tea, determined not to relapse into faint-heartedness when, to my surprise, Miss Kelly made an astonishing comment. 'I've had some thoughts and it seems better if I was to be handed to these people.' I threw down my napkin and my stern disapproval must have been comical in effect because she suddenly let out a peal of laughter. Altogether, my recollections of Mary Kelly are of that; a gentle, playful soul with Ireland's spirit of mirth and melancholy intertwist. How hollow these words must seem now, to those who read these paltry words. Holmes checked his watch against the Naval chronometer he kept in a drawer, announced it to be two o'clock and went across to stand by the side of the window to look surreptitiously down on the bus street below. After a few minutes, he had identified two watchers; one was a Special Branch man, the other-and better concealed from attention, was a lanky youth of perhaps seventeen.

What happened next was rather odd as Holmes took down an old flintlock blunderbuss from the wall, blew the dust from the lock and checked the flint. Next, he went to his chemical bench and began grinding a mixture of powders in an old-fashioned pestle and mortar. Curious, I watched as he poured this mixture into the comical barrel and then tamped it using-of all things, my reflex hammer, which I had left lying on my desk and only just noticed his purloining of same. The next ingredient in this odd mix was a paper folded around an alarmingly large pile of magnesium powder mixed with oxide of lead, some copper powder and-most worrying of all, fulminate of silver. This, I knew from my college days, produces a most frightful effect and my suggestion to Miss

Kelly that we retire to the stairs was met with grateful assent. The sound of the window sliding upwards and the sounds of Baker Street at the height of the day was suddenly drowned out by the most God-awful noise I have ever encountered. To describe it at all seems a task for a fool, but as Holmes' own Boswell, I am impelled to attempt it. First, there was a **BAROOMPH** loud enough to shake the fillings from your teeth, followed by the sound of glass shattering and the door behind which we were cowering rattling. Next came a roar as if a hundred express trains were thundering over our heads, followed by a crackling as if the sky had been rent. Just audible below this barrage were the startled shouts and screams of bystanders caught up in the sudden storm, followed by an impossible silence which lasted nearly a full minute.

Stepping gingerly into the sitting-room I saw Holmes taking the cotton wool from his ears, his expression one of beautific stupefaction such as I had never seen before or since. The blunderbuss was quite demolished, split and rendered useless. Likewise our windows, which were now bereft of glass, as was the display cabinet which contained my prize specimens. Even the ceiling above the firing point had not escaped, with the plaster cracked and scorched. 'Holmes!. This is... this is...Mrs. Hudson will murder you!.' His face still vague, the detective's only reply was 'What?. What did you say?.'

Still rather deaf from his novel signalling attempt, Holmes sat, briar in hand, puffing away gently. The Constable had been, issued a stern warning and then left shaking his head, so too, the glazing contractor, whose estimate Holmes cheerfully accepted. Less cheerfully, Mrs. Hudson had finally accepted the bunch of flowers I had hastened to fetch and was quite refusing to have anything to do with Holmes until the damage was made good. Now, our small party was joined by Wiggins, who had heard his intended call even though he was in Hyde Park at the time 'Buzzing', or picking pockets with some of his ragamuffins. 'Word of truth, Mister 'Olmes, the pidgens thought the sky 'ad fallen in. Fair ruined business, you did, Buster was halfway into a gent's pocket when that bang scared him and he was lucky to get away without a hiding.' 'Tell Buster he will be recompensed.' The street arab's brow furrowed briefly. 'Eh?, oh, you mean he'll get a tickle.' Miss Kelly turned her head to one side as she spoke; 'Why away with yourself you cheeky monkey-you won't get a penny.' Without missing a heartbeat, the urchin had answered back. 'Ease up, Duchess, you'll break a stay like that.' Holmes held up a hand to placate Miss Kelly. 'Please, Wiggins and his Irregulars are the unofficial branch of the Baker Street Detective force and as such their service is indispensable. Now, Wiggins, here is a shilling, go and fetch Danny the Boy, but tell him the work is dangerous and the pay accordingly higher.' A broad smile creased Wiggins' features then as he palmed the silver and scampered down the stairs.

Danny 'the Boy' was the oldest of Wiggin's circle of friends, at a stately eighteen, yet his features were that of an angelic cherub. Originally, he had railed at Holmes' suggestions, with a mortified exhortation to Holmes to wander and prosper. However, the twin lures of coinage and danger proved too much and he now stood before us pretty as a picture in bonnet and shawl, worn over a French dress that Mrs. Hudson had found amongst a trunk her sister had left with her for safekeeping. Miss Kelly had applied some rouge and the effect-from any distance over five feet, was convincing. Turning from his creation, Holmes asked what I thought. 'He needs a wig.' 'I ain't wearing no bleedin' wig. I swears Mister 'Olmes, you breathe a word of this to Wiggy or any of 'em and I'll do a stretch for yer.' 'Now, now, Danny-you have my word as a Gentleman on it.' Staring daggers, Danny wanted further assurance. 'Swear.' 'What's that?, oh nonsense.' Seeing the lad's discomfit was not appeased, Holmes assumed a look of mock severity, placed his hand on his chest and swore his oath. That and a guinea did the trick. Holmes went over his instructions with us once more.

CHAPTER XXXIV
THE MARSHAL'S DANCE

Hard by the sprawling bulk of Oliver's Wharf and flanked by the houses of Pier Head, the Town of Ramsgate Inn was the obvious place for Holmes to loiter. Guised as a docker, he blended in well with the locals, a rough crowd who were enjoying the end of another long day working the many docks and wharves. Warehouse men rubbed shoulders with ruffians and the 'Dollymops', the prostitutes that enticed the unwary into a back alley for a 'knee trembler' or a whack to the head from an accomplice. Needless to say, both activities would leave the customer rather poorer than before. It was below this very pub that prisoners had been kept before transportation and the place was a stone from the notorious execution dock where pirates such as Kidd were hung, legs dancing the macabre 'Marshal's Dance' in the death agony and their bodies left for three tides to wash over them before the final ignominy that was the gibbet.

I was waiting a few streets away in a carriage driven by Phipps, 'Lightning Len' himself. With me was poor Danny, whose queer apparel had caused no little amount of amusement on Phipp's part. Miss Kelly had remained in the care of our landlady at Baker Street. My watch had ten to eleven, we were to move at precisely five minutes before midnight. With little better to do, we passed the time in a surprisingly lively game of Pharaoh, in which Phipps lost his shirt, Danny the Boy cheated shamelessly and I only managed to win by coppering my bet after spotting him using a tiny piece of mirror as a 'shiner' and deducing he was stacking the deck. Holmes, meanwhile had been busily establishing his identity and had been pressganged into an arm wrestling contest. As a docker, he should have been one of the strongest in the room, but a gentleman is hardly likely to spend his days in physical activity. This was Holmes, however, and his knowledge of anatomy, however eccentric, came to his aid, as did his peculiar habit of strengthening his limbs with the Jahn Regimen; this involved a lot of huffing and puffing and sweating, which did not appeal to me however much Holmes lauded its virtues. By turning his wrist, he was able to dominate his opponent, using both gravity and leverage to force their arm to the table. At the same time as he was collecting his prize; the accumulated stake money and a large whisky, he noticed he was not the only interloper present; the lanky lout he had spotted watching our lodgings earlier that day was loitering by the door-doubtless one of the 'Professor's' lookouts.

It was time; Phipps took the carriage slowly round to a halt beneath a gas lamp opposite the *Town of Ramsgate*. From the window, we could see the pub and the narrow ginnel leading down to the Wapping Steps. There were a very few people going about and I could not see Holmes, but trusted him to be in place. Checking my revolver, I saw the look of alarm on Danny's face and reassured him I was a fair shot and if there was any shooting he was to lay flat on the ground and allow me a free field of fire. Helping 'Miss Kelly' down from the carriage-I was acutely aware that hidden eyes might be abroad-I escorted 'her' across to the alley, hissing a reminder to walk 'like a lady'. We passed through the passageway unmolested, but on reaching the head of the steps a shape detached itself from the darkness. I strode forth and demanded to see Mary. 'She's in the boat.' Came the gruff response. Indeed I had noticed the steam launch at anchor some twenty feet offshore, her sole illumination her navigation lights, which seemed to me purposefully dimmed. The river was unusually free of fog and for a moment I thought I could see my Mary in the wheelhouse. Afraid of trickery, I repeated my demand, stating 'Miss Kelly' was not to be handed over until Mary was safely ashore. The man stepped forward, and I recognised Lenny from the Arches. A malignant smile came across his evil features. 'Why don't we ask the slut?, what do yer say, gel?.' Holmes had warned us of this; under no account was Danny to speak, for fear of exposing the deceit.

Suddenly, Lenny bent forwards and shouted back to the launch; 'It's moody! nommus!.' I didn't have to be a cockney to know what this meant, lunging forwards I struck the fellon down with my leaded stick. He fell with a grunt like a slaughtered pig. All at once came the sound of police whistles and as the steam launch began hauling anchor, two others lit up and began converging on it from astern. With a start I realised Holmes had joined us, as he hauled the prostrate Lenny to his knees and placed handcuffs upon him. By now the patrons of the pub were spilling out to see what the hullabaloo was about, two hefty Constables shouldering through the throng to take hold of Lenny. One of the launches pulled up to the steps and we went down to board, but to my surprise, Danny insisted on coming along, hitching his skirts and jumping across. One of the pub-goers let out a loud whistle and let out a coarse exclamation of endearment at the 'Lady's pluck'-in rhyme. His shock at being answered with his own language, but in a distinctly un-ladylike tone produced roars of laughter from his compatriots. 'Blimey!-ee's a bleedin' fairy!.'

Our launch, named the *Mercury* was the fastest on the Thames; not a standard police vessel, this was a streamlined affair with an exceptionally shallow draft and a large engine originally intended for an omnibus. It had been hoped these would replace the horse, but this one now gave the *Mercury* her wings, with a top-speed of some seventeen knots. Lestrade was aboard *Hotspur*, the other craft, with a complement of his men, with both launches crewed by men of the Thames Division. The tide was racing to the east, towards the far estuary and we were racing upstream, *Mercury's* unique feature-twin screws, biting into the filthy water. We passed Hermitage Stairs and the basin, the stoker frantically shovelling coal into the firebox as the work that would soon become Tower Bridge loomed ahead, the going somewhat choppier here as a Sou'wester was beginning to blow across. Ahead, we could see the running lights of *Hotspur*, but of the Professor's launch, all that could be seen was the odd smudge against the night.

It was as we passed the Tower of London that we also passed Lestrade in *Hotspur, Mercury's* powerful steam engine more than a match for the standard engine in Lestrade's craft. Now we could see the pale lights of the Professor's launch more clearly and even the odd glimpse of the people aboard, the lights of the city reflected on the water providing tantalisingly brief outlines. If the Professor had hoped to outrun us, he was to be disappointed. Hawkins, our coxswain estimated that we would overtake the fleeing launch in under ten minutes and a crewman added emphasis to this by lighting a carbon arc lamp, a thing I had never seen before. This remarkable device instantly threw a light of the most pure and dazzling white over the river ahead, and was soon concentrated on the launch. From our vantage point, crouched in the bow, Holmes and myself could see clearly the figures in the boat, Indian Joe easily recognisable because of his absurd headgear, another seemed to be struggling with... yes!, it was Mary!. I am a temperate man, but by God I tell you I would have swung for these men. Still too far for a revolver shot, I held my fire and waited for the distance to decrease further. Suddenly, one of the men hefted a long dark object and a shot rang out, narrowly missing Holmes. A second hit the woodwork by my head with a *THWOCK* and a third crashed into the lamp, which exploded with an alarming cracking and fizzing sound.

On the approaches to London Bridge, we passed a coal barge travelling downstream and from the bridge itself another light had been set into operation, although weaker than our destroyed lamp, it was enough to throw the launch we were chasing into stark silhouette-and I saw that we were no more than twenty-five feet to stern. Taking the most careful aim of my life and a deep breath, I braced my left hand on the prow, my revolver in my right. I exhaled partially and held my remaining breath, exactly as taught on the firing range at Bisley. My first shot was wide of the mark, blasting off into the darkness. My second, however, caught the rifleman-we later found that I had caught him in the ribs, puncturing a lung-and he fell backwards from sight. I would have fired again had Holmes not stayed my hand. 'No, Watson, it's too dangerous!, wait until we board her!.' At that moment, however, my poor Mary was lifted bodily by Indian Joe and hurled overboard into the stinking Thames!. A fusilade of shots from above; the Constables there had opened fire on the launch on seeing my love's predicament. A cloud of steam and smoke rose from the launch and we could see it had lost all power and I threw aside my Ulster and jacket. The moment we had reached the spot where Mary had vanished, I was over the side, with one thought alone. I *must* save her!. I must!.

Barely had I submerged myself into the cold, foul waters when another splash announced a second diver; it was

Holmes, who, typically of himself had no thought for his own safety. Pulling myself down with powerful strokes, I found I could see, thanks to the lamp that still shone down into the waters. Thankfully, the operator had the wit to aim his beam at the spot where Mary had gone under and by this I saw her, struggling to regain the surface. Hampered by her own wedding gown, she was unable to extricate herself from certain doom, but somehow I had managed to reach her and grasped at her dress, pulling her towards me. Something-I never found out what, had caught my leg, however and I found myself unable to pull her up any further. I am not a great swimmer and my lungs were burning for the lack of precious oxygen, my vision dimming as I realised that my life and hers were over. The last thing I saw was Holmes swimming past me as I began to lose consciousness.

CHAPTER XXXV
THE LETTER THAT NEVER WAS

I had to get up from the cold darkness. I had to get...up. My arms were moving, but not of their own accord-up and down... up-down. Gradually the darkness became light and I was looking up at a Constable holding a lamp, Holmes was there, too and holding my wrists. On seeing me revived, he let go and pulled me over as the first of the feculent water I had ingested found its way back up, my system in revolt at the revolting liquid. I was soon upright, wrapped in a blanket and being given a stiff tot of the brandy from my own flask. As my faculties returned my first thought was to Mary, but Holmes would only say she was in safe hands on her way to St. Barts-my *alma mater* and one of the finest of it's kind in Europe. When pressed, he would say only that she was alive, but had not recovered consciousness and I fought to my feet at once, demanding to see her. Knowing it was of no use to argue, Holmes agreed to fetch a cab and after thanking the crews of our launches we were soon on our way.

As luck would have it, both Mary and the rifleman I had shot were being treated on our arrival and I immediately sought out a familiar face, finding one in the excellent Dr. Alfred Garrold, properly *Sir.* Alfred-though he rarely used the title. Although youthful, I knew of his reputation and had seen his career blossom. Pulling him aside, I asked him to form an opinion on Mary's case and he so agreed. I waited by the door as this eminent physician made his diagnosis. Gravely, he informed me that she had suffered considerable shock and was likely to be comatose for some time. He feared the prolonged lack of air combined with the cold water may have produced the onset of cerebral damage-this, combined with the septic effects of the water might prove fatal. Toxicity of

211

the lungs or even cholera might be expected. Thanking him for his excellent work, I went to her, kissed her forehead, then turned my face to the wall so no-one would see the only tears I had yet cried as an adult.

Holmes was there, as I knew he would be. Without a word, we walked to the church where, for the first time in many a long year, I knelt to pray. With surprising gentleness, Holmes suggested we should retire to Baker Street so I could have a hot bath and a change of clothes. Despondent, I allowed him to lead me from the second church I had visited that appalling day. The journey must have taken only twenty minutes, yet it seemed to me a lifetime.

Nor was the day done with us yet; on our arrival, Mrs. Hudson assured Holmes Miss Kelly had received his note. Needless to say, he had sent none. The girl herself had gone, of course and it suddenly seemed so obvious; just as we had tried to deceive the Professor he had successfully gulled us- and with a simple trick a schoolboy should have seen through. I was for finding her, but Holmes knew better. Kelly would not be found-this Professor would be far too resourceful and any clue would doubtless lead into a trap. With this in mind, Holmes tipped out on to the table a small jumble of chattels, trinkets and the like. These he had craftily purloined from the wounded rifleman's clothes whilst he was in the care of the surgeons at St. Barts. The man had been saved from immediate death, but any wound in the vicinity of such a noxious body of water as the Thames would almost certainly lead to septic shock, or worse. If he lived, he would hang.

The man's possessions seemed paltry; a pocket-knife, a

small sewing-kit of the kind known to soldier's and sailors everywhere as a 'hussif', a key on a string, a few coins in a leather purse and little else. I saw nothing to indicate any kind of advancement of our cause and satisfied myself with my pipe and thoughts of Mary. I did not share these with Holmes, because-and I am ashamed of it-they concerned the deaths of those involved and in a manner far removed from the legality with with Holmes would wish them prosecuted. My companion, naturally, had removed the small, sad collection to his bench and his glass. Scrutiny under the magnifying lens led him to immerse the knife in a solution of alcohol, the sediment which remained left to dry over a flame. The key was examined against his pattern-books and identified as a Price-type model, not usually associated with simple mortice-locks. Consulting his Hobbs Guide he discovered that this was a safe key, American made by the Atlas Strongbox Company of Chicago.

Next, Holmes turned his keen eye to the hussif, turning it out to find the expected usual paltry collection of needles, thread, wool and buttons. There was, though a thimble, a battered old tin thing of no obvious merit. Only Sherlock Holmes would have taken the ordinary as a sign of the un-ordinary and delved further, finding the cap, when twisted, opened out to reveal a minuscule stanhope lens. I had heard of these curiosities, such things usually in the form of miniature novelties with a tiny lens. On close inspection the device shows a miniature photograph of some landmark the buyer is visiting. Holmes remarked that his brother Mycroft had something of a collection of such items, but was more interested in the optical possibilities than the subjects, which were invariably lurid. Holding the thimble to the light, Holmes could see three words, which seemed unfathomable to say the least. *DOG . WATER . BULLSEYE .* Asked his opinion of this curio, Holmes set it aside and steepled his fingers. 'Oh, nothing. Everything, perhaps.' Going to his slipper, I saw him glance at the hated leather case and he caught my scrutiny. 'Do not worry, Watson-this case provides enough mental stimulation to keep me from the needle.' Filling his pipe, he went to the window to survey the street below as he lit it. It was only then that we both realised the filthy state we were both still in and, rather than ring, I went down to knock Mrs. Hudson up. Despite her protestation, I insisted on filling the baths myself, it being no hour for a woman to trudge the stairs, and was quite exhausted by the time I had drawn a bath for Holmes, then myself. It was with a profound weariness that I found my bed and was asleep before I had time to replace Mary's picture on the dresser.

CHAPTER XXXVI
CONVALESCENCE AND THE MAGICIAN

It was a long week before Mary was able to leave hospital, initially for the Langham, then-at her brother Thaddeus' insistence at the familial home in Upper Norwood. Pondicherry Lodge will be instantly familiar to readers of *The Sign of Four* and, apart from the repairs being conducted to the lawns was much as I remembered it. To my lasting relief, Mary instantly agreed to my calling on her and I was received in the conservatory, a hot-house of India, McMurdo the prize fighter answering the door. There, amongst the bougainvillea, the orchids and lotus flowers we sat, drinking tea, my concern for her health hopefully hidden behind a rather strained smile and the smell of jasmine that clung to my clothes for the drive back to Baker Street that afternoon. Jeakins, the local Doctor had hovered nearby until he pronounced Miss Morstan's strength was fading and it was time for her to, as he put it, 'Convalesce! Convalesce!'. With heavy heart, I kissed her cheek and walked to the hall for my hat and stick, Jeakins accompanying me for a subdued and rushed conference. His opinion tallied with my own, that there was no sign of cholera, her brain was not fevered, but the effects of her ordeal were taxing her terribly and rest, combined with nourishment and clean air were the key to her recuperation. I left her in his hands with the instruction to send his bills to me at Baker Street, McMurdo prowling the grounds with a rather alarming lead cosh in his gnarled hands.

With little to occupy me, I resumed my practice, furnishing it and setting out to accumulate a list of patients. My days passed industriously, with twice-weekly visits to Mary at Norwood. Holmes, however, had progressed his case admirably, with the result that he had made preparations regarding the impending 'Party' at Highgate and even made a surreptitious reconnaissance of the place. Further-he had visited Maskelyne the Magician and enlisted his aid to attempt to foil the Professor's robbery of the Crown Jewels. As to Mary Kelly, she would not be found anywhere in London. Despite the energetic search Holmes had put into place, even the Irregulars had not managed to earn the guineas promised to them and Tobias Webb's efforts had not borne fruit. It was becoming increasingly desperate as it was already November the Seventh, with the Highbury affair due in two nights. Over a hurried breakfast, Holmes apprised me of the Professor's scheme, at least the details of it which he had so far unveiled.

It seemed the prostitute known as 'Pearly Poll' who had identified Guardsmen as the murderers of Martha Tabram had done so on the orders of the Professor, or one of his confederates. Using the very real murder committed by two soldiers, she had blackmailed a subaltern with access to the Tower, his fear of being associated with such a loathsome crime such he had agreed to lend some keys to her for an hour, during which, doubtless, copies had been made. Clearly, Holmes felt the Professor would use the uniforms made at the tailor Green's shop. Doubtless these were the uniforms worn by the Yeomen Warders at the Tower and fitted for the Professor's gang, perhaps even the Professor himself, Holmes hoped. As for Indian Joe, he was awaiting trial for his part in Mary's kidnapping, in a damp cell in Newgate gaol. Hopefully, he would offer information about the Professor-as yet only his appearance was known, but my recollection of him had been sparse in detail and of his comings and goings, nothing was known save that he seemed to have the usage of a private coach, implying that he kept a house with stables and therefore lived in some luxury. The bell rang, with that familiar measured tread on the stair that announced Lestrade had arrived for some purpose. Grabbing his top hat and a frock coat, Holmes' actions suggested I should follow suit and no more than a minute after his arrival, the Inspector was met with the sight of us ready for the town.

Our carriage rolled up to the impressive stone edifice, coming to a halt in the fog that swirled up from the great river that so recently had nearly claimed two lives. At our approach to the Tower of London the massive and ancient gate became clearer; the heavy wooden door swinging inwards to reveal a pair of armed Guardsmen, a third figure standing expectantly behind. Following this person, we first ascended a set of steps, then crossed a grassy square to an open doorway, lit dimly from within. The gait and bearing seemed oddly familiar, the man was evidently dressed for the town in fashionable tails and tightly fitted trousers above a pair of sparkling patent leather shoes that spoke of a monied position. The sound of the door closing was followed by the scrape and crash of heavy bolts being thrust home, hollow footsteps resonating in what I perceived to be a short tunnel. The tunnel opened to reveal a low-ceilinged vault, perhaps a disused storage room. My curiosity about our nameless benefactor was stilled in a heartbeat; it was Maskelyne the Magician!. 'Good morning Gentlemen. Please forgive the intrusion, but you are to be searched... strictly necessary I am afraid.' Maskelyne stepped back apologetically to allow four grim-faced Guardsmen to step forward from the shadows. We were indeed most closely searched from top to bottom-even Lestrade was not spared a fingertip examination from hair to the soles of his shoes. A small pile of effects was formed on the table; nothing that could be conceivably used by a criminal or arsonist was left on our persons and, at length we were apparently approved safe to proceed deeper into the Tower.

Evidently, our conjuror was something of an amateur historian, as he regaled us with a brief outline of its terrible and awe-inspiring existence. The Tower-in actuality, a series of fortifications surrounding an original palace, had served various purposes since the first flag was laid; Royal residence and symbol of Regal primacy, prison and, until recently, the home to the Royal Mint. The lights along the walls only seemed to add to the feeling of being at the very heart of our Nation's history – there, across the courtyard was the White Tower, the very heart of the fortress and the first part to be built; it had stood nearly eight hundred years. A wooden sign stood on a small platform, but the script was illegible in the dark-Lestrade asked what it was and was answered with a morbid grin; it was the site of the scaffold. 'Doubtless should we fail in our endeavour the carpenters will be busy.'

I shall, of course, refrain from detailing the measures taken to ensure the security of the Crown Jewels themselves-whilst I am sure, my honest reader, you would not think of such a grievous crime as to attempt their removal, you will understand that not all are so upright or trustworthy. Suffice to say, we found ourselves in a dimly-lit vault of ancient stone blocks with a heavy curtain of purple velvet covering a large area of one wall. To either side stood a Yeoman Warder-the famous 'Beefeaters', each armed with an old-fashioned partisan. There were two silken ropes at either side of the entranceway so that the visitor was drawn towards the curtain-I could not grasp the reasoning at work, deciding on the prudence of silence. Turning to face us, with a glimmer in his eye, Maskelyne addressed us. 'Well, there really is no effective way to prepare you for this-so, Gentlemen, the Crown Jewels.' With a pull of a silken cord, we stood in silence, simply stunned and quite unable to speak. For there, in front of our eyes, arrayed on velvet-covered plinths of crimson sat all the wonder of the World with only a grille of rather thin ironwork between the dazzling display and ourselves. I have not the wit nor word to convey the majesty and splendour of that privileged chamber-yet I must try. Maskelyne waved his arm across the display and detailed each treasure from his impressive memory.

'The St. Edward's Crown; gold inlaid with precious stones-that is used for Coronations. The Imperial Crown, the lighter and more comfortable Queens Crown; the Ampulla-the flask used to anoint the new sovereign; the Sovereign's Orb, The Sovereign's Sceptre and Sceptre with Dove.The Imperial Mantle-made for The Queen's father of cloth of gold; the Swords of Temporal Justice, Spiritual Justice and of Mercy-along with the anointing spoon the only pre-Reformation pieces of Regalia to survive. Various rings, spurs and bracelets... and then there is the Koh-i-Nur diamond. At over a hundred carats it is, quite literally, a mountain of light. Once the prize of the Mugal Emperor's jewels it passed to Duleep Singh and was presented to Her Majesty in 1850. Legend has it, only a woman can possess it; it is certain death for any man to wear it.'

Not unsurprisingly, Holmes was the first to break himself free of the spell. 'Mr. Maskelyne, I presume my brother Mycroft used his not inconsiderable influence within government to arrange all this.' 'He rather wanted his name kept out of the business, Mr. Holmes... but you are of course, quite correct.' Holmes let his eye run over the incomparable splendour once more before putting voice to his thoughts. 'None of us can ever claim the slightest credit or connection should we succeed-the confidence in the Monarchy depends on stability; the Regalia must be safe and *seen* to be so. I am aware of Colonel Blood's attempted theft of the jewels in the seventeenth Century. Has there ever been any further attempt made?.' 'Not any made public-your brother was reluctant to furnish me with more information on *that* matter. Anyway, if you are satisfied, I shall proceed-the two gentlemen with their armaments are, of course, to remain *in situ* throughout, but I have included them in my- *performance* tonight and so they shall add conviction to the illusion by acting out a melodrama I have scripted for them, perhaps of the kind planned by this mysterious Professor of which you spoke. I must ask that you leave us, gentlemen, Inspector. Once outside the door, wait one minute and return.' Exchanging questioning looks of curiosity and uncertainty we three found ourselves outside the Jewel room-I consulted the minute hand of my watch as closely as had I been taking a patient's pulse.

The sweeping hand seemed to creep around the dial as if a mere minute was an age. At my nod, Holmes led the way, grasping the iron handle and throwing the large doors open. The scene was the same; the Yeomen stood impassively beside the curtain, but of Maskelyne there was no sign. There being no Maskelyne, it was one of the Warders who now turned and pulled the cord. As a man, we gasped; the jewels were gone!. I must detail the scene; the bars, sawn through, the velvet plinths, quite empty. The lighting was, perceivably lower-yet apart from these facts the scene was as before. Both the Yeomen sprang into action; one dashing off as if for help, leaving the other to detain our group at the point of his halberd. 'Dear God, Holmes-the man has done it!, he has stolen the... we must stop him!, aren't you going to...' my voice tailed off as I caught the look in the great detective's face. 'Remarkable-convincing in every aspect and impressive. Yet, if I step across to stand here...' Holmes stepped over the cord. 'Yes, as I thought. You may put down your weapon, Maskelyne-I believe you have proved the point!.'

It was indeed so; the 'Beefeater' who had detained us was none other than the uncanny wizard Maskelyne. On closer inspection, it was as thus; the 'sawn-through' bars were merely wrapped in an imperceptibly lighter shade of red velvet than the deeper crimson of the display itself. The jewels were where they had rested all along; on the same plinths. What we saw were merely a series of identical velvet draperies, formed into shape by a thin wire framework that had been threaded through the bars from one side. On first inspection, the impossible was facilitated by insinuating and turning a previously formed framework of wire through the grille, the velvet already wrapped around this form and unfurled by simple twisting. From the front, the deception was completed by a simple lowering of the gas-lights and the use of the silken ropes was soon apparent; one of the 'walls' was a simple piece of canvas stretched across a wooden frame. Painted to resemble the stone blocks it was invisible from the distance afforded by the ropes-and it was behind this contrivance that the wire contraption had been concealed, along with the Yeoman that walked from behind the hideaway with a broad grin on his face.

Lestrade was the first to laugh. 'Well, I'll be... I'd thought my career over. And you did all this, in one minute...' As ever, Holmes retained his logical faculty. 'The uniform you've got on-how did you effect the change in one minute?.' Maskelyne jerked his thumb at the returning Yeoman. 'Simple misdirection-as he made his commotion I made my switch-stepping out from behind my screen and taking the Halberd from him as he passed me behind the screen. I already had the breeches on beneath my trousers-I had the rest on hooks behind the canvas. Not my finest work, incidentally, but time was pressing. By the way-the switch itself was incidental; a Conjurers trick of adding superfluous layers to a performance so that by the time the witnesses are asked for their recollection of events, their memories are confused and therefore unreliable. What may seem a simple trick becomes, through application of chicanery and subtle changes to perception, almost miraculous.'

Standing outside on the parapet at the edge of the river wall, we stood, Holmes and I. Silently we watched the river that was the lifeblood of London run past below us. The faint light of the false dawn limned the clouds to the East and it was time to leave this place of Kings and Conquerors. Already, Maskelyne had departed by carriage and we were to make a journey of our own as soon as our launch came for us. 'I cannot understand why none of us recognised the man sooner' said I. 'He was, after all standing right before us.' 'It all hangs on that remark of his about perception, Watson-the brain really is a most remarkable tool, capable of un-paralleled feats of achievement-yet with a simple, yet sudden string of events it cannot cope with the facts of the situation. Our perception is what separates us from the primate, Watson, yet it is the easiest thing to fool it.' 'I can see how the deception regarding the jewels worked so well, Holmes. The fellow didn't even wear a disguise and yet I would have sworn to it the Warder was holding us there.'

Spinning round, Holmes grasped my shoulders and spoke in a rapid staccato; 'The Curtain opens and the Jewels are gone!-A Yeoman runs for help!-the other thrusts his point under our chins and all in a moment!. The sequence of events is so plain it cannot be otherwise, yet a substitution was made as we were caught off balance by the hullabaloo-and that's the beauty of this remarkable counter-plan Watson-anyone reporting back to their Master that the jewels were gone, therefore lost to them, would be so flummoxed by all the hoo-ha and the hue and cry surrounding such a theft that it is highly unlikely they would possess the sang-froid to make more than the most cursory examination of the apparently bereft vault to discover the jewels intact.' Lighting his cigarette, Holmes leant back against the stonework and inhaled, eyes closed for a long moment of silent thought. My thoughts, however, rested with Mary, but I shook them away. 'And then?.' 'And then. And then, Watson, the gang makes their getaway, *without* the treasure and most likely by boat. We shall explore this now as I perceive the running lights of our old friend *The Mercury.'*

We spent the next four hours examining the most likely places, quiet wharves and jetties that could be used to unload a priceless haul away from prying eyes. Finally, Holmes pronounced himself satisfied that he had the three most likely premises and we headed for Waterloo Pier. As we passed beneath London Bridge I suppressed a shudder as the memories returned unbidden. A hand on my shoulder, it was Lestrade, with a gesture of simple generosity. Not for the first time I had cause to thank this man, who may not have possessed Holmes' intellect, but was of good and kind heart. Holmes and Lestrade agreed a simple plan; at short notice the latter was to present himself to the Thames Division boatyard at Wapping, with a complement of his best men. They would intercept the fleeing criminals as they departed from the Tower. I had wondered why they did not simply clap the men in irons on their arrival at the Tower, but Lestrade explained the charges against them would easily be dismissed by any reasonably competent lawyer. No, better to catch them *in flagrante* and *a posteriori*.

CHAPTER XXXVII
A WARREN OF INTRIGUE

'Have you seen this, Holmes?.' My enquiry brought little response, so I handed over the copy of *Murray's Magazine,* the 'Home and Colonial Periodical for the General Reader.' Taking it up, his eternal briar extinguished for the moment, my friend read the article which was to set the final seal on the fate of Sir. Charles Warren's Police career. Written by Sir. Charles himself, it began thus; *London has for many years past been subject to the sinister influence of a mob stirred up into spasmodic action by restless demagogues. Their operations have exercised undue influence on the Government of the day, and year by year the Metropolis of our Empire has become more and more prone to dangerous panics, which, if permitted to increase in intensity, must certainly lead to disastrous consequences...* the article continued in mixed vein, both moderate and wildly incautious. Discussion of the constitution of the Metropolitan force gave way to attacks on the government, especially Mr. Matthews the Home Secretary. These were of a veiled nature, but the veil was rather thinly woven. Finally, he seemed to advocate the assistance of Vigilance Committees to aid the undermanned official force. It seemed irrelevant now whether the Twelve O'Clock Committee had sought to relieve Sir. Charles of his duties and Holmes agreed with me there would be no choice, but to remove the man.

Holmes had spent some time investigating the ownership of the three places, the two wharves and the steps that we had examined from the river and a curious co-incidence had emerged. Horsleydown Stairs were reached through the Courage Brewery building and the passageway led through to Gainsford Street, where a warehouse of dubious origin was to be found. This was the warehouse of the brewery company whose design Holmes had seen on the vans hidden at the Arches. All the brigands had to do was load their boat, cross the river unseen-Holmes was certain the attempt would take place at night-and load their plunder onto the vans where they would be hidden or moved on in other ways, perhaps in apparently innocent barrels of beer. It all seemed so simple, yet fate makes fools of us all.

The first we heard of the death of Tobias Webb was a call from Detective Constable Walter Dew, a most energetic official who later rose to prominence as the man who arrested Crippin, the basement murderer. In his plain, Northern tone, he informed us of the finding of a body in the Thames, which had hung by a rope around the ankles. It had been found when a barge collided with the suspended corpse below London Bridge. The initial finding was murder, with death occasioned by drowning. It seemed to have been a gruesome warning to informers. Already on the order of Lestrade the murder was hushed up and reporters kept away; the fear being, not unnaturally that if it were known the Professor's organisation were capable of such retribution, the already paltry stream of information would altogether dry up. It was useless to pursue the matter further as the clock chimed midnight and the date of the next orgy of sadism was upon us.

CHAPTER XXXV
THE RIDDLE OF ANUBIS

The night of Friday, November the Ninth will remain embedded in the memory of the Nation. I regret to say that until this account reaches the public, it shall be for false reasons. Doubtless many of you read with mounting horror the news that Mary Jane Kelly was found at her miserable little room in Millers Court, a tiny appendage to the rear of Twenty-Six, Dorset Street-the very street we had passed through in search of her. She did not die there... and only now is the truth reaching you. I beg of you to fortify yourselves with whatever methods you have to hand.

At six-fifty in the evening, we stepped down quietly from our carriage, leaving 'Lightning Len' to keep his mare calm. Although Lestrade had made generous offers, we refused his aid and were alone, Holmes and myself. Both armed, we had chosen our finest clothes, hoping to pass as members of the sinister hunting club we in turn were hunting. With no particular date in mind for the Tower robbery, Holmes had felt it best to alert Lestrade to be in position for that night with his men-this Professor had outwitted him before and it seemed not beyond the bounds that he might choose this night, had he an inkling of our discoveries. Highgate Cemetery loomed large, dark and menacing before us. The clouds hung low overhead after a wet morning which left the place steaming slightly into a low fog. My memories of London are always filled with the stuff.

The great cemetery at Highgate is divided into two sections, East and West. The only lights we could see shone from the window at the side of the Superintendent's Lodge and we stole cautiously past, anxious lest the sound of our shoes on the gravel path cause any disturbance. From here onwards, the sole illumination came from the half-moon that hung somewhere above the clouds and the broad stone steps up the hill seemed to lead into the next life. Eventually, we found ourselves descending towards an extraordinary sight. There, through the trees was a tunnel straight from the land of the Pharaohs themselves. Torches affixed to the walls lit the way and above the cornice we saw a winged serpent which Holmes quietly informed me was Wadjet, protector of the Pharoahs and Guardian of the Nile. As we approached, suddenly Holmes' steely fingers were at my wrist and we froze as a couple of older men approached the Avenue from across the grass. The two seemed in cheery high spirits, though retained caution enough to moderate their laughter. Clearly, this occasion was known only to a select few-and ourselves.

The entranceway led through a narrow stone passageway which opened out to reveal, amongst various 'ancient' ornaments and pillars, the doorways to the tombs at either side. These now reflected the flames from small braziers ranged along the length of the Avenue itself, all of which culminated in a massive iron door flanked with large statues of Egyptian deities, perhaps Sphinxes-from this distance I could not be sure. Our two gentlemen had reached this door and a cowled figure crossed the small courtyard to them, at which Holmes shrank back into the shadows. Joining him was impossible, so I retreated to the recess offered by a sunken doorway across from him and waited while the be-robed figure admitted the two, a process which seemed oddly ritualistic-the man hunched over one of the statues as if in prayer, before reaching forwards to turn something in the iron door, which swung inwards to allow the two men to enter, presumably after some secret sign or password had been exchanged. Infuriatingly, we were at such a distance that it was impossible to discern these. The figure then stepped out as the door shut beside him and he returned to his vigil out of sight.

We stepped forwards, moving as quietly as possible. At out approach to the small yard, however, my foot dislodged a small stone, which clattered off the wall with a stomach-lurching reverberation, the sound echoing back and forth the length of the tunnel that was the true nature of the 'avenue'. At once, Holmes sprang forwards, to meet the capistrate form that lunged at him from the shadows. I saw the glint of steel and heard a terrible groan, at which the man folded up at the detective's feet. Feeling for a pulse and finding none, I exclaimed 'You've killed him!.' 'But with his own blade. Damn it!, we must move quickly before his death is discovered.' At Holmes' insistence, we moved the body into a shadowed recess where he was able to search it, finding nothing of interest save a tin mug of the type used by our soldiers in India. I was about to discard this when Holmes suddenly remembered the odd inscription printed in the rifleman's stanhope and began pulling off the unfortunate sentry's cowl, wrapping himself in it so that no-one would know the difference. 'Here, you'd best have this, Watson.' Handing me his sword-cane, I laid my own stick with the body.

Grabbing the mug, Holmes went to the door, which was securely locked, an embossed torch at the centre, the cast iron device flush with the smooth metal of the door. This must have been turned by the guard, yet now it was stuck fast-no amount of wisting and prying by both of us could persuade it to move an inch. There had to be another way!. Casting around for anything that might aid us, my eye fell upon a bowl set on a pedestal, which was filled with water. 'Holmes!, the bowl!.' 'Quite.' Stepping over to the statue the robe's original owner had stooped at, Holmes began examining it's surface for any clue. 'You remember it, Watson-*Dog, Water, Bullseye...*' 'Hardly Egyptian words.' 'Yes... more the sort of *aide memoire* an educated man might prepare for a lackey from the slums.' He tapped the head of the statue, which was a dog-like carving identical to its companion, both seated on pedestals carved with hieroglyphic symbols. 'This is Anubis, guardian, protector of the dead. Usually depicted as a dog. Here!.' He had found something, pressing both of the statue's eyes together, he was able to twist the head to face downwards, at which the head of the correspondent statue followed suit, some hidden mechanism linking the two. 'Holmes!-they're bowing!.' 'No-drinking!.' Matching actions to words, Holmes ran to the bowl, scooped some water and placed it at the dog-statue's muzzle. Fantastically, the water started to disappear, drawn into the stone figure by some arcane wizardry. Now Holmes looked for a 'bullseye', finding it among the inscriptions on the base. 'I might have known-the symbol of Ra, the chief among Egyptian gods!.' Pressing the small circle within a circle, the moulded torch moved out from the iron door by a fraction of an inch, with a barely audible click. Grasping it, Holmes twisted it so that the torch faced the ground... and the door swung open.

The short passageway was pitch-black, but Holmes had elected to bring along a rather ingenious folding contraption, containing a phosphorescent material-which when opened out began to emit a dullish, green-hued light through a lens. This provided just enough light to see the tomb of a Lord and Lady some-one or some-such, now laid side by side for eternity in a large elaborate, if dusty double-widthed sarcophagi. Finding ourselves in such a small chamber seemed to cause Holmes some perturbation at first, but he soon shook this off to examine the walls for signs that would aid our progress further. At first I began to suspect an awful trap had been set for us, but we had seen two men enter this place-and where they had travelled, so could we. Striking a match, I held it aloft to survey my surroundings better, seeing the chamber had four identical columns at each corner, with walls of inlaid tile, more hieroglyphs covering these. The floor was pitted with indentations of a purpose I could not fathom, rather reminding me of the old cribbage board I had seen an Uncle use in his club once. Our recent acquaintance Anubis was represented, as was Ra the sun god, but pry and prod at these as I might, no door was opened or portal unveiled. Another match and I was no nearer to enlightenment, with perhaps ten or so remaining in the vesta. I decided to spare the matches, to let Holmes search with his eerie light. It was then that I looked upwards.

What neither of us had thought to look for was something only visible *without light.* The ceiling was done out as stars, depicting another ancient and long-forlorn deity. I had seen as much on entering the crypt. However, without light, the muted glow from one of the stars was dimly, yet clearly visible. Seeing this, I hissed out to Holmes, suddenly fearful lest my voice carry in this horrible place. He found me pointing with my cane, took it from me and went across to stand beneath it, at which he suddenly went down to his knees to make a closer examination of the odd floor-stones there. Finding one that was directly beneath the star, he remarked that it was worn, as if by recent insertion of some kind. Fishing inside his pocket, he produced a silver pencil and experimentally jabbed it into the aperture, at which the sarcophagi-startlingly-began to rise towards the ceiling, in almost total silence. Clearly, this mechanism was new, designed and installed at the behest of the Professor!. As the empty pretence of the coffins was revealed, so too was the spiral iron stairway running down beneath it. Down we went, but how I wish we had not.

CHAPTER XXXVI
DEATH IN A CEMETARY

Clearly, someone of vast resources had spent freely of them, such vast the vastness of the subterranean chamber we now entered. In place of torchlight, gas-lamps ranged the walls of what could have been a fashionable club in St. James's. Comfortable chairs and plush carpeting led us onwards, past the discreet nods from several members, none of whom were masked. I thought of our own masks, safe in our pockets and was glad we had neglected them thus far. At the far end, two passageways led off, both guarded by a cowled thug. From the corner of my mouth, I muttered to Holmes 'What now?. We don't know the sign!.' This was, of course, the 'Sign of the Hunter' mentioned in the pamphlet Holmes had decoded. 'Steady, old fellow-you are a neophyte and I the sentry bringing you for your first meeting. Don't be surprised if I have to return to my post outside, merely keep your eyes and ears open and say as little as possible.' I had not bargained for this and would have objected, but Holmes was already stepping up to the guardian on the right.

Holmes bowed and indicated me. 'A new Brother.' Regarding me curiously, the man beckoned me over. 'Has he the sign?.' 'I shall give it to him.' replied Holmes, making a curious gesture, opening the finger and thumb of his left hand to form the shape of a bow and curling the index finger of his right hand, he moved it to meet the left, drawing back an imaginary arrow. Copying this, I waited for the guard to speak, my heart fairly in my mouth. Something of this must have shown, as the man smiled and clapped me on the shoulder with a sudden familiarity. 'Don't worry, Sir-first parties are always to be cherished-you'll be fine. Have you your mask?.' Nodding, I reached for the mask-hoping it would do.

233

Apparently, it was acceptable as I was shown through into another parlour, Holmes leaving me with an almost imperceptible nod of complicity.

The first room contained a well-stocked bar and was currently host to perhaps a dozen 'gentlemen' of various ages, all dressed in well-tailored suits, their shoes hand-made. All wore masks, unlike the 'ladies' present, who wore next to nothing. My keeper waved one of these harlots over, explaining in hushed tones that I was an initiate. A handsome brunette, she attached herself to my arm and guided me over to the bar as if I were senile or a child. Resisting every urge to detach myself from this woman, I nevertheless allowed myself to be refreshed with an exquisite brandy, the woman whispering in my ear that this was all part of the membership fees and I need not proffer payment. The woman was really rather pretty, and I estimated her age to be in the early thirties, her lustrous hair in fashionable curls that failed to cover her breasts. In fact, *nothing* was covering her breasts, her corset, negligible undergarment and stockings all she wore over a pair of Parisian heels. Despite my vows to Mary, I found it hard to ignore this woman's undoubted charms and it was a relief-of sorts, when she suggested we try the next parlour.

Only later did Holmes tell me of his increasingly frantic search for the exit he was certain lay concealed about the cemetery, the near-miss he had when a pair of guards almost uncovered his temporary refuge behind a tomb-stone and his eventual discovery of what might be called the 'tradesmen's entrance', concealed inside another tomb in a gloomy crescent. This was where, under cover of darkness or fog, doubtless with the paid complicity of some minor officials, the women and the furniture ,victuals and suchlike were brought in. Finding it propitiously unguarded, it was simple for the cloaked Holmes to enter, finding himself in a basic storeroom from which a door opened into the kitchen of a bar. This was not the same one I had recently vacated as he was beyond the left-hand passageway. Leaving the cowl behind some crates, he donned his mask and waited for the barman to leave his position for more supplies or for a call of nature in the small, but fully-fitted bathroom that adjoined each bar.

'What should I call you, then?.' I placed my hand on the nape of her neck as I asked the question, hoping to be taken for a salubrious degenerate. 'I'm a slave, Mister Tally-Ho. Slaves don't have names, they have numbers.' 'And what, pray, is yours?.' Somewhat unnecessarily, she whispered it into my ear. 'There are that many of you?.' She shook her head, revealing her fine chest fully. 'No, Sir. It's my speciality.' Even beneath the mask I could feel that I had blushed and she let out a delightfully coquettish giggle. The next chamber was laid out as a boudoir and I could see, illuminated by the occasional red lamp, couples in the act of congress. This was all most educational, but not what I had come to see. I knew from Miss Kelly's description that there would be worse to come, perhaps on the other side of this, the most exclusive and certainly most dis-respectful of all London clubs. Affecting an air of jaded *ennui,* I enquired whether something more *recherché* was available. With a look of ill-concealed alarm, the girl tightened her grip on my arm. 'Don't. Please, Sir, don't ask. Stay in this room with me. The others...' But the approach of another hooded guard stayed her tongue and in a conspicuous voice she announced that 'Mister Tally-Ho' wished to tread the 'Sinister' path.

I was taken, alone across the excavated labyrinth to the Left-Handed, or Sinister side. Here the first chamber was guarded by a heavy oaken door which must have been proofed against sound escaping-the moment it was opened a faint scream reached my ears and I suppressed the shudder that ran through me. This room was comparable to it's opposite, again with a bar, more patrons and girls, but these latter were all wearing masks that prevented speech, leather gags that denoted the subservient role of these wretched courtesans. One was kneeling at her Master's feet as he lolled in a leather chair, his feet crossed on her back using her as a human foot-stool. The urge to strike a fellow man had rarely been stronger. Another brandy was offered to me and I gulped it gratefully.

A thin blonde girl approached me shyly, bowing formally from the neck. Realising this poor creature could not reply, conscious of the guard who had remained loitering suspiciously, I adopted what I hoped was a commanding voice. 'Slave, fetch me another. And a cigar!.' Taking my glass, the girl hurried to fulfil my command, but the guard drew closer and, reaching into the folds of his robe produced a small riding crop. 'Here, Brother. Teach her not to spill any.' I had no choice; if I was to escape detection as an intruder here I would have to abandon any remaining pretence at decency. I tried to moderate the blow, please, please believe this. Still, it left a welt on the pitiable girl's backside, she let out a stifled moan at the outrage and had Holmes seen this I should have expired from shame. Satisfied at my debauched nature, the guard let out a low chuckle and went back out to his post. I would have strangled the life from the swine if I had not a duty to fulfil.

The next chamber-again the baffled door-was a scene

from Dante; more of the same torture devices and contrivances that I remembered from the Abbey, women being flogged, beaten and whipped, their screams of pain through their gags agonising to the ears. The girl whom I had struck had followed me docilely, carrying my snifter and cigar on a silver tray. Still another chamber!. What horrors did it contain?. I was about to find out when another of the masked men came across to me from the torture racks. 'Fine night, what?.' It took a moment before I recognised him, but of course it was Holmes. For a long moment I stood, gawping like an idiot, but then took hold of myself and responded jovially. 'Thought I'd take this one into the next room, teach her some manners, eh?.' 'A fine idea, I shall join you.' At which we led the girl into the very deepest pit in all Hell.

There were five of them and no more. They stood round some twisted version of a Gynaecologist's chair, much like the one in the basement at the Abbey. This one, however, was occupied and by Mary Kelly. Naked, the poor child was strapped in and barely conscious, the smell of ether in the air explanation enough. Perhaps this was better, she had already sustained several grievous wounds to her breasts, face and lower abdomen. Behind the chair a board had been affixed to the wall with a basic diagram of the female form, each limb, each organ assigned a number. The game was simplicity itself. A cowled figure would spin the Devil's very own roulette wheel, numbered correspondent to the diagram. A '1' was the Head, '2' The Eyes... and so on and so on. The higher numbers seemed particularly prized. Each masked Gentleman would bid for the pleasure of inflicting the next torment. The highest bidder established, he would select an instrument from the trolley placed next to the chair.

I have written as much as I can bear, but I now confess for the first time that I failed Holmes; when the number '13' came up my self-control was washed away by the hatred and bile that had been rising since I entered this godforsaken hole. Handing Holmes his sword-stick, I snatched up a scalpel and an amputation knife, then charged as an enraged bull does, swinging the knife I created a space and used the scalpel to try to cut the poor girl free. Holmes had retrieved his sword from its hiding place and now wielded it in one hand, with the metal sheath in his left keeping the men at bay while I worked to free the terribly injured girl.

It was for naught; the men were cowards, but the guards who came running proved to have pistols and pluck both. One of the masked men, however, had caught my eye; something about his manner seemed familiar, but the leer on his face was too familiar by half. Throwing the scalpel at him I was rewarded with a screech of pain as the blade sank deep into his shoulder. 'Take that, you _____! I roared, drawing my revolver and blasting away at the be-robed thugs who were even then taking their own aim. One bullet found its mark, smashing into a guard's face and destroying it, but his colleague was no fool, grabbing ahold of his dying counterpart and using his body as a shield to send a fusilade of shots slamming into the wall behind me, shattering a gas-lamp, only Holmes' presence of mind saving me-as he shoved me bodily aside with his scabbard, before ducking down and pushing the trolley into the gunman's legs, instruments flying everywhere at the impact. Dashing forward, my friend threw out his arm, blade at full stretch. It was not enough. The man had, by my estimate, one or two shots left-I had none and Holmes was a dead man.

Suddenly, I saw my chance; my snifter of brandy!; somehow-and most inexplicably, the girl who had carried it was still holding it on its tray. The girl must have been literally frozen with fear. The man was taking his time, enjoying his moment of victory over Holmes-surely he would be well rewarded for his brave actions!. Indeed he was-I had taken my glass-held it to the flame of the shattered gas-lamp to warm it-lit it-and hurled it, the blazing liquid spreading its blue fire over the cowled figure's face and upper body. The fire caught. His screams are with me to this day, but despite my oath to Hippocrates I stood and watched him burn. Any final attempt to pass myself off as a gentleman will be lost as I tell you I took my cigar from that damned tray and I lit it from his burning corpse, watched by Holmes and the slave girl-the others had fled-in unyielding silence. Expecting a protest from my friend at my reprehensible behaviour, I turned and regarded him through the smoke, but Holmes merely asked after the taste of the cigar. Grimly, my reply was that no cigar had ever tasted finer. Clapping me on the shoulder, Holmes reminded me that we were far from safe and Miss Kelly-clearly already dying, needed the urgent medical help of a surgeon. Which is when the bottle of ether shattered at our feet.

CHAPTER XXXVII
A MONSTER UNMASKED

We awoke to find ourselves bound hand and foot in a cellar, shelves containing dusty bottles of wine on the far wall and only a rat for company. Presently, however, we heard steps descending wooden stairs and then the door to the cellar creaked open, an extraordinary figure entering, covered from head to foot in white muslin, a child's toy blackboard in his hand. Scratching at this, he wrote and showed us both the words; 'Where are the Jewels?.' At this, to my surprise, Holmes let out a chuckle and spoke, his voice rich with delight that I could not share. 'Really, Sir. Bernard-this is just too comical for words. Why not remove that ludicrous sheet and speak properly?.' I could not believe it-but it was so!; pulling off the muslin, the features of Sir. Bernard Gibson were revealed to us. At once I realised that this was the fiend which my scalpel had found-the eyes!. It was he!. Joining Holmes in what might be my final moment of humour, I asked after Sir. Bernard's shoulder, to which the reply was a stinging blow from the back of his left hand.

'It's all over, Sir. Bernard-though I doubt you'll have a knighthood after tonight.' Holmes' stinging words drew our captor's attention from me and I began working on my bonds, using my strength as unobtrusively as possible. Unfortunately, our bonds were of hempen rope and had been soaked first, which made them shrink to form tight, unbreakable ligatures that even now were cutting off my circulation at wrist and ankle. Holmes, however, continued with his philippic, determined to goad our host into some sort of admission or error, I could not be sure which. 'By now, of course, you know that the gang was seized on their exit from the Tower-they should be... pardon me, *Sir*. Bernard, could you please tell me the time?.' Icily, Gibson consulted his watch. 'It is somewhat after One.' 'Thank You. By now, they should be in the less than capable hands of Sir. Charles Warren, who doubtless will take the credit for smashing the Professor's organisation.'

With a short, high-pitched laugh suited to a maniac, Sir. Bernard took a step backwards. 'You think so?. I can tell you, Mister Sherlock Snooper that at this very moment the gang are headed for the Continent, albeit without the Jewels. As for Sir. Charles, I hope to replace him as he has tendered his resignation unexpectedly. So I ask you again; where are they?. I'll not hesitate to do to you what you saw us do to the Kelly whore, so please be compendious in your reply.' 'It's too late for that, I'm afraid.' The voice came from the foot of the stairs, a sibilant, malevolent voice I had heard before. The sound that followed was oddly like a wet glove smacking onto wood, Sir. Bernard's body falling soundlessly to the stone floor, the life gone from it. 'Gentlemen. I take my leave of you. We will, however, be discussing this at a later date-however distant.' With that, the sound of soft footsteps ascending the stairs announced the mysterious figure's departure. Holmes began wriggling his way towards the distant wine rack for some suitable glass to cut ourselves free.

EPILOGUE

Of course, the fate of poor Mary Kelly is well established, at least in the fiction that stands in for the journalistic press these days, nor too, was there any robbery at the Tower of London, despite the odd rumours concerning the dirigible that accidentally lost height and was seen brushing against the ramparts briefly before being seen to head out to sea. Of the gang, nothing more was heard, though rumours persist of course. Also, you may have read of the fate of the gallant Sir.

Bernard Gibson, shot down by common burglars after his collection of silver plate-said to be uncommon even amongst the finer museums of Europe. Sir. Charles Warren's resignation is a matter of public record, as is the Home Secretary's response in the House, which co-incidentally included this reference to official Home Office policy;

'The Secretary of State, having had his attention called to the question of allowing private publication, by officers attached to the Department, of books on matters relating to the Department, is of opinion that the practice may lead to embarrassment, and should in future be discontinued. He desires, therefore, that it should be considered a Rule of the Home Department that no officer should publish any work relating to the Department, unless the sanction of the Secretary of State has been previously obtained for the purpose.' With this strict admonition in mind, it seems unlikely Sir. Charles' memoirs will contain anything but the vaguest attempt at the truth. This prohibition also served to gag several officers from both London forces who had hoped to shed some light on the truth someday, such being their outrage at the falsehoods evident in the official account.

As for Holmes' sponsor, he had been part of it all along, something that Holmes regretted until his retirement, upon which he vowed never to speak of the matter-or the case again. That he has allowed this narrative to emerge into the light of public scrutiny is something I can only marvel at. Perhaps he feels he should be excoriated for his perceived failings, yet he not only prevented the theft of the most famous jewels in the World, he brought justice and retribution to those evil and twisted souls behind the most ghastly and notorious of all crimes, those attributed to a mythical figure-'Jack the Ripper.' Only the killer of Sir. Bernard remained uncaught, though the public still believes in a savage phantom who cruelly slaughtered five women, the last in a dismal hovel named Millers Court. Mary Jane Kelly was just twenty-five at the time of her death, but she did not die in her room as so many millions now believe, she was placed there, further injuries were made to her *post-mortem* and a significant amount of blood-whether animal or otherwise, splashed about.

Then what, you might ask, of the scenes of debauchery themselves?-you have already read in an aside that Laroche Abbey burned to the ground, but the subterranean workings at Highgate were lost in an unexplained earth tremour, several tombs thought destroyed. A spokesman for the Office of Works said it would take several weeks to fill in all the damage. Of the mysterious Hunting Club, nothing remained, save an obscure paper in Holmes' possession-the work of a crank, no doubt, nothing more.

Mary Morstan became Mary Watson on November the Twenty-Fourth of that year. It was a small ceremony, conducted in the chapel at St. Barts with only Holmes as witness and, of course dear Stamford. The Guard of Honour was a tad unconventional, but Wiggins and his Arabs had at least brushed their shoes and teeth for the occasion. We took our Honeymoon in Brighton and had the best weather possible; it rained nearly constantly, so I'm told.

An odd aside came from the files of Hansard, the Parliamentary Reports office, concerning the debate on the resignation of the Commissioner, a brief excerpt of which follows;

Mr. Henry Du Pré Labouchère, the Member of Parliament for Northampton-
'What is the precise position which Mr. Monro holds now?-
He has been consulted by the Home Secretary.'

Mr. Henry Matthews, Her Majesty's Home Secretary-
'Mr. Monro holds no office of any kind...
and is in no way connected with the Department.'

How odd, then, that James Monro, the prickly Scottish Solicitor's son and head of the C.I.D., who had resigned in September and had been reporting exclusively to the Home Secretary, should be referred to as having no connexion with the Metropolitan force. Odder, still was the fact that after his resignation, such an unofficial personage was given charge of the Special Branch and following Sir. Charles' own departure, the position of Commissioner of Police of the Metropolis itself!. This rankled with Holmes particularly, although he kept much of his feelings to himself. As for myself, life in our new house was a positive salve to my sorely tested nerves and I had never been happier. Then came the day when Mycroft Holmes invited Holmes and myself up to the Diogenes Club for a late lunch.

After a surprisingly rubbery steak and kidney pie, we ate a lemon sponge cake with custard that could have been served in any school. This, I suspected was the point of the cuisine at the Diogenes, to transport it's members back to their days at Harrow or Eton. Retiring with a carafe of port and cigars, we sat by the fire in the Strangers' Room and at last Sherlock was able to unburden himself to us both. 'Watson, my brother Mycroft believes me an abject fool. I happen to share his opinion.' waving down my protest, he continued, waving smoke from his corona as he stood in front of the fire. 'I quite failed to see how high this business reached-or how low it had stooped. While my patron turned out to be a creature of evil character, a monster hiding behind a respectable facade as it were, I knew of his involvement from the time we visited him together that night.' I had raised an eyebrow at this, but

Mycroft both, a fixed half-smile upon his features that challenged his younger sibling to elaborate. 'Sir. Bernard mentioned Extortionists, this stimulated my imagination and I began to question the nature of this gang, that if they extorted money from the poor of Whitechapel they could also turn their attentions to the higher circles of society.'

Holmes took his seat and his glass to continue. 'I began to wonder at the true interest of Sir. Bernard, so I made some simple, but obvious request for him to strengthen security at the Tower, knowing this would not hamper the Professor's attempt in any meaningful way. A man of such resources would hardly neglect to have a lock-picking expert handy or some dynamite to open any recently-installed locks. Likewise any extra men he put in place would be under orders not to try to hamper the thieves.' 'But you had no real cause to doubt him?.' Taking a sip before answering Mycroft, Sherlock shook his head. 'Only later-I had spotted a bronze figure of Artemis in his study-Artemis being the Greek correlative of Diana, this began to assume a sinister aspect. It was only, however, when I discovered Sir. Bernard was the owner of Laroche Abbey that my doubts found a firm basis in fact.' One facet of this extraordinary case had dogged me from the night I had shot at what we then believed to be a lone madman. 'Mister Holmes, I must know; the identity of the man I shot.' 'Ah. I was afraid of this. To give his name would invite ruin to Her Majesty's Government and accordingly, it must never cross my lips. I can assure you, he is being watched. Perhaps it would have been better had your shot taken him from us.'

Miss Carter had mentioned her knowledge of Sir. Bernard's interest in the case and I reminded Holmes of this. He agreed that she had known more than she had let on-and that I was not the only one who should have acted on this information.

'All in all, then, a terrible business.' Mycroft stood and took my hand. 'Doctor, I congratulate you on escaping the freedom of bachelor-hood.' Finishing his port, Holmes rose. 'Of course, not every patron is a murderous lunatic.' 'Whatever do you mean, Sherlock?.' 'Simply this, brother mine. *Yours* has risen to prominence while mine lies in his grave.' The elder Holmes' eyes reddened visibly at this, but he did not reply. 'I wonder, though, if those others at the cemetery, those fine gentlemen safely anonymous behind their masks and finery, will be as keen to reward the man who secured their freedom that night. What assurance have you they will not attempt to resurrect that vile club of theirs?.' In place of an answer, Mycroft merely gave a snort and shook his head ruefully. 'Why, I have *you,* Dear Brother. What better assurance could any man have?.'

This story is respectfully dedicated to the memory of Sir.
Arthur Conan Doyle.
My Thanks and Undying Love go to my Wife Angie, who
helped with my execrable spelling-any errors of grammar
remaining are historical variations and intended to evoke the
feel of a Victorian novel.

About The Author

Photo by Angie Sohn

Mark Sohn was born in Brighton in 1967 and has lived in Sussex for most of his life. After various unusual careers he met his Wife Angie. They live together by the English Channel and enjoy their family and life together. A Conan Doyle fiend of long-standing, Mark also enjoys the works of Chandler, Fleming and Le Carre-as well as his library of Espionage books he loves music and old movies.

Also from MX Publishing

MX Publishing is the world's largest specialist Sherlock Holmes publisher, with over a hundred titles and fifty authors creating the latest in Sherlock Holmes fiction and non-fiction.

From traditional short stories and novels to travel guides and quiz books, MX Publishing cater for all Holmes fans.

The collection includes leading titles such as _Benedict Cumberbatch In Transition_ and _The Norwood Author_ which won the 2011 Howlett Award (Sherlock Holmes Book of the Year).

MX Publishing also has one of the largest communities of Holmes fans on Facebook with regular contributions from dozens of authors.

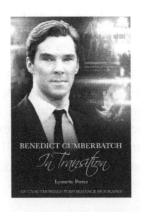

www.mxpublishing.com

Also from MX Publishing

The Missing Authors Series

Sherlock Holmes and The Adventure of The Grinning Cat
Sherlock Holmes and The Nautilus Adventure
Sherlock Holmes and The Round Table Adventure

"Joseph Svec, III is brilliant in entwining two endearing and enduring classics of literature, blending the factual with the fantastical; the playful with the pensive; and the mischievous with the mysterious. We shall, all of us young and old, benefit with a cup of tea, a tranquil afternoon, and a copy of Sherlock Holmes, The Adventure of the Grinning Cat."
Amador County Holmes Hounds Sherlockian Society

www.mxpublishing.com

Lightning Source UK Ltd.
Milton Keynes UK
UKHW02f0741200418
321385UK00009B/605/P